LETTERS WR
SWEDEN, NORWAY,

MARY WOLLSTONECRAFT was born in 1759, the granddaughter of a wealthy Irish manufacturer. Her father spent the fortune he inherited and took to drink, so in 1783 Mary left to keep a school in Newington Green with her sister Eliza. She subsequently became governess to Lord Kingsborough's children, during which time she wrote *Mary: A Fiction* (1788). Her best-known works are *Vindication of the Rights of Men* (1790) and *Vindication of the Rights of Woman* (1792). She left for France in 1792 to witness the progress of the Revolution at first hand. In France she met and lived with an American, Gilbert Imlay, by whom she had a daughter, Fanny. His infidelity drove her to return to England and to an attempted suicide. Soon afterwards she left for Scandinavia on business for Imlay, the journey that produced *Letters written during a short residence in Sweden, Norway, and Denmark*. On her return she found him living with an actress and again attempted suicide. She married William Godwin in 1797, and died a few months later at the birth of her daughter Mary (later to become Shelley's second wife). *The Wrongs of Woman*, a largely autobiographical novel in which she explores the parallels between domestic and political life, private and public morality, was published in 1798.

TONE BREKKE is Visiting Research Fellow at the Centre for Gender Research at the University of Oslo.

JON MEE is Professor of Romanticism Studies at the University of Warwick.

OXFORD WORLD'S CLASSICS

*For over 100 years Oxford World's Classics have brought
readers closer to the world's great literature. Now with over 700
titles—from the 4,000-year-old myths of Mesopotamia to the
twentieth century's greatest novels—the series makes available
lesser-known as well as celebrated writing.*

*The pocket-sized hardbacks of the early years contained
introductions by Virginia Woolf, T. S. Eliot, Graham Greene,
and other literary figures which enriched the experience of reading.
Today the series is recognized for its fine scholarship and
reliability in texts that span world literature, drama and poetry,
religion, philosophy, and politics. Each edition includes perceptive
commentary and essential background information to meet the
changing needs of readers.*

OXFORD WORLD'S CLASSICS

MARY WOLLSTONECRAFT

Letters written during a short residence in Sweden, Norway, and Denmark

Edited with an Introduction and Notes by
TONE BREKKE and JON MEE

OXFORD
UNIVERSITY PRESS

OXFORD

UNIVERSITY PRESS

Great Clarendon Street, Oxford OX2 6DP

Oxford University Press is a department of the University of Oxford.
It furthers the University's objective of excellence in research, scholarship,
and education by publishing worldwide in

Oxford New York

Auckland Cape Town Dar es Salaam Hong Kong Karachi
Kuala Lumpur Madrid Melbourne Mexico City Nairobi
New Delhi Shanghai Taipei Toronto

With offices in

Argentina Austria Brazil Chile Czech Republic France Greece
Guatemala Hungary Italy Japan Poland Portugal Singapore
South Korea Switzerland Thailand Turkey Ukraine Vietnam

Oxford is a registered trade mark of Oxford University Press
in the UK and in certain other countries

Published in the United States
by Oxford University Press Inc., New York

British Library Cataloguing in Publication Data

Data available

Library of Congress Cataloging-in-Publication Data

Wollstonecraft, Mary, 1759-1797.
Letters written during a short residence in Sweden, Norway, and Denmark /
Mary Wollstonecraft ; edited with an introduction and notes by Tone Brekke and Jon Mee.
p. cm. — (Oxford world's classics)
Includes bibliographical references.
ISBN 978-0-19-923063-1
1. Wollstonecraft, Mary, 1759-1797—Travel—Scandinavia. 2. Wollstonecraft, Mary,
1759-1797—Correspondence. 3. Imlay, Gilbert, 1754?-1828?—Correspondence.
4. Scandinavia—Description and travel—Early works to 1800.
5. Authors, English—18th century—Correspondence.
6. Feminists—Great Britain—Correspondence. I. Brekke, Tone. II. Mee, Jon. III. Title.
PR5841.W8Z48 2009
828'.609—dc22
[B]

2008046065

Typeset by Cepha Imaging Private Ltd., Bangalore, India

Printed and bound in Great Britain by Clays Ltd, Elcograf S.p.A.

ISBN 978-0-19-923063-1

14

ACKNOWLEDGEMENTS

THE editors are extremely grateful to the Bodleian Library and the Danish State Archives for permission to reproduce the materials in Appendices 1 and 2.

The introduction and notes have benefited greatly from the advice of Lyndall Gordon and Gunnar Molden, who very generously gave their time and knowledge at short notice to help the editors. Astrid Wind and Luisa Calè also gave valuable help. David Fallon worked tirelessly checking the manuscript and hunting down facts. His enthusiasm, knowledge, and good spirits have been greatly appreciated. Any errors that remain are, of course, the responsibility of the editors.

Jon Mee is grateful for the support of a Philip J. Leverhulme Major Research Fellowship provided by the Leverhulme Trust. Tone Brekke would like to thank the Centre for Gender Research at the University of Oslo for providing a nurturing research environment.

To
S/Z
as it were

CONTENTS

INTRODUCTION

By the time she went to Scandinavia in June 1795, the pioneering feminist Mary Wollstonecraft was an established professional writer, but getting there had been a hard journey, and her ability to survive, never mind her reputation, as a professional writer was far from guaranteed. Although she is still better known for her enthusiastic defence of the French Revolution in *Vindication of the Rights of Men* (1790) and even more famous for the ground-breaking feminism of *Vindication of the Rights of Woman* (1792), *Letters written during a short residence in Sweden, Norway, and Denmark* (1796) was the book best received by her contemporaries and can still claim to be among her greatest achievements. Her future husband William Godwin responded to it with immense eagerness and warmth: 'If ever there was a book calculated to make a man in love with its author, this appears to me to be the book.'[1] Although she also saw the book as revealing Wollstonecraft 'the woman' behind 'the philosopheress', the novelist Amelia Alderson took a more balanced view than Godwin: 'I saw nothing but the interesting creature of feeling, & imagination, & I resolved if possible, to become acquainted with one who had alternately awakened my sensibility & gratified my judgement.'[2] The interplay of 'feeling' and 'judgment' point to the complexity of a text which is full of powerful emotional responsiveness to the natural scenery of Scandinavia, but also an awareness of the precarious nature of the writing self and her relation to the different kinds of societies through which she passes. Wollstonecraft's book is not simply auto-biographical, not simply about her personal situation, but also a reflection on the responsiveness of human beings—with the emphasis very much on the situation of women—to their emotional and historical surroundings. She thinks hard about the options of solitude and social engagement, attracted by the primitive society

[1] See Appendix 4.
[2] Amelia Alderson to Mary Wollstonecraft, 28 August 1796, Bodleian Library, Abinger Collection, Dep. 210/6.

she finds in Norway, but recognizing that the sociable self needs a more developed cultural life, such as she had enjoyed in London and, especially, republican Paris. More generally, *A Short Residence* is a generic tour de force: it includes sentimental travel narrative, reflections on aesthetic theories of the sublime and the picturesque, sociological analysis, a historical record of the effects of the French Revolution in Europe, disquisitions on natural theology, and feminist polemic. The literary accomplishment is even more extraordinary when placed in the context of the real reasons behind Wollstonecraft's journey: the attempt to discover what had happened to the shipment of silver sent to Sweden by her lover Gilbert Imlay in defiance of the British naval blockade of revolutionary France.

Mary Wollstonecraft's Life and Career

Mary Wollstonecraft was the eldest of seven children born to an Irish mother and a volatile, often violent, English father. This unstable background meant from early on in life she had to fend for herself and assume much of the responsibility for her siblings. During her teenage years, she developed a passionate friendship with a young woman, Fanny Blood, whose own family she also ended up trying to support. Wollstonecraft's first attempt at economic independence was running a school for girls in Islington, north London, soon moved to nearby Newington Green, which involved both Fanny and the other Wollstonecraft sisters. The arrangement was broken up when Fanny accepted a marriage proposal from a British merchant in Lisbon, Hugh Skeys, and sailed for Portugal early in 1785. Wollstonecraft followed her out to help with the birth of her child, but Fanny passed away soon afterwards. The intensity of their relationship is still recalled over twenty years later as one of the voices from the past that haunt the Scandinavian landscape of *A Short Residence*: 'the grave has closed over a dear friend, the friend of my youth; still she is present with me, and I hear her soft voice warbling as I stray over the heath' (p. 39). When Wollstonecraft returned to London, she found her sisters quarrelling over the management of the school.

Economic necessity forced her to take up work as a governess in Ireland for Lady Kingsborough at the end of 1786, but she had to return to London in 1787 after being dismissed; the grounds seem to have been the encouragement she had given the eldest daughter, Margaret, in rebelling against her parents.

When Wollstonecraft had moved to Newington Green, a stronghold for religious dissenters (those Protestants who were not part of the established Church into which Wollstonecraft herself was born), she came into contact with progressive nonconformist thinkers such as the minister Richard Price. Although not actively persecuted by the state in the late eighteenth century, religious nonconformists created a powerful literary culture that frequently expressed their unhappiness at legal exclusion from full civil rights, and played an important role in political and other reform movements from the 1760s. Through Price and other dissenting contacts, Wollstonecraft met the publisher Joseph Johnson, who was to publish *A Short Residence*, as he also published her other early writings—mainly concerned with the education of women— *Thoughts on the Education of Daughters* (1787), *Original Stories from Real Life* (1788), and *The Female Reader* (1789). After she was dismissed by Lady Kingsborough, Wollstonecraft was supported by Johnson, who provided her with accommodation and work for his new journal the *Analytical Review*, which extended her knowledge both of new ideas and the varieties of writing in London's rapidly expanding print culture. She also produced a novel, *Mary: A Fiction* (1788), partly drawing on her experience in Ireland, but it was events in France in 1789 that transformed Mary's reputation and ambitions. Hitherto primarily an educational writer, an interest that never left her, Wollstonecraft turned her attention towards the political events of her time. Most of the writers of Johnson's circle welcomed the French Revolution as a major change in the course of human affairs. Many dissenters thought of it as the realization of a providential plan for human history. Price published one of the most striking responses as a *Discourse on the Love of one's Country* (1789), which provided the immediate target for Edmund Burke's *Reflections on the Revolution in France*, published in November 1790. Amazingly Mary managed to get out a reply to Burke, *Vindication of the Rights of Men*, before the end of the same year. By the end of 1791, she was becoming well known to radical intellectuals such as William Godwin and Thomas Paine, although Godwin, her future husband, was famously disappointed to hear her opinions dominate at a dinner he attended to hear what Paine had to say. This confidence in the right of women to articulate their point of view was expressed with brilliance in her *Vindication of the Rights of Woman* (1792). Developing her long concern with issues of education, Wollstonecraft tied them to the question of what made a good citizen, countering the opinions of Jean-Jacques Rousseau, whom she otherwise admired in many ways. For Wollstonecraft, unlike Rousseau, it was the need actively to develop women's talents, particularly their intellectual abilities, which made their plight central to any consideration of how to foster republican virtue.

By the time *Vindication of the Rights of Woman* was published, Mary was in the aftermath of a complicated relationship with another member of the Johnson circle, the painter Henry Fuseli, and had decided to travel to Paris to witness the Revolution at first hand. There she met the American writer and entrepreneur Gilbert Imlay, with whom she began a passionate but troubled affair, the cause of two suicide attempts in the next four years.[3] Their child Fanny was born in Le Havre in 1794, where Imlay had arranged for civil recognition of their relationship. Via his American citizenship, Imlay's name provided Wollstonecraft with protection from the anti-British policies adopted by the Jacobin government in France over 1793–4. By the time Fanny was born, however, Imlay was already showing signs of restlessness. Wollstonecraft followed Imlay back to London in 1795, where Johnson published her account of the early years of the Revolution, *A Historical and Moral View* (1794), but her relationship with Imlay was deteriorating, and she made a suicide attempt with an overdose of laudanum. On her recovery, Wollstonecraft agreed to make the trip to Scandinavia in pursuit of Imlay's business affairs, but she returned only to find him living openly with another

---

[3] The first full-length biography of Imlay is Wil Verhoeven's *Gilbert Imlay: Citizen of the World* (London, 2008).

woman in London. Her efforts at reconciliation failed and she attempted suicide again, this time by drowning in the Thames. Rescued by boatmen, her recovery was assisted by another woman writer, Mary Hays, who reintroduced her to William Godwin in 1796. Hays became one of Wollstonecraft's most stalwart supporters and regarded her explicitly as a role model for a woman trying to make a career in the republic of letters. Together with Godwin, they became part of a vibrant progressive writing community centred on North London, very close to what is now the British Library in St Pancras. Godwin and Wollstonecraft became lovers after an uncertain courtship. Despite Godwin having written against marriage and even cohabitation, they were married at St Pancras Church at the end of March 1797, although he maintained a separate home for work and some of his literary socializing. Some of their 'respectable' friends, the actress Sarah Siddons and novelist and playwright Elizabeth Inchbald among them, withdrew from their social circle on discovering that Wollstonecraft had never been Mrs Imlay, and that Fanny was illegitimate. Wollstonecraft began writing a second novel, *Maria or The Wrongs of Women*, but it was never finished. She died from complications after giving birth to the future Mary Shelley in August 1797.

Scandinavia and the 'Silver Ship'

Possibly because she wanted to prove her worth to him, perhaps because she just wanted to get away, Wollstonecraft agreed to accept Imlay's commission to go to Scandinavia in pursuit of a dubious business venture that had gone awry.[4] Only two weeks before she left she had taken an overdose in response to his rejection of her. Imlay, like their mutual friend Joel Barlow, was an American of radical political sympathies, who also had a nose for making money out of the turmoil of the French Revolution.

---

[4] The narrative that follows is indebted to two Scandinavian historians in particular: Per Nyström and Gunnar Molden. See Select Bibliography for details of their work. There is also an excellent accessible account in Lyndall Gordon's *Vindication: A Life of Mary Wollstonecraft* (London, 2006), 256–90.

Imlay had served as an officer in the War of Independence, a character he traded upon in the new republic, where he was involved in land speculation. To encourage migrants to the backwoods of Kentucky, he had published a pamphlet, *A Topographical Description of the Western Territory of North America* (1792), followed by a novel, *The Emigrants* (1793), which painted an attractive picture of the possibilities to be found in the new world. Imlay was also trying to get the French republican government to involve itself in the jockeying between the old powers in the new world, as well as looking for ways to make money by circumventing the British naval blockade of revolutionary France. From 1792 France was at war with most of monarchical Europe. Britain joined the coalition against the new republic in January 1793, soon after the execution of Louis XVI. The Scandinavian countries, Sweden, where the King had been assassinated in 1792, and the joint monarchy of Denmark and Norway, had declared their neutrality in 1794 in the face of protests from Britain and Russia, and some of their merchants were growing rich out of their unique trading position.

Imlay was attempting to make money through trade with France by employing Scandinavian merchants as commercial agents. Among these was Elias Backman of Gothenburg. The immediate background for Wollstonecraft's trip was Backman and Imlay's scheme of licensing a French ship—renamed the *Maria and Margaretha*—with Norwegian papers and loading it with a treasure of French silver to take to Gothenburg, where it could be used in payment for Scandinavian grain to feed the embattled new republic. The ship sailed under the command of its Norwegian captain Peder Ellefsen in August 1794, but it failed to arrive in Gothenburg. Exactly what happened is still not clear. Recent research by Norwegian and Swedish historians shows that the ship was harboured on the Norwegian coast near Arendal, where Ellefsen left it in the hands of the first mate, after taking at least some of the silver ashore. Although Imlay may have later recovered some of his money, what happened to the cargo as a whole is still uncertain. The fate of the silver ship itself is equally difficult to discern among competing testimonies at various trials held to investigate its fate, but its course over the next few months—as it sailed around the coast of Scandinavia in an attempt to make it through difficult waters to Gothenburg—determined the route Wollstonecraft took on her travels. The scandal over the fate of the ship reached the highest levels of society in Denmark and Sweden. Backman's connections in Sweden, Norway, and Denmark pressed the Danish government to set up a Royal Commission at the end of January 1795, and in February Ellefsen the captain was arrested and only released after his wealthy family stood an enormous bail.

Wollstonecraft's commission from Imlay was to act as his representative in the case against Ellefsen that was begun in January 1795.[5] She was empowered to receive any monies disbursed by the Ellefsen family, regardless of the outcome of the legal proceedings. Imlay also gave her the authority to use her own judgement as to the appropriate amount of damages that ought to be paid and either to seek an out-of-court settlement or begin litigation for damages. Making such a judgement would involve investigating both what had happened to the ship and the ability of the Ellefsen family to pay. Whatever the vicissitudes of their relationship, Imlay clearly recognized Wollstonecraft's practical abilities, placing his faith, as the commission puts it, in her 'talent zeal and earnestness'. Mary began her voyage from Hull, accompanied by her 13-month-old daughter Fanny and a French nursemaid, Marguerite. Originally Wollstonecraft was to have landed at Arendal in Norway, a base for the powerful Ellefsen family presided over by Peder's formidable mother, where the silver, or at least some of it, was supposed to have been taken ashore, but bad weather forced the captain to make for a lighthouse just south of Gothenburg. They were rowed ashore by sailors from the ship, where they found the district pilot chief, who turned out to be an English-speaking retired naval officer. Wollstonecraft's letter to Imlay describing her arrival on shore shows that she later fainted from the exertions, although, in one of the striking differences between *A Short Residence* and her letters home, no mention is made of it in the published account. 'I am not well', she told Imlay, 'and yet you see I cannot die' (p. 140). Her response to the dramatic

---

[5] The commission is reproduced in Appendix 1.

Norwegian landscape was almost immediately to feel the contrast its grandeur provided with revolutionary France: 'I forgot the horrors I had witnessed in France, which had cast a gloom over all nature' (p. 10). The next day she set out for Gothenburg, lodging with Backman, Imlay's associate. She was unimpressed by the city, not least by the women of polite society. Her published comments created great offence there after *A Short Residence* was quickly translated into Swedish, her unpopularity gleefully reported in his own travel book by the anti-republican French traveller Henri Marie de Bougrenet de La Tocnaye.[6] Leaving her daughter and the maid behind, Wollstonecraft headed for Norway in Backman's company. En route they stayed in the frontier town of Strömstad, where the ship had been sailed for repairs after failing to make Gothenburg. Following a sightseeing trip to the fortress where Charles XII had met his death near modern-day Halden, she then crossed from Strömstad into Norway by open boat to Larvik, where she consulted with the lawyers acting on the case, and then by carriage into Tønsberg, where Jacob Wulfsberg, a local magistrate and one of the members of the Royal Commission, lived. She stayed in the comfortable inn by the sea for over three weeks before sailing for Risør (Ellefsen's home port). There she confronted Ellefsen and seems to have extracted some sort of confession from him. After a few days, she turned back, visiting Oslo (Letters XIII and XIV), enjoying the hospitality, like most foreign visitors, of the powerful Anker family, before returning to Gothenburg to be reunited with her daughter and her nursemaid. After a sightseeing trip to the falls at Trollhättan, she was taken to Helsingborg, from where she was rowed over to Elsinore, and then Copenhagen. There she met the Danish Prime Minister, Bernstorff, to put Imlay's case directly to him, but without success. She then sailed for Hamburg, a free port, but also one of the seamiest cities in Europe, full of aristocratic émigrés from revolutionary France, and, consequently, a centre of espionage and intrigue. She stayed for the most part in nearby Altona, a Danish

---

[6] See his *Promenade d'un Français en Suède et en Norvège* (1801), mentioned again at the end of this Introduction in the context of other early responses to Wollstonecraft's book.

town on the German mainland, where Joel Barlow and his wife Ruth, a friend of Wollstonecraft's, had lived over the winter of 1794–5. Barlow, who was working as a shipping agent, left a couple of months before Wollstonecraft arrived, having made one of those 'mushroom fortunes' Wollstonecraft condemns at the end of her book. Money was certainly to be made from disposing of the gold, silver, and other valuables of displaced French aristocrats. Wollstonecraft's book records disgust at Hamburg's commercial bustle, 'an ill, close-built town, swarming with inhabitants' (p. 125), and its influence on the character of her lover. Receiving no news of Imlay's intentions for their relationship, she left abruptly to confront him in London.

Letters written during a short residence

Little or nothing of this murky commercial background and its influence on Wollstonecraft's itinerary makes it into her book, unless one counts the intensifying attacks on the corrupting power of commerce as it nears its conclusion. The brilliance of *A Short Residence* lies in its exploitation of the language of sentiment, which marks an important change from the rhetoric of the vindications, but also in the way it combines the sense of a self responding to personal and political disappointment with a refusal to abandon her political and intellectual commitments, not least her concern with the condition of women. Perhaps the most obvious way, however, in which the book inspired its first readers was in its brilliant descriptions of the dramatic landscape of Scandinavia. The region was not unknown to British readers. Indeed Wollstonecraft refers several times to William Coxe's *Travels into Poland, Russia, Sweden and Denmark* (1784), which had gone into four editions by the time of her journey. Although her book continues to ask '*men's questions*' (p. 11) about social and political conditions, always with a republican inflection very different from Coxe's, the most striking contrast comes with her impassioned narrative voice and her emphasis on the 'effect different objects had produced on my mind and feelings' (p. 3). Wollstonecraft does not simply describe the scenery, she gives a vivid sense of its interaction with a living human mind, and uses these reactions to think about the nature of human psychology more generally:

When a warm heart has received strong impressions, they are not to be effaced. Emotions become sentiments; and the imagination renders even transient sensations permanent, by fondly retracing them. I cannot, without a thrill of delight recollect views I have seen, which are not to be forgotten,—nor looks I have felt in every nerve which I shall never more meet. (p. 39)[7]

Paradoxically, however, her 'desultory' style, as she calls it in her 'Advertisement', seems to have won through only after a struggle with her own anxieties about the egotism of a first-person narrative. Indeed in a review of Hester Lynch Piozzi's *Observations and Reflections, made in the Course of a Journey through France, Italy, and Germany* (1789), written for Joseph Johnson's *Analytical*, we get a sense of why she might have felt some reluctance about this manner of proceeding:

These travels are very desultory, and have all the lax freedom of letters without that kind of insinuating interest, which slightly binds a nosegay of unconnected remarks, and throws a thin, but graceful veil over egotism; the substitution of *one* for I, is a mere cobweb.[8]

Few readers of Wollstonecraft's *Short Residence* have not felt the pull of 'insinuating interest' in her own style, the continual reference back to the viewing subject and her experiences, and the projection forward of the political question of the future for herself, her child, and the societies in which she moves.

In the process of examining her own responsiveness to her environment, Wollstonecraft also investigates some of the key aesthetic categories used in the period to think about nature and art. By the time Wollstonecraft wrote, ideas about the sublime and the beautiful had been given an influential statement in

---

[7] Nigel Leask, *Curiosity and the Aesthetics of Travel Writing 1770–1840: 'From an Antique Land'* (Oxford, 2002), 42, has suggested that such 'affective realism' was becoming increasingly prevalent in the travel writing of the time, influenced, in part, by the novel of sensibility.

[8] See *The Works of Mary Wollstonecraft*, ed. Janet Todd and Marilyn Butler (London, 1989), vii. 109.

Edmund Burke's *Philosophical Inquiry on our Ideas of the Sublime and the Beautiful* (1757). Burke had famously defined beauty as the more sociable category, identifying it, for instance, with feminine softness. The sublime he associated with what inspires awe and towers over us. Wollstonecraft had rejected Burke's gendering of these categories in her vindications, and insisted on the possibility of a woman displaying a 'masculine' understanding capable of grasping sublimity. Certainly the Scandinavian scenery gives her ample opportunities to display her own responsiveness to the sublime and the way it provokes the human senses to an intuition of something beyond the powers of the eye or ear to comprehend. Perhaps the most striking instance is her reaction to the falls outside Fredrikstad:

Reaching the cascade, or rather cataract, the roaring of which had a long time announced its vicinity, my soul was hurried by the falls into a new train of reflections. The impetuous dashing of the rebounding torrent from the dark cavities which mocked the exploring eye, produced an equal activity in my mind: my thoughts darted from earth to heaven, and I asked myself why I was chained to life and its misery? Still the tumultuous emotions this sublime object excited, were pleasurable; and, viewing it, my soul rose, with renewed dignity, above its cares—grasping at immortality—it seemed as impossible to stop the current of my thoughts, as of the always varying, still the same, torrent before me—I stretched out my hand to eternity, bounding over the dark speck of life to come. (p. 89)

God was Burke's ultimate example of sublimity, and writers of the time regularly used the sublime in nature as an occasion to praise the hand of God in creating nature. In the 1790s, however, such issues were likely to be closely scrutinized by readers for signs of unorthodoxy, especially where they seemed to break free of institutional religion and received morality. Wollstonecraft herself had been born into the Church of England, but much of her intellectual life had been shaped by her conversations with religious dissenters. Godwin himself was a lapsed dissenter who was routinely regarded as an atheist by his political opponents. In his *Memoirs* of Wollstonecraft, Godwin represents her religious sense as an instrinsic part of her emotional response to nature, 'almost entirely of her own creation . . . the growth of her own moral taste': 'But nature itself, she thought, would be no better than a vast blank, if the mind of an observer did not supply it with an animating soul.'[9] For all the enthusiastic drama of the sublime in Wollstonecraft's writing, however, *A Short Residence* also places a great deal of emphasis on the picturesque. Picturesque travel writing usually pitched itself between the symmetry associated with beauty and the awestruck reverence of the sublime. Its leading principle was energy and, Wollstonecraft's contemporary Uvedale Price suggested, 'curiosity'.[10] So Wollstonecraft's responsiveness to the grandeur of the Scandinavian landscape may occasion a series of brilliant reveries, but these serve only as stopping points before she reorients herself towards the 'active principle' (p. 11) and re-engagement with society.[11]

A Short Residence is not only a travelogue and hymn to natural religion. Before leaving London, Wollstonecraft had left her *Historical and Moral View of the French Revolution* with the printers, and everywhere she goes in Scandinavia her interest in contemporary European affairs is evident. She records the enthusiasm for the French Republic in Norway and describes the assassination of the reactionary Swedish King Gustav III as a blessing for his country. She was also particularly interested in the story of Queen Matilda (pp. 102–3), an Englishwoman, sister of George II, wife of King Christian VII, and her lover Struensee, whose fate she would have read about in Coxe before she arrived in Scandinavia. Wollstonecraft's attitude to Struensee and Matilda is much more sympathetic than Coxe's. Christian VII had sunk into mental illness after a life of debauchery and, as a consequence, his physician Johann Frederick Struensee (1731–72) rose

---

[9] Godwin, *Memoirs of the Author of a Vindication of the Rights of Woman* (1798), 34 and 33. The section of chapter 8 of the *Memoirs* describing the period in Scandinavia is reproduced in Appendix 4.

[10] Uvedale Price, *An Essay on the Picturesque, as Compared with the Sublime and the Beautiful*, new edn. (London, 1796), as quoted in Leask, *Curiosity*, 42.

[11] Mary Favret suggests that many of the reveries in the book are self-consciously aware of Rousseau's *Reveries of a Solitary Walker*. Just as with her treatment of Rousseau's *Emile* in *Vindication of the Rights of Woman*, Wollstonecraft reorients her model, here 'in order to critique his isolation and egocentrism'. See Favret, *Romantic Correspondence: Women, Politics, and the Fiction of Letters* (Cambridge, 1993), 105.

in political influence, encouraging the King to introduce liberal reforms. Matilda supported Struensee and the pair were believed to have begun an affair, resulting in the birth of a daughter in 1771. The unpopularity of their reforms led to his arrest in 1772. Struensee was horribly executed. Matilda was divorced and then deported to Hanover, where she died aged only 24. For Wollstonecraft, Matilda was a victim of counter-revolution, someone vilified for her supposed sexual conduct primarily because she supported political reforms, but typically Wollstonecraft also pays attention to the Queen's attempt to introduce refinement in Danish manners, a process that she implicitly suggests creates a wider orbit for female freedom. This 'morals and manners' approach to historical change, also evident in her *Historical and Moral View*, influenced by historians of the Scottish Enlightenment and emphasizing the role of social and cultural progress in politics, plays an important part in *A Short Residence*, where she constantly maps her personal response to what she sees onto the social development of the places she visits. Resisting the emphasis on climate in determining national character that was associated with the French philosopher Montesquieu, Wollstonecraft's approach uses political institutions and the development of social life to explain the differences between societies. So, for instance, she largely favours Norway in her account, because its distance from the Danish monarchy, the lack of a strong nobility, and the sturdy independence of the landowning farmers (a kind of equivalent of the yeomanry Wordsworth celebrated in the Lake District) made its people among the freest in the world. Later she also acknowledges the importance of commercial development in relation to social conditions, perhaps reflecting a self-consciousness about her own position as a professional writer in a rapidly developing print culture: 'To be born here, was to be bastilled by nature—shut out from all that opens the understanding, or enlarges the heart' (p. 69). For Wollstonecraft some degree of refinement, predicated on economic development, is necessary, especially if women are to be treated as more than drudges. In fact, her interest in manners, as one would expect of the author of *Vindication of the Rights of Woman*, is continually indexed against the position of women in their societies, and the issue of the nurturing and education of children (an important point in her appreciation of Queen Matilda). David Hume and many other eighteenth-century thinkers took the development of polite sociability in commercial societies to be key to human progress. For Hume, this refinement was the product of a courtly culture based on 'mutual deference or civility, which leads us to resign our own inclinations to those of our companion, and to curb and conceal that presumption and arrogance so natural to the human mind'.[12] Although Wollstonecraft sees the development of commercial society as bringing with it improvements of this kind, she is also sceptical of its benefits. Her emphasis is much more rational and much more republican than Hume's. Hume thought women were the 'sovereigns of the empire of conversation'; that is, the company of women polished and refined the manners of men.[13] Although she acknowledges that commercial society and 'luxury' produced conditions that created more opportunities for women, Wollstonecraft thought this kind of gallantry could only debase the rationality of women (and mankind more generally).[14] In its emphasis on rationality, candour, and sincerity, her idea of manners has more in common with the dissenters she moved among from the later 1780s. Where commerce brings with it duplicity and exploitation, then it vitiates the benefits of refinement it brings to developing societies. A countervailing critique of commercial society intensifies as the book nears its conclusion:

But you will say that I am growing bitter, perhaps, personal. Ah! shall I whisper to you—that you—yourself, are strangely altered, since you have entered deeply into commerce—more than you are aware of—never allowing yourself to reflect, and keeping your mind, or rather passions, in a continual state of agitation. (p. 126)

The reflection on Imlay's treatment of her is obvious, but to emphasize this biographical aspect only would be to underestimate the seriousness of Wollstonecraft's thinking about issues of social and

---

[12] David Hume, 'Of the Rise and Progress of the Human Sciences', in *Selected Essays*, ed. Stephen Copley and Andrew Edgar (Oxford, 1996), 69.

[13] Hume, 'Of Essay Writing', *Selected Essays*, 3.

[14] See the excellent discussion in Greg Claeys, 'The Divine Creature and the Female Citizen', in Glenn Burgess and Matthew Festenstein (eds.), *English Radicalism, 1550–1850* (Cambridge, 2007), 115–34.

economic change and their effects on human morals and manners
that runs throughout the book.[15]

Reception and Afterlife

A Short Residence was immediately popular, and translated into
several European languages, including Swedish, with an American
edition quickly appearing, shepherded through the press by her
friend the Irish radical Archibald Hamilton Rowan. The personal
aspects of the book have always been emphasized by later scholars
and readers, and there remains a strong urge to read it as straight-
forwardly autobiographical.[16] Naively treating *A Short Residence*
as a map of Wollstonecraft's heart, however, risks underplaying
the serious work she did back in England on making her journey
into a book, never mind falling into the trap of identifying women's
writing purely with sensibility, an elision that Wollstonecraft
spent her entire career resisting. For all that the book announces
itself as anchored in Wollstonecraft's personal responses, those
responses are continually reflected upon and directed out towards
the world in which they participate (the 'you' addressed in the book
cannot simply be translated into the 'Imlay' of the private letters).
Nevertheless, there is no doubt that Wollstonecraft's contemporaries were themselves eager to read the book in terms of the access it
gave them to what was perceived as her personality and feelings.

Partly this response was itself predicated on the idea, developed further by Godwin, that the book did represent a reorientation from masculine questions of politics and philosophy in the
vindications to a language rooted in the affections. This point is
made to a greater or lesser extent in nearly all the early reviews of

[15] Useful analyses of the cross-currents of Wollstonecraft's critiques of commerce,
and their implications for the condition of women discussed in the next paragraph, are
to be found in Favret, *Romantic Correspondence*, and in Harriet Guest's *Small Change:
Women, Learning, Patriotism* (Chicago, 2000), 303–12.

[16] The letters to Imlay in Appendix 3 are reproduced from the *Posthumous Works*
(1798), edited by Godwin, primarily to enable the reader to judge for herself as to the
differences from *A Short Residence*. The manuscripts no longer exist. Godwin seems to
have cut all references to the business reasons behind Wollstonecraft's journey from the
versions he published. The chapter from Godwin's *Memoirs* which covers Wollstonecraft's
time in Scandinavia is reproduced in Appendix 4.

Wollstonecraft's book, although it is given most emphasis in the more conservative journals, including the *British Critic*, where it is welcomed as a corrective to an inappropriate interest in politics and philosophy, 'joining to a *masculine* understanding, the finer sensibilities of a female'. Obviously unaware of the exact nature of her relationship to Imlay, which was at the centre of the general outcry against Wollstonecraft after the revelations in Godwin's *Memoir*, the same journal seems to give its limited approval to the fact that the book records the experiences of a wife and mother (even if it notes the latter have not been without their trials): 'The thrilling sensation of maternal tenderness has been excited towards an infant; and the pang of misplaced affection inflicted by a husband.' Even so the espousal in the book of a religion of nature with little mention of institutions prevented either the *British Critic* or the *Monthly Mirror* giving Wollstonecraft's book their endorsement. For the *British Critic* the fears and anxieties about the future expressed throughout the book would find a better '*refuge from sorrow*, in feelings and in hopes, prompted by something better than *a strong imagination, the only solace* she now *knows for a bleeding heart*'. The more liberal reviews also recognized the turn towards feeling in the book, but do not so obviously render it in terms of a softening of her '*masculine*' understanding. Indeed the *Monthly Review* regarded the book as an affirmation of her previous strength of mind: 'We have on several former occasions paid our willing tribute of respect to the strong—or, if the fair traveller will accept the epithet as a compliment, the *masculine*—mind of this female philosopher; and these Letters furnish us with new inducements to repeat it.' The *Analytical*, for which Wollstonecraft had effectively been a staff writer, also recognized the personal and desultory nature of the book, but noted that 'from a mind so well stored, and exercised, as this writer's, the easy unsolicited effusions of the moment, in a work of this kind, are preferable to artificial arrangements'. For both of these journals the imaginative and sentimental aspects of the book did not take precedence over its reflections on history and society.[17]

---

[17] Appendix 5 reproduces excerpts from a number of contemporary reviews, including all those quoted above.

The series of striking reveries running through the book certainly hit home with many readers, not least in the imaginations of the poets Samuel Taylor Coleridge and Robert Southey. In April 1797 Southey wrote to his brother Tom: 'Have you ever met with Mary Wollstonecroft's [*sic*] letters from Sweden and Norway? She has made me in love with a cold climate, and frost and snow, with a northern moonlight.'[18] Typically his friend Coleridge's first response was about the question of religion, which always troubled his relationship with writers with whom—at this time at least—he might have otherwise been in sympathy politically. A notebook entry written some time in the autumn of 1796 suggests he had read the qualms of reviews like the one in the *British Critic*, but perhaps not the book itself: 'Epistle to Mrs Wolstoncraft [*sic*] urging her to Religion. Read her Travels'.[19] For a long time now it has been thought that the moonlit scenes admired by Southey made their way into Coleridge's 'Rime of The Ancient Mariner'.[20] The opening of another Coleridge poem 'Frost at Midnight'—first published in 1798 by Wollstonecraft's publisher Joseph Johnson—seems indebted to the striking reverie in Letter I, where Wollstonecraft moves from watching her baby under a moonlit sky to a consideration of the operations of a sympathy that link her to the whole of mankind:

I have then considered myself as a particle broken off from the grand mass of mankind;—I was alone, till some involuntary sympathetic emotion, like the attraction of adhesion, made me feel that I was still a part of a mighty whole, from which I could not sever myself. (p. 12)[21]

Coleridge's poem takes off from the same quiet domestic scenario, before turning into a reflection on the operations of 'dim sympathies', which in turn expands into an affirmation of God's hand in nature:

[18] 'To Thomas Southey, April 28, 1797', *The Life and Correspondence of the Late Robert Southey*, ed. C. C. Southey, 6 vols. (London, 1849), i. 311.

[19] *The Notebooks of Samuel Taylor Coleridge*, ed. Kathleen Coburn, i: *1794–1804*, Fo. 76. This interpretation depends on 'read' being an imperative.

[20] See John Livingston Lowes, *The Road to Xanadu: A Study in the Ways of the Imagination*, 2nd rev. ed. (London, 1951), 161–2.

[21] The connection is made by Guest, *Small Change*, 309–10.

Of that eternal language, which thy God
Utters, who from eternity doth teach
Himself in all, and all things in himself.

Except, of course, Wollstonecraft's reverie is more sceptical and exploratory, and does not come to rest in religious affirmation. Perhaps, therefore, among many other things, 'Frost at Midnight' could be understood as Coleridge's epistle to Wollstonecraft on religion.

Coleridge's poem was written a month or so after Godwin's hurriedly composed memoir of his wife was published. Godwin's account is committed to the idea of *A Short Residence* as the autobiographical record of a tortured soul: 'The occasional harshness and ruggedness of character, that diversify her Vindication of the Rights of Woman, here totally disappear' (pp. 155–6). Godwin was heavily invested in an idea of his former wife as primarily a creature of sensibility. Not everyone was happy with this account, including Mary Hays and Joseph Johnson, but it was enormously influential. Godwin's memoir played an important part in fixing an image of Mary as a wounded heart, supported by details of (and letters from) her relationships with Fuseli and Imlay. The response was far from sympathetic; it was mostly one of outrage, overturning all the positive responses to her travel book, and fixing her in the public imagination as the republican virago of satires in the *Anti-Jacobin* newspaper and Richard Polwhele's vicious poem *The Unsex'd Females* (1798). Godwin's *Memoirs* and the reaction against them had a double consequence for *A Short Residence*. He obscured the experimental brilliance and diversity in the book in order to produce the idea of its author as a creature of throbbing sensibility. Worse, the reaction against the personal details used to flesh out Godwin's portrait ensured that the initial positive response to Wollstonecraft's book was sunk with the reputation of the author. Indeed, even twenty years later, Godwin's account was still influential enough to inspire an entire poem on the theme: Thomas Brown's *The Wanderer in Norway* (1816), written for 'a female friend, who had expressed a desire of reading [Wollstonecraft's book]'. Brown rewrites Wollstonecraft's reveries as a study of 'the first great misery of having yielded to guilty passion' in defence of those 'high principles of conduct, which no mind, however ardent in its general admiration of virtue, can abandon with impunity, and without the strength of which no powers are strong'. [22]

Even so, later literary travellers to Scandinavia felt they had at least to acknowledge Wollstonecraft's presence there before them. The Frenchman de La Tocnaye, no friend either of Wollstonecraft's politics or her experiment with sentimental travel writing à la Sterne, showed a malicious delight at the scandal her book had caused among the women of polite society in Gothenburg.[23] When Thomas Malthus visited Scandinavia in 1799, his travelling companion Edward Clarke almost certainly took a copy of Wollstonecraft's book with him. His published account attempts to rebut some of her critiques of the 'domestic slavery' suffered by women in Norway, but even he noticed that her signature was to be seen on the walls of the ancient house owned by Peder Anker, among those of the great and the good.[24] Evidently much more thrilled to be treading after Wollstonecraft was the artist J. W. Edy, who on adding his own name to the others on the wall of the house 'perceived that of Mary Wolstencraft not very distant'.[25] Others had even more reason to be proud of following in Wollstonecraft's footsteps, even if only metaphorically. Travelling through France in 1814, towards the sublime landscapes of Switzerland, where Wollstonecraft had hoped to meet Imlay after the trip to Scandinavia, Percy Shelley read aloud from *A Short Residence* to Wollstonecraft's daughter Mary Shelley.[26] The book must have provided a dramatic and compelling introduction to the personality of the mother she never knew. For two young

[22] Thomas Brown, *The Wanderer in Norway, with Other Poems*, 2nd edn. (London, 1816), 23, 25. A footnote, p. 14, makes it clear that Brown's poem was based on Godwin's memoir as much as on Wollstonecraft's book itself.

[23] Tocnaye, *Promenade*, 25.

[24] Edward Daniel Clarke, *Travels in Various Countries of Europe, Asia and Africa*, part 3, section 2 (London, 1823), 30 and 22.

[25] *Boydell's Picturesque Scenery of Norway; with the Principal Towns from the Naze by the Route of Christiania, to the Magnificent Pass of the Swinesund; from Original Drawings made on the spot, and engraved by John William Edy, with Remarks and Observations Made in a Tour through the Country* (London, 1820), plate 48 [n.p.].

[26] *The Journals of Mary Shelley 1814–1844*, ed. Paul R. Feldman and Diana Scott-Kilvert, 2 vols. (Oxford, 1987), i. 22.

radicals still searching for signs of progress in a Europe coming to terms with the defeat of the French Revolution, it would have provided the example of a mind still committed to freedom of enquiry and hope for the future in the face of political defeat and personal despair. For modern readers it still provides the most immediate introduction to the experimental mind of Mary Wollstonecraft.

NOTE ON THE TEXT

THIS edition is based on the 1796 first edition. Changes are by and large restricted to what are probably typesetter's errors. Spelling and place names have been left as they were in the first edition, except where they might cause confusion. The notes give most modern English equivalents for Scandinavian place names. Wollstonecraft's habit of putting adjectives derived from proper nouns in lower case—as in 'swedish'—has been brought into line with modern conventions. Quotation marks have been standardized to single throughout.

Imlay's commission (Appendix 1) has been transcribed from the original in the Abinger Collection of the Bodleian Library by the editors. We are grateful for the permission of the Bodleian Library to produce it here. Wollstonecraft's letter to the Danish Prime Minister (Appendix 2) is transcribed from a copy generously provided by Gunnar Molden. Any errors are the fault of the editors. Wollstonecraft's letters to Imlay (Appendix 3) are taken from the first edition of the *Posthumous Works* (details are given at the start of the Appendix). For Godwin's editorial practice and a recent edition of Wollstonecraft's letters, see *The Collected Letters of Mary Wollstonecraft*, ed. Janet Todd, esp. p. xiv.

All footnotes are by Wollstonecraft. Asterisks in the text indicate an editorial note at the back of the book.

SELECT BIBLIOGRAPHY

Critical Editions

Poston, Carol H. (ed.), *Letters Written During a Short Residence in Sweden, Norway, and Denmark* (Lincoln, Nebr., 1976).

Holmes, Richard (ed.), *A Short Residence in Sweden, Norway and Denmark and Memoirs of the Author of A Vindication of the Rights of Woman* (Harmondsworth, 1987).

Todd, Janet, and Butler, Marilyn (eds.), *The Works of Mary Wollstonecraft*, 7 vols. (London, 1989), volume vi.

Related Writings by Wollstonecraft

Todd, Janet (ed.), *The Collected Letters of Mary Wollstonecraft* (Harmondsworth, 2003).

——and Butler, Marilyn (eds.), *The Works of Mary Wollstonecraft*, 7 vols. (London, 1989).

Wardle, Ralph M. (ed.), *Collected Letters of Mary Wollstonecraft* (Ithaca, NY, 1979).

Biography and General Criticism

Barker-Benfield, G. J., 'Mary Wollstonecraft: Eighteenth-Century Commonwealthwoman', *Journal of the History of Ideas*, 50 (1989), 95–115.

Claeys, Greg, 'The Divine Creature and the Female Citizen', in Glenn Burgess and Matthew Festenstein (eds.), *English Radicalism, 1550–1850* (Cambridge, 2007), 115–34.

Conger, Syndy McMillen, *Mary Wollstonecraft and the Language of Sensibility* (Rutherford, NJ, 1994).

Emerson, Oliver Farrar, 'Notes on Gilbert Imlay, Early American Writer', *PMLA: Publications of the Modern Language Association of America*, 39 (1924), 406–39.

Falco, Maria J. (ed.), *Feminist Interpretations of Mary Wollstonecraft* (University Park, Pa., 1996).

Ferguson, Frances, 'Wollstonecraft our Contemporary', in Linda Kauffman (ed.), *Gender and Theory: Dialogues in Feminist Criticism* (Oxford, 1989), 51–62.

Godwin, William, *Memoirs of the Author of A Vindication of the Rights of Woman*, ed. Pamela Clemit and Gina Luria Walker (Peterborough, 2001).

Gubar, Susan, 'Feminist Misogyny: Mary Wollstonecraft and the Paradox of "It Takes One to Know One"', *Feminist Studies*, 20 (1994), 453–73.

Hays, Mary, 'Memoirs of Mary Wollstonecraft', *Annual Necrology, 1797–8* (London, 1800), 411–60.

Johnson, Claudia L. (ed.), *The Cambridge Companion to Mary Wollstonecraft* (Cambridge, 2002).

Jones, Chris, 'Mary Wollstonecraft's Vindications and their Political Tradition', in Johnson (ed.), *Cambridge Companion*.

Jump, Harriet Devine, *Mary Wollstonecraft: Writer* (Brighton, 1994).

——*Lives of the Great Romantics: Mary Wollstonecraft* (London, 1999).

——*Mary Wollstonecraft and the Critics, 1790–2001*, 2 vols. (London, 2003).

Kaplan, Cora, 'Mary Wollstonecraft's Reception and Legacies', in Johnson (ed.), *Cambridge Companion*.

Kay, Carol, 'Canon, Ideology, and Gender: Mary Wollstonecraft's Critique of Adam Smith', *New Political Science*, 15 (1986), 63–76.

Kelly, Gary, *Revolutionary Feminism: The Mind and Career of Mary Wollstonecraft* (New York, 1992).

Khin Zaw, Susan, 'The Reasonable Heart: Mary Wollstonecraft's View of the Relation between Reason and Feeling in Morality, Moral Psychology, and Moral Development', *Hypatia*, 13 (1998), 78–117.

Moore, Jane, *Mary Wollstonecraft* (Plymouth, 1999).

Poovey, Mary, *The Proper Lady and the Woman Writer: Ideology as Style in the Works of Mary Wollstonecraft, Mary Shelley and Jane Austen* (Chicago, 1984).

Sapiro, Virginia, *A Vindication of Political Virtue: The Political Theory of Mary Wollstonecraft* (Chicago, 1992).

Swift, Simon, 'Mary Wollstonecraft and the "Reserve of Reason"', *Studies in Romanticism*, 45 (2006), 3–24.

Taylor, Barbara, *Mary Wollstonecraft and the Feminist Imagination* (Cambridge, 2003).

Todd, Janet, *Mary Wollstonecraft: A Revolutionary Life* (London, 2000).

Tomalin, Claire, *The Life and Death of Mary Wollstonecraft* (London, 1974; rev. edn. Harmondsworth, 1992).

Wardle, Ralph M., *Mary Wollstonecraft: A Critical Biography* (Lawrence, Kan., 1951).

——'Mary Wollstonecraft: *Analytical Reviewer*', *PMLA* 62 (1947), 1000–9.

Criticism on A Short Residence

Adickes, Sandra, *The Social Quest: The Expanded Vision of Four Women Travelers in the Era of the French Revolution* (New York, 1991).

Bohls, Elizabeth A., 'Mary Wollstonecraft's Anti-Aesthetics', in her *Women Travel Writers and the Language of Aesthetics, 1716–1818* (Cambridge, 1995).

Buss, Helen M., Macdonald, D. L. and McWhir, Anne (eds.), *Mary Wollstonecraft and Mary Shelley: Writing Lives* (Waterloo, Ont., 2001).

Buus, Stephanie, 'Bound for Scandinavia: Mary Wollstonecraft's Promethean Journey in *Letters Written during a Short Residence in Sweden, Norway, and Denmark*', *Scandinavica: An International Journal of Scandinavian Studies*, 40 (2001), 241–61.

Chaney, Christine, 'The Rhetorical Strategies of "Tumultuous Emotions": Wollstonecraft's *Letters Written in Sweden*', *Journal of Narrative Theory*, 34 (2004), 277–303.

Conger, Syndy M., 'The Sentimental Logic of Wollstonecraft's Prose', *Prose Studies*, 10 (1987), 143–58.

—— 'Three Unlikely Fellow Travellers: Mary Wollstonecraft, Yorick, Samuel Johnson', *Studies on Voltaire and the Eighteenth Century*, 305 (1992), 1667–8.

—— 'The Power of the Unnamed You in Mary Wollstonecraft's *Letters Written during a Short Residence in Sweden, Norway, and Denmark*', in Helen M. Buss, D. L. Macdonald, and Anne McWhir (eds.), *Mary Wollstonecraft and Mary Shelley: Writing Lives* (Waterloo, Ont., 2001), 43–53.

Ebert, Antje, 'I May Be a Little Partial ("Je suis peut-être un peu partiale"): Constructions d'images nationales de soi et des autres dans les *Letters Written during a Short Residence in Sweden, Norway and Denmark* de Mary Wollstonecraft', *Revue germanique internationale*, 16 (2001), 27–45, 186–7.

Favret, Mary, *Romantic Correspondence: Women, Politics and the Fiction of Letters* (Cambridge, 1993).

Furniss, Tom, 'Mary Wollstonecraft's French Revolution', in Johnson (ed.), *Cambridge Companion*.

Guerra, Lia, 'Unexpected Symmetries: Samuel Johnson and Mary Wollstonecraft on the Northern Road', *Textus: English Studies in Italy*, 18 (2005), 93–106.

Guest, Harriet, *Small Change: Women, Learning, Patriotism, 1750–1810* (Chicago, 2000).

Harper, Lila Marz, *Solitary Travelers: Nineteenth-Century Women's Travel Narratives and the Scientific Vocation* (Madison, NJ, 2001).

—— 'The Stigma of Emotions: Mary Wollstonecraft's Travel Writing', *Journeys: The International Journal of Travel and Travel Writing*, 2 (2001), 45–63.

Heng, Mary, 'Tell Them No Lies: Reconstructed Truth in Wollstonecraft's *A Short Residence in Sweden*', *Journal of Narrative Technique*, 28 (1998), 366–87.

Holmes, Richard, 'Introduction', *A Short Residence in Sweden, Norway and Denmark and Memoirs of the Author of A Vindication of the Rights of Woman* (Harmondsworth, 1987).

Jacobus, Mary, 'In Love with a Cold Climate: Traveling with Wollstonecraft', in *First Things: Reading the Maternal Imaginary* (New York, 1995).

—— 'Intimate Connections: Scandalous Memoirs and Epistolary Indiscretion', in Elizabeth Eger, Charlotte Grant, Clíona Ó Gallchoir, and Penny Warburton (eds.), *Women, Writing and the Public Sphere, 1700–1830* (Cambridge, 2001), 274–89.

Jones, Angela D., ' "When a Woman so Far Outsteps her Proper Sphere": Counter-Romantic Tourism', in Linda S. Coleman (ed.), *Women's Life-Writing: Finding Voice/Building Community* (Bowling Green, OH, 1997), 209–38.

Juengel, Scott, 'Countenancing History: Mary Wollstonecraft, Samuel Stanhope Smith, and Enlightenment Racial Science', *ELH*, 68 (2001), 897–927.

Kautz, Beth Dolan, 'Mary Wollstonecraft's Salutary Picturesque: Curing Melancholia in the Landscape', *European Romantic Review*, 13 (2002), 35–48.

Kennard, Lawrence R., 'Reveries of Reality: Mary Wollstonecraft's Poetics of Sensibility', in Buss, Macdonald, and McWhir (eds.), *Mary Wollstonecraft and Mary Shelley: Writing Lives*, 55–68.

Khalip, Jacques, 'A Disappearance in the World: Wollstonecraft and Melancholy Skepticism', *Criticism: A Quarterly for Literature and the Arts*, 47 (2005), 85–106.

Labbe, Jacqueline, 'A Family Romance: Mary Wollstonecraft, Mary Godwin, and Travel', *Genre: Forms of Discourse and Culture*, 25 (1992), 211–28.

Mills, Sara, 'Written on the Landscape: Mary Wollstonecraft's *Letters Written during a Short Residence in Sweden, Norway, and Denmark*', in Amanda Gilroy (ed.), *Romantic Geographies: Discourses of Travel, 1775–1844* (Manchester, 2000), 19–34.

Molden, Gunnar, 'Sølvbriggen Maria Margrete: ut av historiens mørke', *Norsk Sjøfartsmuseum: Årsberetning. 1995* (Oslo, 1996), 139–54.

Moore, Jane, 'Plagiarism with a Difference: Subjectivity in "Kubla Khan" and *Letters Written during a Short Residence in Sweden, Norway and Denmark*', in Stephen Copley and John Whale (eds.), *Beyond Romanticism: New Approaches to Texts and Contexts 1780–1832* (London, 1992), 140–59.

Moskal, Jeanne, 'The Picturesque and the Affectionate in Wollstonecraft's *Letters from Norway*', *Modern Language Quarterly*, 52 (1991), 263–94.

Myers, Mitzi, 'Wollstonecraft's *Letters Written . . . in Sweden*: Towards Romantic Autobiography', *Studies in Eighteenth-Century Culture*, 8 (1979), 165–85.

Nyström, Per, *Mary Wollstonecraft's Scandinavian Journey*, Acts of the Royal Society of Arts and Letters of Gothenburg, Humaniora 17 (Gothenburg, 1980).

Parks, George B., 'The Turn to the Romantic in the Travel Literature of the Eighteenth Century', *Modern Language Quarterly*, 25 (1964), 22–33.

Perkins, Pam, 'Mary Wollstonecraft's Scandinavian Journey', *Scandinavian-Canadian Studies*, 10 (1997), 1–21.

Richards, Cynthia, 'Fair Trade: The Language of Love and Commerce in Mary Wollstonecraft's *Letters Written during a Short Residence in Sweden, Norway, and Denmark*', *Studies in Eighteenth-Century Culture*, 30 (2001), 71–89.

Ryall, Anka, 'A Vindication of Struggling Nature: Mary Wollstonecraft's Scandinavia', *Nordlit: Arbeidstidsskrift i litteratur*, 1 (1997), 127–49.

—— and Sandbach-Dahlström, Catherine, *Mary Wollstonecraft's Journey to Scandinavia: Essays* (Stockholm, 2003).

Swaab, Peter, 'Romantic Self-Representation: The Example of Mary Wollstonecraft's *Letters in Sweden*', in Vincent Newey and Philip Shaw (eds.), *Mortal Pages, Literary Lives: Studies in Nineteenth-Century Autobiography* (Aldershot, 1996).

Ty, Eleanor, 'Writing as a Daughter: Autobiography in Wollstonecraft's Travelogue', in Marlene Kadar (ed.), *Essays on Life Writing: From Genre to Critical Practice* (Toronto, 1992), 61–77.

—— ' "The History of my Own Heart": Inscribing Self, Inscribing Desire in Wollstonecraft's *Letters from Norway*', in Buss, Macdonald, and McWhir (eds.), *Mary Wollstonecraft and Mary Shelley: Writing Lives*, 69–84.

Weiss, Deborah, 'Suffering, Sentiment, and Civilization: Pain and Politics in Mary Wollstonecraft's *Short Residence*', *Studies in Romanticism*, 45 (2006), 199–221.

Whale, John, 'Death in the Face of Nature: Self, Society and Body in Wollstonecraft's *Letters Written in Sweden, Norway, and Denmark*', *Romanticism*, 1 (1995), 177–92.

Yousef, Nancy, 'Wollstonecraft, Rousseau and the Revision of Romantic Subjectivity', *Studies in Romanticism*, 38 (1999), 537–57.

Contextual Criticism

Barker-Benfield, G. J., *The Culture of Sensibility: Sex and Society in Eighteenth-Century Britain* (Chicago, 1992).

Barton, H. Arnold, *Scandinavia in the Revolutionary Era 1760–1815* (Minneapolis, 1986).

Benedict, Barbara, *Framing Feeling: Sentiment and Style in English Prose Fiction* (New York, 1994).

Braithwaite, Helen, *Romanticism, Publishing, and Dissent: Joseph Johnson and the Cause of Liberty* (Basingstoke, 2002).

Butler, Marilyn (ed.), *Burke, Paine, Godwin, and the Revolution Controversy* (Cambridge, 1984).

Davidson, Jenny, *Hypocrisy and the Politics of Politeness: Manners and Morals from Locke to Austen* (Cambridge, 2004).

Ellis, Markman, *The Politics of Sensibility: Race, Gender and Commerce in the Sentimental Novel* (Cambridge, 1996).

Evans, Chris, *Debating the Revolution: Britain in the 1790s* (London, 2006).

Hampsher-Monk, Iain (ed.), *The Impact of the French Revolution* (Cambridge, 2005).

Jones, Chris, *Radical Sensibility: Literature and Ideas in the 1790s* (London, 1993).

Kaplan, Cora, *Sea Changes: Essays on Culture and Feminism* (London, 1986).

Leask, Nigel, *Curiosity and the Aesthetics of Travel Writing, 1770–1840: 'From an Antique Land'* (Oxford, 2002).

Todd, Janet, *Sensibility: An Introduction* (London, 1986).

Tyson, Gerald P., *Joseph Johnson: A Liberal Publisher* (Iowa City, 1979).

Verhoeven, Wil, *Gilbert Imlay: Citizen of the World* (London, 2008).

Whale, John, *Imagination under Pressure, 1789–1832* (Cambridge, 2000).

Internet Resources

Online texts of *Letters written during a Short Residence in Sweden, Norway and Denmark*:

<http://www.gutenberg.org/dirs/3/5/2/3529/3529.txt>.

<http://ebooks.adelaide.edu.au/w/wollstonecraft/mary/w864l>.

Todd Janet, 'Mary Wollstonecraft: A "Speculative and Dissenting Spirit"':<http://www.bbc.co.uk/history/british/empire_seapower/wollstonecraft>.

Further Reading in Oxford World's Classics

Burke, Edmund, *A Philosophical Enquiry into the Origin of our Ideas of the Sublime and the Beautiful*, ed. Adam Phillips.

Wollstonecraft, Mary, *Mary* and *The Wrongs of Woman*, ed. Gary Kelly.

——*A Vindication of the Rights of Men* and *A Vindication of the Rights of Woman*, ed. Janet Todd.

A CHRONOLOGY OF MARY WOLLSTONECRAFT

1759 (27 April) born in Spitalfields, London, second of seven children, to John and Elizabeth (Dickson) Wollstonecraft.

1765 Family moves to another part of the outskirts of London; frequent moves thereafter. American colonists resist British taxation.

1768 Family moves to Beverley in Yorkshire; educated at a day-school; friendship with Jane Arden. Riots in London over the trial of popular MP John Wilkes.

1775 Family moves to Hoxton, outskirts of London; befriended by Mr Clare, retired clergyman, and his wife; through them meets Fanny Blood, aged 18, and develops intense friendship with her. War of American Independence begins.

1776 (Spring) family moves to Laugharne, Carmarthenshire. American Declaration of Independence; Jacques Necker made finance minister in France.

1777 (Spring) family moves to Walworth, outskirts of London. French troops arrive to support American colonists; Habeas Corpus suspended in Britain to repress political protest.

1778 Finds home life disagreeable and leaves to be paid companion of Sarah Dawson, merchant's widow, at Bath and Windsor, for two years; suffers from depression and illness. France allies with American colonists; British forces capture French posts in India.

1781 (Autumn) called home by mother's deteriorating health. British army surrenders to Americans at Yorktown; British forces advance in India.

1782 (Spring) mother dies; (October) sister Eliza marries Meredith Bishop and bears a daughter, but develops mental illness. Whig government comes to power in Britain; Ireland granted an independent parliament.

1784 (January) persuades Eliza to leave her husband and child; with Fanny Blood, they start a school at Newington Green, outskirts of London; meets Richard Price and Samuel Johnson. William Pitt heads government after parliamentary election.

1785 (February) Fanny Blood marries Hugh Skeys, merchant, in Lisbon, Portugal; (summer) MW possibly has a suitor; (November) goes to Lisbon to attend Fanny in childbirth, but Fanny and the child die; while voyaging home forces ship's captain to assist another ship in a storm. Pitt's motion for parliamentary reform is defeated.

1786 (Summer) school closed; suffers from depression; accepts position as governess to daughters of Lord and Lady Kingsborough; (September) joins the family at their estate in Mitchelstown, county Cork, Ireland; spends winter season with them in Dublin; friendships with Henry Gabell and John Hewlett, clergymen, and George Ogle, MP for Wexford. Pitt establishes sinking fund to reduce the national debt.

1787 *Thoughts on the Education of Daughters* published early in the year by Joseph Johnson; (summer) during stay at Bristol Hot Wells with the Kingsboroughs writes *Mary: A Fiction* and an incomplete philosophical tale, 'The Cave of Fancy'; (August) dismissed by the Kingsboroughs, ostensibly because of their daughter Margaret's attachment to MW; becomes assistant editor and reviewer for Johnson's periodical, the *Analytical Review*; joins Johnson's circle of artists, writers, and intellectuals. Beginning of impeachment of Warren Hastings for maladministration in India; United States Constitution signed.

1788 Publishes *Mary: A Fiction* and *Original Stories from Real Life*, an education manual in fictional form; translates and adapts Necker's *On the Importance of Religious Opinions*; meets Swiss artist Henry Fuseli, Johnson's close friend. Parliamentary motion to abolish slavery; Regency crisis.

1789 Johnson publishes MW's literature anthology, *The Female Reader*, including 'some original pieces', ostensibly by 'Mr. Cresswick, Teacher of Elocution'; with most in Johnson's circle, welcomes French Revolution. (May) French States-General meet to deal with financial crisis and public grievances; (14 July) Parisian crowd seize Bastille prison; (August) French feudal regulations abolished; Declaration of the Rights of Man adopted; (October) Parisian crowd led by women force royal family and court to return to Paris; London Revolution Society congratulates French.

1790 Johnson publishes MW's adaptation of a French translation of de Cambon's education novel, *Young Grandison*; (November) Edmund Burke's *Reflections on the Revolution in France* instigates intense political debate and numerous replies; MW's *A Vindication of the Rights of Men* (published anonymously by Johnson) is one of the first replies to Burke; well received until second edition carries MW's name on the title-page; Richard Price thanks her for it; MW now a public figure; adapts C. G. Salzmann's book of philosophy for youth, *Elements of Morality* (published by Johnson 1790–1). Defeat of parliamentary bill giving civil rights to religious dissenters; nationalist United Irishmen formed.

1791 Meets William Godwin, with Tom Paine and others, at Johnson's; powerful intellectual infatuation with Fuseli; friendship with William Roscoe, Liverpool banker, reformer, and intellectual; begins writing book on female education in response to French government proposal for national education system marginalizing girls. Girondin party lead the French Revolution; new French constitution.

1792 (January) Johnson publishes MW's *A Vindication of the Rights of Woman*; well received; (June) plans excursion of political tourism to Paris with Fuseli, his wife, and Johnson; violence in Paris in late summer and autumn causes postponement of trip; (8 December) leaves alone for Paris. War between France and Prussia and Austria; (August) Parisian crowd attacks Tuileries palace; (September) French citizen army defeats Prussian-Austrian allies; French republic proclaimed, offers assistance to revolutionaries everywhere.

1793 In Paris joins circle of expatriate Britons around Johnson's friend Thomas Christie; meets Helen Maria Williams and others engaged in business with the French government, or engaging in political journalism; plans to meet Girondin political faction, led behind the scenes by Marie Roland; (February) outbreak of war between France and Britain puts MW in danger; she begins an affair with an American businessman, Gilbert Imlay; registered as his wife at the American embassy to avoid being arrested as an enemy alien; moves to outskirts of Paris for greater safety. (January) Louis XVI tried and executed for treason in Paris; (February) France declares war on Britain; Jacobin faction overthrow Girondins and initiate the Terror against counter-Revolutionaries; (October) Christianity abolished in France; Queen Marie Antoinette executed; Girondins guillotined.

1794 (14 May) daughter Fanny born; relationship with Imlay, often away on business, foundering; she suspects him of other affairs; Johnson publishes MW's *An Historical and Moral View of the French Revolution*; it causes little stir. Polish rebellion against Russian rule is suppressed; (July) Jacobins overthrown and many guillotined; demands for peace in British parliament; France abolishes slavery in its colonies; moderate French government formed; leading British political reformers tried for treason.

1795 Imlay living in London; (April) MW leaves France to join him there; discovers his infidelities; (May) attempts suicide but prevented by Imlay; to regain him, she undertakes journey to Scandinavia to recover money owed him by business associates; to meet with Imlay in Germany; plans book of her observations there; (summer) travels through Norway, Sweden, Denmark, and northern Germany, accompanied by daughter Fanny and French servant Marguerite; Imlay reneges on meeting; (October) arrives in London to find Imlay living with an actress; (November) attempts suicide by jumping from Putney Bridge, but rescued by passers-by. (April) food riots in Paris; severe food shortages in parts of Britain; French armies advance in surrounding countries; (November) Directory governs France; Pitt government passes measures to suppress political dissent; Austria withdraws from the war.

1796 (January) Johnson publishes MW's political and feminist travelogue, *Letters written during a short residence in Sweden, Norway, and Denmark*; well received and widely admired; meets Godwin, his friend Thomas Holcroft, Anna Laetitia Barbauld, Sarah Siddons, and other artists, intellectuals, writers, and actors; resumes friendships with Mary Hays and others; resumes reviewing for the *Analytical Review*; (April) calls on Godwin; they see each other frequently thereafter; (summer) begins work on a feminist novel; MW and Godwin become lovers; (December) finds herself pregnant. Pitt negotiates for peace with France; Napoleon assumes command of French armies in Italy, wins spectacular victories; Spain declares war on Britain; formal separation of Prince and Princess of Wales and public dispute over control of their daughter, born in January; parliament votes to pay Prince of Wales's enormous debts.

1797 (March) marries Godwin to avoid public notoriety and damage to profession as a writer; works on 'Letters on the Management of Children'; (30 August) daughter Mary born; (10 September) MW dies of complications of childbirth; friends rally to Godwin; he works on MW's literary remains and a biography of her. (April and June) British naval mutinies; French armies advance in Europe.

1798 Godwin publishes his edition of *Posthumous Works of the Author of A Vindication of the Rights of Woman* (4 vols.) along with *Memoirs* of MW; both are seized on by conservative critics to pillory MW and Godwin; her reputation does not recover for decades.

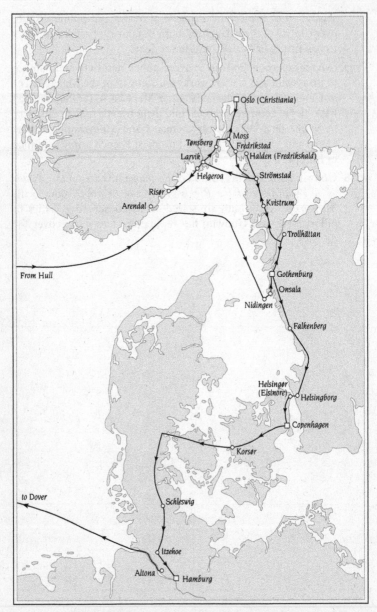

Mary Wollstonecraft's journey through Scandinavia

LETTERS WRITTEN DURING A SHORT RESIDENCE IN SWEDEN, NORWAY, AND DENMARK

ADVERTISEMENT

THE writing travels, or memoirs, has ever been a pleasant employment; for vanity or sensibility always renders it interesting.* In writing these desultory letters, I found I could not avoid being continually the first person—'the little hero of each tale.'* I tried to correct this fault, if it be one, for they were designed for publication; but in proportion as I arranged my thoughts, my letter, I found, became stiff and affected: I, therefore, determined to let my remarks and reflections flow unrestrained, as I perceived that I could not give a just description of what I saw, but by relating the effect different objects had produced on my mind and feelings, whilst the impression was still fresh.

A person has a right, I have sometimes thought, when amused by a witty or interesting egotist, to talk of himself when he can win on our attention by acquiring our affection. Whether I deserve to rank amongst this privileged number, my readers alone can judge—and I give them leave to shut the book, if they do not wish to become better acquainted with me.

My plan was simply to endeavour to give a just view of the present state of the countries I have passed through, as far as I could obtain information during so short a residence; avoiding those details which, without being very useful to travellers who follow the same route, appear very insipid to those who only accompany you in their chair.

LETTER I

ELEVEN days of weariness on board a vessel not intended for the accommodation of passengers have so exhausted my spirits, to say nothing of the other causes, with which you are already sufficiently acquainted, that it is with some difficulty I adhere to my determination of giving you my observations, as I travel through new scenes, whilst warmed with the impression they have made on me.

The captain, as I mentioned to you, promised to put me on shore at Arendall,[1] or Gothenburg, in his way to Elsineur;* but contrary winds obliged us to pass both places during the night. In the morning, however, after we had lost sight of the entrance of the latter bay, the vessel was becalmed; and the captain, to oblige me, hanging out a signal for a pilot, bore down towards the shore.

My attention was particularly directed to the light-house;* and you can scarcely imagine with what anxiety I watched two long hours for a boat to emancipate me—still no one appeared. Every cloud that flitted on the horizon was hailed as a liberator, till approaching nearer, like most of the prospects sketched by hope, it dissolved under the eye into disappointment.

Weary of expectation, I then began to converse with the captain on the subject; and, from the tenour of the information my questions drew forth, I soon concluded, that, if I waited for a boat, I had little chance of getting on shore at this place. Despotism, as is usually the case, I found had here cramped the industry of man.* The pilots being paid by the king, and scantily, they will not run into any danger, or even quit their hovels, if they can possibly avoid it, only to fulfil what is termed their duty. How different is it on the English coast, where, in the most stormy weather, boats immediately hail you, brought out by the expectation of extraordinary profit.

Disliking to sail for Elsineur, and still more to lie at anchor, or cruise about the coast for several days, I exerted all my rhetoric to prevail on the captain to let me have the ship's boat; and though

---

[1] In Norway.

I added the most forcible of arguments, I for a long time addressed him in vain.

It is a kind of rule at sea, not to send out a boat. The captain was a good-natured man; but men with common minds seldom break through general rules. Prudence is ever the resort of weakness; and they rarely go as far as they may in any undertaking, who are determined not to go beyond it on any account. If, however, I had some trouble with the captain, I did not lose much time with the sailors; for they, all alacrity, hoisted out the boat, the moment I obtained permission, and promised to row me to the light-house.

I did not once allow myself to doubt of obtaining a conveyance from thence round the rocks—and then away for Gothenburg—confinement is so unpleasant.

The day was fine; and I enjoyed the water till, approaching the little island, poor Marguerite,* whose timidity always acts as a feeler before her adventuring spirit, began to wonder at our not seeing any inhabitants. I did not listen to her. But when, on landing, the same silence prevailed, I caught the alarm, which was not lessened by the sight of two old men, whom we forced out of their wretched hut. Scarcely human in their appearance,* we with difficulty obtained an intelligible reply to our questions—the result of which was, that they had no boat, and were not allowed to quit their post, on any pretence. But, they informed us, that there was at the other side, eight or ten miles over, a pilot's dwelling; two guineas tempted the sailors to risk the captain's displeasure, and once more embark to row me over.

The weather was pleasant, and the appearance of the shore so grand, that I should have enjoyed the two hours it took to reach it, but for the fatigue which was too visible in the countenances of the sailors who, instead of uttering a complaint, were, with the thoughtless hilarity peculiar to them, joking about the possibility of the captain's taking advantage of a slight westerly breeze, which was springing up, to sail without them. Yet, in spite of their good humour, I could not help growing uneasy when the shore, receding, as it were, as we advanced, seemed to promise no end to their toil. This anxiety increased when, turning into the most picturesque bay* I ever saw, my eyes sought in vain for the vestige of a human habitation. Before I could determine what step to take in such a dilemma, for I could not bear to think of returning to the ship, the sight of a barge relieved me, and we hastened towards it for information. We were immediately directed to pass some jutting rocks when we should see a pilot's hut.

There was a solemn silence in this scene, which made itself be felt. The sun-beams that played on the ocean, scarcely ruffled by the lightest breeze, contrasted with the huge, dark rocks, that looked like the rude materials of creation forming the barrier of unwrought space, forcibly struck me; but I should not have been sorry if the cottage had not appeared equally tranquil. Approaching a retreat where strangers, especially women, so seldom appeared, I wondered that curiosity did not bring the beings who inhabited it to the windows or door. I did not immediately recollect that men who remain so near the brute creation, as only to exert themselves to find the food necessary to sustain life, have little or no imagination to call forth the curiosity necessary to fructify the faint glimmerings of mind which entitles them to rank as lords of the creation.—Had they either, they could not contentedly remain rooted in the clods they so indolently cultivate.

Whilst the sailors went to seek for the sluggish inhabitants, these conclusions occurred to me; and, recollecting the extreme fondness which the Parisians ever testify for novelty, their very curiosity appeared to me a proof of the progress they had made in refinement. Yes; in the art of living—in the art of escaping from the cares which embarrass the first steps towards the attainment of the pleasures of social life.

The pilots informed the sailors that they were under the direction of a lieutenant retired from the service, who spoke English; adding, that they could do nothing without his orders; and even the offer of money could hardly conquer their laziness, and prevail on them to accompany us to his dwelling. They would not go with me alone which I wanted them to have done, because I wished to dismiss the sailors as soon as possible. Once more we rowed off, they following tardily, till, turning round another bold protuberance of the rocks, we saw a boat making towards us, and soon learnt that it was the lieutenant himself, coming with some earnestness to see who we were.

To save the sailors any further toil, I had my baggage instantly removed into his boat; for, as he could speak English, a previous parley was not necessary; though Marguerite's respect for me could hardly keep her from expressing the fear, strongly marked on her countenance, which my putting ourselves into the power of a strange man excited. He pointed out his cottage; and, drawing near to it, I was not sorry to see a female figure, though I had not, like Marguerite, been thinking of robberies, murders, or the other evil* which instantly, as the sailors would have said, runs foul of a woman's imagination.

On entering, I was still better pleased to find a clean house, with some degree of rural elegance. The beds were of muslin, coarse it is true, but dazzlingly white; and the floor was strewed over with little sprigs of juniper (the custom, as I afterwards found, of the country), which formed a contrast with the curtains and produced an agreeable sensation of freshness, to soften the ardour of noon. Still nothing was so pleasing as the alacrity of hospitality—all that the house afforded was quickly spread on the whitest linen. —Remember I had just left the vessel, where, without being fastidious, I had continually been disgusted. Fish, milk, butter, and cheese, and I am sorry to add, brandy, the bane of this country, were spread on the board. After we had dined, hospitality made them, with some degree of mystery, bring us some excellent coffee. I did not then know that it was prohibited.*

The good man of the house apologized for coming in continually, but declared that he was so glad to speak English, he could not stay out. He need not have apologized; I was equally glad of his company. With the wife I could only exchange smiles; and she was employed observing the make of our clothes. My hands, I found, had first led her to discover that I was the lady. I had, of course, my quantum of reverences; for the politeness of the north seems to partake of the coldness of the climate, and the rigidity of its iron sinewed rocks. Amongst the peasantry, there is, however, so much of the simplicity of the golden age* in this land of flint—so much overflowing of heart, and fellow-feeling, that only benevolence, and the honest sympathy of nature, diffused smiles over my countenance when they kept me standing, regardless of my fatigue, whilst they dropt courtesy after courtesy.

The situation of this house was beautiful, though chosen for convenience. The master being the officer who commanded all the pilots on the coast, and the person appointed to guard wrecks,* it was necessary for him to fix on a spot that would overlook the whole bay. As he had seen some service, he wore, not without a pride I thought becoming, a badge to prove that he had merited well of his country. It was happy, I thought, that he had been paid in honour; for the stipend he received was little more than twelve pounds a year.—I do not trouble myself or you with the calculation of Swedish ducats. Thus, my friend, you perceive the necessity of *perquisites*.* This same narrow policy runs through every thing. I shall have occasion further to animadvert on it.

Though my host amused me with an account of himself, which gave me an idea of the manners of the people I was about to visit, I was eager to climb the rocks to view the country, and see whether the honest tars had regained their ship. With the help of the lieutenant's telescope I saw the vessel underway with a fair though gentle gale. The sea was calm, playful even as the most shallow stream, and on the vast bason I did not see a dark speck to indicate the boat. My conductors were consequently arrived.

Straying further, my eye was attracted by the sight of some heart's-ease that peeped through the rocks. I caught at it as a good omen, and going to preserve it in a letter* that had not conveyed balm to my heart, a cruel remembrance suffused my eyes; but it passed away like an April shower. If you are deep read in Shakspeare, you will recollect that this was the little western flower tinged by love's dart, which 'maidens call love in idleness.'* The gaiety of my babe was unmixed; regardless of omens or sentiments, she found a few wild strawberries more grateful than flowers or fancies.

The lieutenant informed me that this was a commodious bay. Of that I could not judge, though I felt its picturesque beauty. Rocks were piled on rocks, forming a suitable bulwark to the ocean. Come no further, they emphatically said, turning their dark sides to the waves to augment the idle roar. The view was sterile:

still little patches of earth, of the most exquisite verdure, enamelled with the sweetest wild flowers, seemed to promise the goats and a few straggling cows luxurious herbage. How silent and peaceful was the scene. I gazed around with rapture, and felt more of that spontaneous pleasure which gives credibility to our expectation of happiness, than I had for a long, long time before. I forgot the horrors I had witnessed in France,* which had cast a gloom over all nature, and suffering the enthusiasm of my character, too often, gracious God! damped by the tears of disappointed affection, to be lighted up afresh, care took wing while simple fellow feeling expanded my heart.

To prolong this enjoyment, I readily assented to the proposal of our host to pay a visit to a family, the master of which spoke English, who was the drollest dog in the country, he added, repeating some of his stories, with a hearty laugh.

I walked on, still delighted with the rude beauties of the scene; for the sublime often gave place imperceptibly to the beautiful,* dilating the emotions which were painfully concentrated.

When we entered this abode, the largest I had yet seen, I was introduced to a numerous family; but the father, from whom I was led to expect so much entertainment, was absent. The lieutenant consequently was obliged to be the interpreter of our reciprocal compliments. The phrases were awkwardly transmitted, it is true; but looks and gestures were sufficient to make them intelligible and interesting. The girls were all vivacity, and respect for me could scarcely keep them from romping with my host, who, asking for a pinch of snuff, was presented with a box, out of which an artificial mouse, fastened to the bottom, sprung. Though this trick had doubtless been played time out of mind, yet the laughter it excited was not less genuine.

They were overflowing with civility; but to prevent their almost killing my babe with kindness, I was obliged to shorten my visit; and two or three of the girls accompanied us, bringing with them a part of whatever the house afforded to contribute towards rendering my supper more plentiful; and plentiful in fact it was, though I with difficulty did honour to some of the dishes, not relishing the quantity of sugar and spices put into every thing. At supper my host told me bluntly that I was a woman of observation, for I asked him *men's questions.**

The arrangements for my journey were quickly made; I could only have a car with post-horses,* as I did not chuse to wait till a carriage could be sent for to Gothenburg. The expense of my journey, about one or two and twenty English miles, I found would not amount to more than eleven or twelve shillings, paying, he assured me, generously. I gave him a guinea and a half. But it was with the greatest difficulty that I could make him take so much, indeed any thing for my lodging and fare. He declared that it was next to robbing me, explaining how much I ought to pay on the road. However, as I was positive, he took the guinea for himself; but, as a condition, insisted on accompanying me, to prevent my meeting with any trouble or imposition on the way.

I then retired to my apartment with regret. The night was so fine, that I would gladly have rambled about much longer; yet recollecting that I must rise very early, I reluctantly went to bed: but my senses had been so awake, and my imagination still continued so busy, that I sought for rest in vain. Rising before six, I scented the sweet morning air; I had long before heard the birds twittering to hail the dawning day, though it could scarcely have been allowed to have departed.

Nothing, in fact, can equal the beauty of the northern summer's evening and night; if night it may be called that only wants the glare of day, the full light, which frequently seems so impertinent; for I could write at midnight very well without a candle. I contemplated all nature at rest; the rocks, even grown darker in their appearance, looked as if they partook of the general repose, and reclined more heavily on their foundation.—What, I exclaimed, is this active principle* which keeps me still awake?—Why fly my thoughts abroad when every thing around me appears at home? My child was sleeping with equal calmness—innocent and sweet as the closing flowers.—Some recollections, attached to the idea of home, mingled with reflections respecting the state of society I had been contemplating that evening, made a tear drop on the rosy cheek I had just kissed; and emotions that trembled on the brink of extacy and agony gave a poignancy to my sensations, which made me feel more alive than usual.

What are these imperious sympathies? How frequently has melancholy and even mysanthropy taken possession of me, when the world has disgusted me, and friends have proved unkind. I have then considered myself as a particle broken off from the grand mass of mankind;—I was alone, till some involuntary sympathetic emotion, like the attraction of adhesion,* made me feel that I was still a part of a mighty whole, from which I could not sever myself—not, perhaps, for the reflection has been carried very far, by snapping the thread of an existence which loses its charms in proportion as the cruel experience of life stops or poisons the current of the heart. Futurity, what hast thou not to give to those who know that there is such a thing as happiness! I speak not of philosophical contentment, though pain has afforded them the strongest conviction of it.

After our coffee and milk, for the mistress of the house had been roused long before us by her hospitality, my baggage was taken forward in a boat by my host, because the car could not safely have been brought to the house.

The road at first was very rocky and troublesome; but our driver was careful, and the horses accustomed to the frequent and sudden acclivities and descents; so that not apprehending any danger, I played with my girl, whom I would not leave to Marguerite's care, on account of her timidity.

Stopping at a little inn to bait the horses, I saw the first countenance in Sweden that displeased me, though the man was better dressed than any one who had as yet fallen in my way. An altercation took place between him and my host, the purport of which I could not guess, excepting that I was the occasion of it, be it what it would. The sequel was his leaving the house angrily; and I was immediately informed that he was the custom-house officer. The professional had indeed effaced the national character, for living as he did with these frank hospitable people, still only the exciseman appeared,—the counterpart of some I had met with in England and France. I was unprovided with a passport,* not having entered any great town. At Gothenburg I knew I could immediately obtain one, and only the trouble made me object to the searching my trunks. He blustered for money; but the lieutenant was determined to guard me, according to promise, from imposition.

To avoid being interrogated at the town-gate, and obliged to go in the rain to give an account of myself, merely a form, before we could get the refreshment we stood in need of, he requested us to descend, I might have said step, from our car, and walk into town.

I expected to have found a tolerable inn, but was ushered into a most comfortless one; and, because it was about five o'clock, three or four hours after their dining hour, I could not prevail on them to give me any thing warm to eat.

The appearance of the accommodations obliged me to deliver one of my recommendatory letters, and the gentleman, to whom it was addressed,* sent to look out for a lodging for me whilst I partook of his supper. As nothing passed at this supper to characterize the country, I shall here close my letter.

Your's truly.

LETTER II

GOTHENBURG is a clean airy town, and having been built by the Dutch, has canals running through each street,* and in some of them there are rows of trees that would render it very pleasant were it not for the pavement, which is intolerably bad.

There are several rich commercial houses,* Scotch, French, and Swedish; but the Scotch, I believe, have been the most successful. The commerce and commission business with France since the war,* has been very lucrative, and enriched the merchants, I am afraid, at the expence of the other inhabitants, by raising the price of the necessaries of life.

As all the men of consequence, I mean men of the largest fortune, are merchants, their principal enjoyment is a relaxation from business at the table, which is spread at, I think, too early an hour (between one and two) for men who have letters to write and accounts to settle after paying due respect to the bottle. However, when numerous circles are to be brought together, and when

neither literature nor public amusements furnish topics for conversation, a good dinner appears to be the only centre to rally
round, especially as scandal, the zest of more select parties, can
only be whispered. As for politics, I have seldom found it a subject of continual discussion in a country town in any part of the
world. The politics of the place being on a smaller scale, suits better with the size of their faculties; for, generally speaking, the
sphere of observation determines the extent of the mind.

The more I see of the world, the more I am convinced that
civilization is a blessing not sufficiently estimated by those who have
not traced its progress; for it not only refines our enjoyments, but
produces a variety which enables us to retain the primitive delicacy
of our sensations. Without the aid of the imagination all the pleasures of the senses must sink into grossness, unless continual novelty
serve as a substitute for the imagination, which being impossible, it
was to this weariness, I suppose, that Solomon alluded when he
declared that there was nothing new under the sun!*—nothing for
the common sensations excited by the senses. Yet who will deny that
the imagination and understanding have made many, very many
discoveries since those days, which only seem harbingers of others
still more noble and beneficial. I never met with much imagination
amongst people who had not acquired a habit of reflection; and
in that state of society in which the judgment and taste are not
called forth, and formed by the cultivation of the arts and sciences,
little of that delicacy of feeling and thinking is to be found characterized by the word sentiment. The want of scientific pursuits perhaps
accounts for the hospitality, as well as for the cordial reception
which strangers receive from the inhabitants of small towns.

Hospitality has, I think, been too much praised by travellers as
a proof of goodness of heart, when in my opinion indiscriminate
hospitality is rather a criterion by which you may form a tolerable
estimate of the indolence or vacancy of a head; or, in other words,
a fondness for social pleasures in which the mind not having its
proportion of exercise, the bottle must be pushed about.

These remarks are equally applicable to Dublin,* the most
hospitable city I ever passed through. But I will try to confine my
observations more particularly to Sweden.

It is true I have only had a glance over a small part of it; yet of its present state of manners and acquirements I think I have formed a distinct idea, without having visited the capital, where, in fact, less of a national character is to be found than in the remote parts of the country.

The Swedes pique themselves on their politeness; but far from being the polish of a cultivated mind, it consists merely of tiresome forms and ceremonies. So far indeed from entering immediately into your character, and making you feel instantly at your ease, like the well-bred French, their over-acted civility is a continual restraint on all your actions. The sort of superiority which a fortune gives when there is no superiority of education, excepting what consists in the observance of senseless forms, has a contrary effect than what is intended; so that I could not help reckoning the peasantry the politest people of Sweden, who only aiming at pleasing you, never think of being admired for their behaviour.

Their tables, like their compliments, seem equally a caricature of the French. The dishes are composed, as well as theirs, of a variety of mixtures to destroy the native taste of the food without being as relishing. Spices and sugar are put into every thing, even into the bread; and the only way I can account for their partiality to high-seasoned dishes, is the constant use of salted provisions. Necessity obliges them to lay up a store of dried fish, and salted meat, for the winter; and in summer, fresh meat and fish taste insipid after them. To which may be added the constant use of spirits. Every day, before dinner and supper, even whilst the dishes are cooling on the table, men and women repair to a side-table, and to obtain an appetite, eat bread and butter, cheese, raw salmon, or anchovies, drinking a glass of brandy. Salt fish or meat then immediately follows, to give a further whet to the stomach. As the dinner advances, pardon me for taking up a few minutes to describe what, alas! has detained me two or three hours on the stretch, observing, dish after dish is changed, in endless rotation, and handed round with solemn pace to each guest: but should you happen not to like the first dishes, which was often my case, it is a gross breach of politeness to ask for part of any other till its turn comes. But have patience, and there will be eating enough.

Allow me to run over the acts of a visiting day, not overlooking the interludes.

Prelude a luncheon—then a succession of fish, flesh and fowl for two hours; during which time the desert, I was sorry for the strawberries and cream, rests on the table to be impregnated by the fumes of the viands. Coffee immediately follows in the drawing-room; but does not preclude punch, ale, tea and cakes, raw salmon, &c. A supper brings up the rear, not forgetting the introductory luncheon, almost equalling in removes the dinner. A day of this kind you would imagine sufficient—but a to-morrow and a to-morrow*—A never ending, still beginning feast may be bearable, perhaps, when stern winter frowns, shaking with chilling aspect his hoary locks; but during a summer, sweet as fleeting, let me, my kind strangers, escape sometimes into your fir groves, wander on the margin of your beautiful lakes, or climb your rocks to view still others in endless perspective; which, piled by more than giant's hand, scale the heavens to intercept its rays, or to receive the parting tinge of lingering day—day that, scarcely softened into twilight, allows the freshening breeze to wake, and the moon to burst forth in all her glory to glide with solemn elegance through the azure expanse.

The cow's bell has ceased to tinkle the herd to rest; they have all paced across the heath. Is not this the witching time of night?* The waters murmur, and fall with more than mortal music,* and spirits of peace* walk abroad to calm the agitated breast. Eternity is in these moments: worldly cares melt into the airy stuff that dreams are made of;* and reveries, mild and enchanting as the first hopes of love, or the recollection of lost enjoyment, carry the hapless wight into futurity, who, in bustling life, has vainly strove to throw off the grief which lies heavy at the heart. Good night! A crescent hangs out in the vault before, which woos me to stray abroad:—it is not a silvery reflection of the sun, but glows with all its golden splendour. Who fears the falling dew? It only makes the mown grass smell more fragrant.

Adieu!

LETTER III

THE population of Sweden* has been estimated from two millions and a half to three millions; a small number for such an immense tract of country: of which only so much is cultivated, and that in the simplest manner, as is absolutely necessary to supply the necessaries of life; and near the seashore, from whence herrings are easily procured, there scarcely appears a vestige of cultivation. The scattered huts that stand shivering on the naked rocks, braving the pitiless elements, are formed of logs of wood, rudely hewn; and so little pains are taken with the craggy foundation, that nothing like a pathway points out the door.

Gathered into himself by the cold, lowering his visage to avoid the cutting blast, is it surprising that the churlish pleasure of drinking drams* takes place of social enjoyments amongst the poor, especially if we take into the account, that they mostly live on high-seasoned provisions and rye bread? Hard enough, you may imagine, as it is only baked once a year. The servants also, in most families, eat this kind of bread, and have a different kind of food from their masters, which, in spite of all the arguments I have heard to vindicate the custom, appears to me a remnant of barbarism.

In fact, the situation of the servants in every respect, particularly that of the women, shews how far the Swedes are from having a just conception of rational equality. They are not *termed* slaves; yet a man may strike a man with impunity because he pays him wages; though these wages are so low, that necessity must teach them to pilfer, whilst servility renders them false and boorish. Still the men stand up for the dignity of man, by oppressing the women.* The most menial, and even laborious offices, are therefore left to these poor drudges. Much of this I have seen. In the winter, I am told, they take the linen down to the river, to wash it in the cold water; and though their hands, cut by the ice, are cracked and bleeding, the men, their fellow servants, will not disgrace their manhood by carrying a tub to lighten their burden.

You will not be surprised to hear that they do not wear shoes or stockings, when I inform you that their wages are seldom more than twenty or thirty shillings per annum. It is the custom, I know, to give them a new year's gift, and a present at some other period; but can it all amount to a just indemnity for their labour? The treatment of servants in most countries, I grant, is very unjust; and in England, that boasted land of freedom, it is often extremely tyrannical. I have frequently, with indignation, heard gentlemen declare that they would never allow a servant to answer them; and ladies of the most exquisite sensibility, who were continually exclaiming against the cruelty of the vulgar to the brute creation, have in my presence forgot that their attendants had human feelings, as well as forms. I do not know a more agreeable sight than to see servants part of a family. By taking an interest, generally speaking, in their concerns, you inspire them with one for yours. We must love our servants, or we shall never be sufficiently attentive to their happiness; and how can those masters be attentive to their happiness, who living above their fortunes, are more anxious to outshine their neighbours than to allow their household the innocent enjoyments they earn.

It is, in fact, much more difficult for servants who are tantalized by seeing and preparing the dainties of which they are not to partake, to remain honest, than the poor, whose thoughts are not led from their homely fare; so that, though the servants here are commonly thieves, you seldom hear of house-breaking, or robbery on the highway. The country is, perhaps, too thinly inhabited to produce many of that description of thieves termed footpads,* or highwaymen. They are usually the spawn of great cities; the effect of the spurious desires generated by wealth, rather than the desperate struggles of poverty to escape from misery.

The enjoyment of the peasantry was drinking brandy and coffee, before the latter was prohibited, and the former not allowed to be privately distilled.* The wars carried on by the late king rendering it necessary to increase the revenue, and retain the specie* in the country by every possible means.

The taxes before the reign of Charles the twelfth* were inconsiderable. Since then, the burden has continually been growing heavier, and the price of provisions has proportionably increased; nay, the advantage accruing from the exportation* of corn to France, and rye to Germany, will probably produce a scarcity in both Sweden and Norway, should not a peace put a stop to it this autumn; for speculations of various kinds have already almost doubled the price.

Such are the effects of war, that it saps the vitals even of the neutral countries, who, obtaining a sudden influx of wealth, appear to be rendered flourishing by the destruction which ravages the hapless nations who are sacrificed to the ambition of their governors. I shall not, however, dwell on the vices, though they be of the most contemptible and embruting cast, to which a sudden accession of fortune gives birth, because I believe it may be delivered as an axiom that it is only in proportion to the industry necessary to acquire wealth, that a nation is really benefited by it.

The prohibition of drinking coffee, under a penalty, and the encouragement given to public distilleries, tend to impoverish the poor, who are not affected by the sumptuary laws; for the regent* has lately laid very severe restraints on the article of dress,* which the middling class of people found grievous because it obliged them to throw aside finery that might have lasted them for their lives.[1]

These may be termed vexations; still the death of the king, by saving them from the consequences his ambition would naturally have entailed on them, may be reckoned a blessing.

Besides, the French revolution has not only rendered all the crowned heads more cautious,* but has so decreased every where (excepting amongst themselves) a respect for nobility, that the peasantry have not only lost their blind reverence for their seigniors, but complain, in a manly style, of oppressions which before they did not think of denominating such, because they were taught to consider themselves as a different order of beings. And, perhaps, the efforts which the aristocrats are making here, as well as in every other part of Europe, to secure their sway, will be the most effectual mode of undermining it; taking into the calculation, that the king of Sweden, like most of the potentates

---

[1] The ladies are only allowed to wear black and white silks, and plain muslins, besides other restrictions of a like nature.

of Europe, has continually been augmenting his power by encroaching on the privileges of the nobles.

The well-bred Swedes of the capital are formed on the ancient French model; and they in general speak that language; for they have a knack at acquiring languages, with tolerable fluency. This may be reckoned an advantage in some respects; but it prevents the cultivation of their own, and any considerable advance in literary pursuits.

A sensible writer[1]* has lately observed, (I have not his work by me, therefore cannot quote his exact words) 'that the Americans very wisely let the Europeans make their books and fashions for them.' But I cannot coincide with him in this opinion. The reflection necessary to produce a certain number even of tolerable productions, augments, more than he is aware of, the mass of knowledge in the community. Desultory reading is commonly merely a pastime. But we must have an object to refer our reflections to, or they will seldom go below the surface. As in travelling, the keeping of a journal excites to many useful enquiries that would not have been thought of, had the traveller only determined to see all he could see, without ever asking himself for what purpose. Besides, the very dabbling in literature furnishes harmless topics of conversation; for the not having such subjects at hand, though they are often insupportably fatiguing, renders the inhabitants of little towns prying and censorious. Idleness, rather than ill-nature, gives birth to scandal, and to the observation of little incidents which narrows the mind.* It is frequently only the fear of being talked of, which produces that puerile scrupulosity about trifles incompatible with an enlarged plan of usefulness, and with the basis of all moral principles—respect for the virtues which are not merely the virtues of convention.

I am, my friend, more and more convinced that a metropolis, or an abode absolutely solitary, is the best calculated for the improvement of the heart, as well as the understanding; whether we desire to become acquainted with man, nature, or ourselves. Mixing with mankind, we are obliged to examine our prejudices, and often imperceptibly lose, as we analyze them. And in the country, growing

[1] See Mr. Cooper's Account of America.

intimate with nature, a thousand little circumstances, unseen by vulgar eyes, give birth to sentiments dear to the imagination, and inquiries which expand the soul, particularly when cultivation has not smoothed into insipidity all its originality of character.

I love the country; yet whenever I see a picturesque situation chosen on which to erect a dwelling, I am always afraid of the improvements. It requires uncommon taste to form a whole, and to introduce accommodations and ornaments analogous with the surrounding scene.[1]

I visited, near Gothenburg, a house* with improved land about it, with which I was particularly delighted. It was close to a lake embosomed in pine clad rocks. In one part of the meadows, your eye was directed to the broad expanse; in another, you were led into a shade, to see a part of it, in the form of a river, rush amongst the fragments of rocks and roots of trees; nothing seemed forced. One recess, particularly grand and solemn, amongst the towering cliffs, had a rude stone table, and seat, placed in it, that might have served for a druid's haunt; whilst a placid stream below enlivened the flowers on its margin, where light-footed elves would gladly have danced their airy rounds.

Here the hand of taste was conspicuous, though not obtrusive, and formed a contrast with another abode in the same neighbourhood, on which much money had been lavished: where Italian

---

[1] With respect to gardening in England, I think we often make an egregious blunder by introducing too much shade; not considering that the shade which our climate requires need not be very thick. If it keep off the intense heat of the sun, and afford a solitary retirement, it is sufficient. But in many great gardens, or pleasure-grounds, the sun's rays can scarcely ever penetrate. These may amuse the eye; yet they are not *home walks* to which the owner can retire to enjoy air and solitude; for, excepting during an extraordinary dry summer, they are damp and chill. For the same reason, grottoes are absurd in this temperate climate. An umbrageous tree will afford sufficient shelter from the most ardent heat, that we ever feel. To speak explicitly, the usefulness of a garden ought to be conspicuous, because it ought not to be planted for the season when nature wantons in her prime; for the whole country is then a garden—far sweeter. If not very extensive, I think a garden should contain more shrubs and flowers than lofty trees; and in order to admit the sun-beams to enliven our spring, autumn and winter, serpentine walks, the rage for the line of beauty, should be made to submit to convenience. Yet, in this country, a broad straight gravel walk is a great convenience for those who wish to take exercise in all seasons, after rain particularly. When the weather is fine, the meadows offer winding paths, far superior to the formal turnings that interrupt reflection, without amusing the fancy.

colonades were placed to excite the wonder of the rude craggs; and a stone stair-case, to threaten with destruction a wooden house. Venuses and Apollos condemned to lie hid in snow three parts of the year, seemed equally displaced, and called the attention off from the surrounding sublimity, without inspiring any voluptuous sensations. Yet even these abortions of vanity have been useful. Numberless workmen have been employed, and the superintending artist has improved the labourers whose unskilfulness tormented him, by obliging them to submit to the discipline of rules. Adieu!

Your's affectionately.

LETTER IV

THE severity of the long Swedish winter tends to render the people sluggish; for, though this season has its peculiar pleasures, too much time is employed to guard against its inclemency. Still, as warm cloathing is absolutely necessary, the women spin, and the men weave, and by these exertions get a fence to keep out the cold. I have rarely passed a knot of cottages without seeing cloth laid out to bleach; and when I entered, always found the women spinning or knitting.

A mistaken tenderness, however, for their children, makes them, even in summer, load them with flannels; and, having a sort of natural antipathy to cold water, the squalid appearance of the poor babes, not to speak of the noxious smell which flannel and rugs retain, seems a reply to a question I had often asked—Why I did not see more children in the villages I passed through? Indeed the children appear to be nipt in the bud, having neither the graces nor charms of their age.* And this, I am persuaded, is much more owing to the ignorance of the mothers than to the rudeness of the climate. Rendered feeble by the continual perspiration they are kept in, whilst every pore is absorbing unwholesome moisture, they give them, even at the breast, brandy, salt fish, and every other crude substance, which air and exercise enables the parent to digest.

The women of fortune here, as well as every where else, have nurses to suckle their children; and the total want of chastity in the lower class of women frequently renders them very unfit for the trust.

You have sometimes remarked to me the difference of the manners of the country girls in England and in America; attributing the reserve of the former to the climate—to the absence of genial suns. But it must be their stars, not the zephyrs gently stealing on their senses, which here lead frail women astray.*—Who can look at these rocks, and allow the voluptuousness of nature to be an excuse for gratifying the desires it inspires? We must, therefore, find some other cause beside voluptuousness, I believe, to account for the conduct of the Swedish and American country girls; for I am led to conclude, from all the observations I have made, that there is always a mixture of sentiment and imagination in voluptuousness, to which neither of them have much pretension.

The country girls of Ireland and Wales equally feel the first impulse of nature, which, restrained in England by fear or delicacy, proves that society is there in a more advanced state. Besides, as the mind is cultivated, and taste gains ground, the passions become stronger, and rest on something more stable than the casual sympathies of the moment. Health and idleness will always account for promiscuous amours; and in some degree I term every person idle, the exercise of whose mind does not bear some proportion to that of the body.

The Swedish ladies exercise neither sufficiently; of course, grow very fat at an early age; and when they have not this downy appearance, a comfortable idea, you will say, in a cold climate, they are not remarkable for fine forms. They have, however, mostly fine complexions; but indolence makes the lily soon displace the rose. The quantity of coffee, spices, and other things of that kind, with want of care, almost universally spoil their teeth, which contrast but ill with their ruby lips.*

The manners of Stockholm are refined,* I hear, by the introduction of gallantry; but in the country, romping and coarse freedoms, with coarser allusions, keep the spirits awake. In the article of cleanliness, the women, of all descriptions, seem very deficient; and their dress shews that vanity is more inherent in women than taste.

The men appear to have paid still less court to the graces. They are a robust, healthy race, distinguished for their common sense and turn for humour, rather than for wit or sentiment. I include not, as you may suppose, in this general character, some of the nobility and officers, who having travelled, are polite and well informed.

I must own to you, that the lower class of people here amuse and interest me much more than the middling, with their apish good breeding and prejudices. The sympathy and frankness of heart conspicuous in the peasantry produces even a simple grace-fulness of deportment, which has frequently struck me as very picturesque; I have often also been touched by their extreme desire to oblige me, when I could not explain my wants, and by their earnest manner of expressing that desire. There is such a charm in tenderness!—It is so delightful to love our fellow-creatures, and meet the honest affections as they break forth. Still, my good friend, I begin to think that I should not like to live continually in the country, with people whose minds have such a narrow range. My heart would frequently be interested; but my mind would languish for more companionable society.

The beauties of nature appear to me now even more alluring than in my youth, because my intercourse with the world was formed, without vitiating my taste. But, with respect to the inhabitants of the country, my fancy has probably, when disgusted with artificial manners, solaced itself by joining the advantages of cultivation with the interesting sincerity of innocence, forgetting the lassitude that ignorance will naturally produce. I like to see animals sporting, and sympathize in their pains and pleasures. Still I love sometimes to view the human face divine,* and trace the soul, as well as the heart, in its varying lineaments.

A journey to the country, which I must shortly make, will enable me to extend my remarks.—Adieu!

LETTER V

HAD I determined to travel in Sweden merely for pleasure, I should probably have chosen the road to Stockholm, though convinced, by repeated observation, that the manners of a people are best discriminated in the country. The inhabitants of the capital are all of the same genus; for the varieties in the species we must, therefore, search where the habitations of men are so separated as to allow the difference of climate to have its natural effect.* And with this difference we are, perhaps, most forcibly struck at the first view, just as we form an estimate of the leading traits of a character at the first glance, of which intimacy afterwards makes us almost lose sight.

As my affairs called me to Stromstad* (the frontier town of Sweden) in my way to Norway, I was to pass over, I heard, the most uncultivated part of the country. Still I believe that the grand features of Sweden are the same everywhere, and it is only the grand features that admit of description. There is an individuality in every prospect, which remains in the memory as forcibly depicted as the particular features that have arrested our attention; yet we cannot find words to discriminate that individuality so as to enable a stranger to say, this is the face, that the view. We may amuse by setting the imagination to work; but we cannot store the memory with a fact.

As I wish to give you a general idea of this country, I shall continue in my desultory manner to make such observations and reflections as the circumstances draw forth, without losing time, by endeavouring to arrange them.

Travelling in Sweden is very cheap, and even commodious, if you make but the proper arrangements. Here, as in other parts of the continent, it is necessary to have your own carriage, and to have a servant who can speak the language, if you are unacquainted with it. Sometimes a servant who can drive would be found very useful, which was our case, for I travelled in company with two gentlemen,* one of whom had a German servant who drove very well. This was all the party; for not intending to make a long stay, I left my little girl behind me.*

As the roads are not much frequented, to avoid waiting three or four hours for horses, we sent, as is the constant custom, an *avant courier* the night before, to order them at every post, and we constantly found them ready. Our first set I jokingly termed *requisition* horses;* but afterwards we had almost always little spirited animals that went on at a round pace.

The roads, making allowance for the ups and downs, are uncommonly good and pleasant. The expence, including the postillions and other incidental things, does not amount to more than a shilling the Swedish mile.[1]

The inns are tolerable; but not liking the rye bread, I found it necessary to furnish myself with some wheaten before I set out. The beds too were particularly disagreable to me. It seemed to me that I was sinking into a grave when I entered them; for, immersed in down placed in a sort of box, I expected to be suffocated before morning. The sleeping between two down beds, they do so even in summer, must be very unwholesome during any season; and I cannot conceive how the people can bear it, especially as the summers are very warm. But warmth they seem not to feel; and, I should think, were afraid of the air, by always keeping their windows shut. In the winter, I am persuaded, I could not exist in rooms thus closed up, with stoves heated in their manner, for they only put wood into them twice a day; and, when the stove is thoroughly heated, they shut the flue, not admitting any air to renew its elasticity, even when the rooms are crowded with company. These stoves are made of earthenware, and often in a form that ornaments an apartment, which is never the case with the heavy iron ones I have seen elsewhere. Stoves may be economical; but I like a fire, a wood one, in preference; and I am convinced that the current of air which it attracts renders this the best mode of warming rooms.

We arrived early the second evening at a little village called Quistram,* where we had determined to pass the night; having been informed that we should not afterwards find a tolerable inn until we reached Stromstad.

---

[1] A Swedish mile is nearly six English miles.

Advancing towards Quistram, as the sun was beginning to decline, I was particularly impressed by the beauty of the situation. The road was on the declivity of a rocky mountain, slightly covered with a mossy herbage and vagrant firs. At the bottom, a river, straggling amongst the recesses of stone, was hastening forward to the ocean and its grey rocks, of which we had a prospect on the left, whilst on the right it stole peacefully forward into the meadows, losing itself in a thickly wooded rising ground. As we drew near, the loveliest banks of wild flowers variegated the prospect, and promised to exhale odours to add to the sweetness of the air, the purity of which you could almost see, alas! not smell, for the putrifying herrings, which they use as manure, after the oil has been extracted, spread over the patches of earth, claimed by cultivation, destroyed every other.

It was intolerable, and entered with us into the inn, which was in other respects a charming retreat.

Whilst supper was preparing I crossed the bridge, and strolled by the river, listening to its murmurs. Approaching the bank, the beauty of which had attracted my attention in the carriage, I recognized many of my old acquaintance growing with great luxuriancy.

Seated on it, I could not avoid noting an obvious remark. Sweden appeared to me the country in the world most proper to form the botanist and natural historian:* every object seemed to remind me of the creation of things, of the first efforts of sportive nature. When a country arrives at a certain state of perfection, it looks as if it were made so; and curiosity is not excited. Besides, in social life too many objects occur for any to be distinctly observed by the generality of mankind; yet a contemplative man, or poet, in the country, I do not mean the country adjacent to cities, feels and sees what would escape vulgar eyes, and draws suitable inferences. This train of reflections might have led me further, in every sense of the word; but I could not escape from the detestable evaporation of the herrings, which poisoned all my pleasure.

After making a tolerable supper, for it is not easy to get fresh provisions on the road, I retired, to be lulled to sleep by the murmuring of a stream, of which I with great difficulty obtained sufficient to perform my daily ablutions.

The last battle between the Danes and Swedes, which gave new life to their ancient enmity, was fought at this place 1788;* only seventeen or eighteen were killed; for the great superiority of the Danes and Norwegians obliged the Swedes to submit; but sickness, and scarcity of provisions, proved very fatal to their opponents, on their return.

It would be very easy to search for the particulars of this engagement in the publications of the day; but as this manner of filling my pages does not come within my plan, I probably should not have remarked that the battle was fought here, were it not to relate an anecdote which I had from good authority.

I noticed, when I first mentioned this place to you, that we descended a steep before we came to the inn; an immense ridge of rocks stretching out on one side. The inn was sheltered under them; and about a hundred yards from it was a bridge that crossed the river, whose murmurs I have celebrated; it was not fordable. The Swedish general received orders to stop at the bridge, and dispute the passage; a most advantageous post for an army so much inferior in force: but the influence of beauty is not confined to courts. The mistress of the inn was handsome: when I saw her there were still some remains of beauty; and, to preserve her house, the general gave up the only tenable station. He was afterwards broke for contempt of orders.

Approaching the frontiers, consequently the sea, nature resumed an aspect ruder and ruder, or rather seemed the bones of the world waiting to be clothed with every thing necessary to give life and beauty. Still it was sublime.

The clouds caught their hue of the rocks that menaced them. The sun appeared afraid to shine, the birds ceased to sing, and the flowers to bloom; but the eagle fixed his nest high amongst the rocks, and the vulture hovered over this abode of desolation. The farm houses, in which only poverty resided, were formed of logs scarcely keeping off the cold and drifting snow; out of them the inhabitants seldom peeped, and the sports or prattling of children was neither seen nor heard. The current of life seemed congealed at the source: all were not frozen; for it was summer, you remember; but every thing appeared so dull, that I waited to see ice, in order to reconcile me to the absence of gaiety.

The day before, my attention had frequently been attracted by the wild beauties of the country we passed through.

The rocks which tossed their fantastic heads so high were often covered with pines and firs, varied in the most picturesque manner. Little woods filled up the recesses, when forests did not darken the scene; and vallies and glens, cleared of the trees, displayed a dazzling verdure which contrasted with the gloom of the shading pines. The eye stole into many a covert where tranquillity seemed to have taken up her abode, and the number of little lakes that continually presented themselves added to the peaceful composure of the scenery. The little cultivation which appeared did not break the enchantment, nor did castles rear their turrets aloft to crush the cottages, and prove that man is more savage than the natives of the woods. I heard of the bears, but never saw them stalk forth, which I was sorry for; I wished to have seen one in its wild state. In the winter, I am told, they sometimes catch a stray cow, which is a heavy loss to the owner.

The farms are small. Indeed most of the houses we saw on the road indicated poverty, or rather that the people could just live. Towards the frontiers they grew worse and worse in their appearance, as if not willing to put sterility itself out of countenance. No gardens smiled round the habitations, not a potatoe or cabbage to eat with the fish drying on a stick near the door. A little grain here and there appeared, the long stalks of which you might almost reckon. The day was gloomy when we passed over this rejected spot, the wind bleak, and winter seemed to be contending with nature, faintly struggling to change the season. Surely, thought I, if the sun ever shines here, it cannot warm these stones; moss only cleaves to them, partaking of their hardness; and nothing like vegetable life appears to chear with hope the heart.

So far from thinking that the primitive inhabitants of the world lived in a southern climate, where Paradise spontaneously arose, I am led to infer, from various circumstances, that the first dwelling of man happened to be a spot like this which led him to adore a sun so seldom seen;* for this worship, which probably preceded that of demons or demi-gods, certainly never began in a southern climate, where the continual presence of the sun prevented its being considered as a good; or rather the want of it never being felt, this glorious luminary would carelessly have diffused its blessings without being hailed as a benefactor. Man must therefore have been placed in the north, to tempt him to run after the sun, in order that the different parts of the earth might be peopled. Nor do I wonder that hordes of barbarians always poured out of these regions to seek for milder climes, when nothing like cultivation attached them to the soil; especially when we take into the view that the adventuring spirit, common to man, is naturally stronger and more general during the infancy of society. The conduct of the followers of Mahomet, and the crusaders, will sufficiently corroborate my assertion.

Approaching nearer to Stromstad, the appearance of the town proved to be quite in character with the country we had just passed through. I hesitated to use the word country, yet could not find another; still it would sound absurd to talk of fields of rocks.

The town was built on, and under them. Three or four weather-beaten trees were shrinking from the wind; and the grass grew so sparingly, that I could not avoid thinking Dr. Johnson's hyperbolical assertion 'that the man merited well of his country who made a few blades of grass grow where they never grew before,'* might here have been uttered with strict propriety. The steeple likewise towered aloft; for what is a church, even amongst the Lutherans, without a steeple? But to prevent mischief in such an exposed situation, it is wisely placed on a rock at some distance, not to endanger the roof of the church.

Rambling about, I saw the door open, and entered, when to my great surprise I found the clergyman reading prayers, with only the clerk attending. I instantly thought of Swift's 'Dearly beloved Roger;'* but on enquiry I learnt that some one had died that morning, and in Sweden it is customary to pray for the dead.

The sun, who I suspected never dared to shine, began now to convince me that he came forth only to torment; for though the wind was still cutting, the rocks became intolerably warm under my feet; whilst the herring effluvia, which I before found so very offensive, once more assailed me. I hastened back to the house of a merchant, the little sovereign of the place, because he was by far the richest, though not the mayor.

Here we were most hospitably received, and introduced to a very fine and numerous family.* I have before mentioned to you the lillies of the north, I might have added, water lillies, for the complexion of many, even of the young women seem to be bleached on the bosom of snow. But in this youthful circle the roses bloomed with all their wonted freshness, and I wondered from whence the fire was stolen which sparkled in their fine blue eyes.

Here we slept; and I rose early in the morning to prepare for my little voyage to Norway. I had determined to go by water, and was to leave my companions behind; but not getting a boat immediately, and the wind being high and unfavourable, I was told that it was not safe to go to sea during such boisterous weather; I was therefore obliged to wait for the morrow, and had the present day on my hands; which I feared would be irksome, because the family, who possessed about a dozen French words amongst them, and not an English phrase, were anxious to amuse me, and would not let me remain alone in my room. The town we had already walked round and round; and if we advanced farther on the coast, it was still to view the same unvaried immensity of water, surrounded by barrenness.

The gentlemen wishing to peep into Norway, proposed going to Fredericshall,* the first town, the distance was only three Swedish miles. There, and back again, was but a day's journey, and would not, I thought, interfere with my voyage. I agreed, and invited the eldest and prettiest of the girls to accompany us. I invited her, because I liked to see a beautiful face animated by pleasure, and to have an opportunity of regarding the country, whilst the gentlemen were amusing themselves with her.

I did not know, for I had not thought of it, that we were to scale some of the most mountainous cliffs of Sweden, in our way to the ferry which separates the two countries.

Entering amongst the cliffs, we were sheltered from the wind; warm sun-beams began to play, streams to flow, and groves of pines diversified the rocks. Sometimes they became suddenly bare and sublime. Once, in particular, after mounting the most terrific precipice, we had to pass through a tremendous defile, where the closing chasm seemed to threaten us with instant destruction, when turning quickly, verdant meadows and a beautiful lake relieved and charmed my eyes.

I have never travelled through Switzerland; but one of my companions assured me, that I should not there find any thing superior, if equal to the wild grandeur of these views.*

As we had not taken this excursion into our plan, the horses had not been previously ordered, which obliged us to wait two hours at the first post. The day was wearing away. The road was so bad, that walking up the precipices consumed the time insensibly. But as we desired horses at each post ready at a certain hour, we reckoned on returning more speedily.

We stopt to dine at a tolerable farm. They brought us out ham, butter, cheese, and milk; and the charge was so moderate, that I scattered a little money amongst the children who were peeping at us, in order to pay them for their trouble.

Arrived at the ferry, we were still detained; for the people who attend at the ferries have a stupid kind of sluggishness in their manner, which is very provoking when you are in haste. At present I did not feel it; for scrambling up the cliffs, my eye followed the river as it rolled between the grand rocky banks; and to complete the scenery, they were covered with firs and pines, through which the wind rustled, as if it were lulling itself to sleep with the declining sun.

Behold us now in Norway; and I could not avoid feeling surprise at observing the difference in the manners of the inhabitants of the two sides of the river; for every thing shews that the Norwegians are more industrious and more opulent. The Swedes, for neighbours are seldom the best friends, accuse the Norwegians of knavery, and they retaliate by bringing a charge of hypocrisy against the Swedes. Local circumstances probably render both unjust, speaking from their feelings, rather than reason: and is this astonishing when we consider that most writers of travels have done the same, whose works have served as materials for the compilers of universal histories. All are eager to give a national character; which is rarely just, because they do not discriminate the natural from the acquired difference. The natural, I believe, on due consideration, will be found to consist merely in the degree of vivacity or thoughtfulness, pleasure, or pain, inspired by the climate, whilst the varieties which the forms of government, including religion, produce, are much more numerous and unstable.

A people have been characterized as stupid by nature; what a paradox! because they did not consider that slaves, having no object to stimulate industry, have not their faculties sharpened by the only thing that can exercise them, self-interest. Others have been brought forward as brutes, having no aptitude for the arts and sciences, only because the progress of improvement had not reached that stage which produces them.

Those writers who have considered the history of man,* or of the human mind, on a more enlarged scale, have fallen into similar errors, not reflecting that the passions are weak where the necessaries of life are too hardly or too easily obtained.

Travellers who require that every nation should resemble their native country, had better stay at home. It is, for example, absurd to blame a people for not having that degree of personal cleanliness and elegance of manners which only refinement of taste produces, and will produce every where in proportion as society attains a general polish. The most essential service, I presume, that authors could render to society, would be to promote inquiry and discussion, instead of making those dogmatical assertions which only appear calculated to gird the human mind round with imaginary circles, like the paper globe which represents the one he inhabits.

This spirit of inquiry is the characteristic of the present century, from which the succeeding will, I am persuaded, receive a great accumulation of knowledge; and doubtless its diffusion will in a great measure destroy the factitious national characters which have been supposed permanent, though only rendered so by the permanency of ignorance.

Arriving at Fredericshall, at the siege of which Charles XII. lost his life, we had only time to take a transient view of it, whilst they were preparing us some refreshment.

Poor Charles! I thought of him with respect. I have always felt the same for Alexander;* with whom he has been classed as a madman, by several writers, who have reasoned superficially, confounding the morals of the day with the few grand principles on which unchangeable morality rests. Making no allowance for the ignorance and prejudices of the period, they do not perceive how much they themselves are indebted to general improvement for the acquirements, and even the virtues, which they would not have had the force of mind to attain, by their individual exertions in a less advanced state of society.

The evening was fine, as is usual at this season; and the refreshing odour of the pine woods became more perceptible; for it was nine o'clock when we left Fredericshall. At the ferry we were detained by a dispute relative to our Swedish passport, which we did not think of getting countersigned in Norway. Midnight was coming on; yet it might with such propriety have been termed the noon of night,* that had Young* ever travelled towards the north, I should not have wondered at his becoming enamoured of the moon. But it is not the queen of night alone who reigns here in all her splendor, though the sun, loitering just below the horizon, decks her with a golden tinge from his car, illuminating the cliffs that hide him; the heavens also, of a clear softened blue, throw her forward, and the evening star appears a lesser moon to the naked eye. The huge shadows of the rocks, fringed with firs, concentrating the views, without darkening them, excited that tender melancholy which, sublimating the imagination, exalts, rather than depresses the mind.

My companions fell asleep:—fortunately they did not snore; and I contemplated, fearless of idle questions, a night such as I had never before seen or felt to charm the senses, and calm the heart. The very air was balmy, as it freshened into morn, producing the most voluptuous sensations. A vague pleasurable sentiment absorbed me, as I opened my bosom to the embraces of nature; and my soul rose to its author, with the chirping of the solitary birds, which began to feel, rather than see, advancing day. I had leisure to mark its progress. The grey morn, streaked with silvery rays, ushered in the orient beams,—how beautifully varying into purple!—yet, I was sorry to lose the soft watry clouds which preceded them, exciting a kind of expectation that made me almost afraid to breathe, lest I should break the charm. I saw the sun—and sighed.

One of my companions, now awake, perceiving that the postillion had mistaken the road, began to swear at him, and roused the other two, who reluctantly shook off sleep.

We had immediately to measure back our steps, and did not reach Stromstad before five in the morning.

The wind had changed in the night, and my boat was ready.

A dish of coffee, and fresh linen, recruited my spirits; and I directly set out again for Norway; purposing to land much higher up the coast.

Wrapping my great coat round me, I lay down on some sails at the bottom of the boat, its motion rocking me to rest, till a discourteous wave interrupted my slumbers, and obliged me to rise and feel a solitariness which was not so soothing as that of the past night.

Adieu!

LETTER VI

THE sea was boisterous; but, as I had an experienced pilot, I did not apprehend any danger. Sometimes I was told, boats are driven far out and lost. However, I seldom calculate chances so nicely—sufficient for the day is the obvious evil!*

We had to steer amongst islands and huge rocks, rarely losing sight of the shore, though it now and then appeared only a mist that bordered the water's edge. The pilot assured me that the numerous harbours on the Norway coast were very safe, and the pilot-boats were always on the watch. The Swedish side is very dangerous, I am also informed; and the help of experience is not often at hand, to enable strange vessels to steer clear of the rocks, which lurk below the water, close to the shore.

There are no tides here, nor in the Cattegate;* and, what appeared to me a consequence, no sandy beach. Perhaps this observation has been made before; but it did not occur to me till I saw the waves continually beating against the bare rocks, without ever receding to leave a sediment to harden.

The wind was fair, till we had to tack about in order to enter Laurvig,* where we arrived towards three o'clock in the afternoon. It is a clean, pleasant town, with a considerable iron-work, which gives life to it.

As the Norwegians do not frequently see travellers, they are very curious to know their business, and who they are—so curious that I was half tempted to adopt Dr. Franklin's* plan, when travelling in America, where they are equally prying, which was to write on a paper, for public inspection, my name, from whence I came, where I was going, and what was my business. But if I were importuned by their curiosity, their friendly gestures gratified me. A woman, coming alone, interested them. And I know not whether my weariness gave me a look of peculiar delicacy; but they approached to assist me, and enquire after my wants, as if they were afraid to hurt, and wished to protect me. The sympathy I inspired, thus dropping down from the clouds in a strange land, affected me more than it would have done, had not my spirits been harassed by various causes—by much thinking— musing almost to madness—and even by a sort of weak melancholy that hung about my heart at parting with my daughter for the first time.

You know that as a female I am particularly attached to her—I feel more than a mother's fondness and anxiety, when I reflect on the dependent and oppressed state of her sex. I dread lest she should be forced to sacrifice her heart to her principles, or principles to her heart. With trembling hand I shall cultivate sensibility, and cherish delicacy of sentiment, lest, whilst I lend fresh blushes to the rose, I sharpen the thorns that will wound the breast I would fain guard—I dread to unfold her mind, lest it should render her unfit for the world she is to inhabit—Hapless woman! what a fate is thine!

But whither am I wandering? I only meant to tell you that the impression the kindness of the simple people made visible on my countenance increased my sensibility to a painful degree. I wished to have had a room to myself; for their attention, and rather distressing observation, embarrassed me extremely. Yet, as they would bring me eggs, and make my coffee, I found I could not leave them without hurting their feelings of hospitality.

It is customary here for the host and hostess to welcome their guests as master and mistress of the house.

My clothes, in their turn, attracted the attention of the females; and I could not help thinking of the foolish vanity which makes many women so proud of the observation of strangers as to take wonder very gratuitously for admiration. This error they are very apt to fall into; when arrived in a foreign country, the populace stare at them as they pass: yet the make of a cap, or the singularity of a gown, is often the cause of the flattering attention, which afterwards supports a fantastic superstructure of self-conceit.

Not having brought a carriage over with me, expecting to have met a person where I landed, who was immediately to have procured me one, I was detained whilst the good people of the inn sent round to all their acquaintance to search for a vehicle. A rude sort of *cabriole** was at last found, and a driver half drunk, who was not less eager to make a good bargain on that account. I had a Danish captain of a ship and his mate with me: the former was to ride on horseback, at which he was not very expert, and the latter to partake of my seat. The driver mounted behind to guide the horses, and flourish the whip over our shoulders; he would not suffer the reins out of his own hands. There was something so grotesque in our appearance, that I could not avoid shrinking into myself when I saw a gentleman-like man in the group which crowded round the door to observe us. I could have broken the driver's whip for cracking to call the women and children together; but seeing a significant smile on the face, I had before remarked, I burst into a laugh, to allow him to do so too,—and away we flew. This is not a flourish of the pen; for we actually went on full gallop a long time, the horses being very good; indeed I have never met with better, if so good, post-horses, as in Norway; they are of a stouter make than the English horses, appear to be well fed, and are not easily tired.

I had to pass over, I was informed, the most fertile and best cultivated tract of country in Norway. The distance was three Norwegian miles, which are longer than the Swedish.* The roads were very good; the farmers are obliged to repair them; and we scampered through a great extent of country in a more improved state than any I had viewed since I left England. Still there was sufficient of hills, dales, and rocks, to prevent the idea of a plain from entering the head, or even of such scenery as England and France afford. The prospects were also embellished by water, rivers, and lakes, before the sea proudly claimed my regard; and the road running frequently through lofty groves, rendered the landscapes beautiful, though they were not so romantic as those I had lately seen with such delight.

It was late when I reached Tonsberg;* and I was glad to go to bed at a decent inn. The next morning, the 17th of July, conversing with the gentleman* with whom I had business to transact, I found that I should be detained at Tonsberg three weeks; and I lamented that I had not brought my child with me.

The inn was quiet, and my room so pleasant, commanding a view of the sea, confined by an amphitheatre of hanging woods, that I wished to remain there, though no one in the house could speak English or French. The mayor, my friend, however, sent a young woman to me who spoke a little English, and she agreed to call on me twice a day, to receive my orders, and translate them to my hostess.

My not understanding the language was an excellent pretext for dining alone, which I prevailed on them to let me do at a late hour; for the early dinners in Sweden had entirely deranged my day. I could not alter it there, without disturbing the economy of a family where I was as a visitor; necessity having forced me to accept of an invitation from a private family, the lodgings were so incommodious.

Amongst the Norwegians I had the arrangement of my own time; and I determined to regulate it in such a manner, that I might enjoy as much of their sweet summer as I possibly could;—short, it is true; but 'passing sweet.'*

I never endured a winter in this rude clime; consequently it was not the contrast, but the real beauty of the season which made the present summer appear to me the finest I had ever seen. Sheltered from the north and eastern winds, nothing can exceed the salubrity, the soft freshness of the western gales. In the evening they also die away; the aspen leaves tremble into stillness, and reposing nature seems to be warmed by the moon, which here assumes a genial aspect: and if a light shower has chanced to fall with the sun, the juniper, the underwood of the forest, exhales a wild perfume, mixed with a thousand nameless sweets, that, soothing the heart, leave images in the memory which the imagination will ever hold dear.

Nature is the nurse of sentiment,—the true source of taste;—yet what misery, as well as rapture, is produced by a quick perception of the beautiful and sublime, when it is exercised in observing animated nature, when every beauteous feeling and emotion excites responsive sympathy, and the harmonized soul sinks into melancholy, or rises to extasy, just as the chords are touched, like the æolian harp agitated by the changing wind.* But how dangerous is it to foster these sentiments in such an imperfect state of existence; and how difficult to eradicate them when an affection for mankind, a passion for an individual, is but the unfolding of that love which embraces all that is great and beautiful.

When a warm heart has received strong impressions, they are not to be effaced. Emotions become sentiments; and the imagination renders even transient sensations permanent, by fondly retracing them. I cannot, without a thrill of delight, recollect views I have seen, which are not to be forgotten,—nor looks I have felt in every nerve which I shall never more meet. The grave has closed over a dear friend,* the friend of my youth; still she is present with me, and I hear her soft voice warbling as I stray over the heath. Fate has separated me from another, the fire of whose eyes, tempered by infantine tenderness, still warms my breast; even when gazing on these tremendous cliffs, sublime emotions absorb my soul. And, smile not, if I add, that the rosy tint of morning reminds me of a suffusion, which will never more charm my senses, unless it reappears on the cheeks of my child.

Her sweet blushes I may yet hide in my bosom, and she is still too young to ask why starts the tear, so near akin to pleasure and pain?

I cannot write any more at present. Tomorrow we will talk of Tonsberg.

LETTER VII

THOUGH the king of Denmark be an absolute monarch,* yet the Norwegians appear to enjoy all the blessings of freedom. Norway may be termed a sister kingdom; but the people have no viceroy to lord it over them, and fatten his dependants with the fruit of their labour.

There are only two counts* in the whole country, who have estates, and exact some feudal observances from their tenantry. All the rest of the country is divided into small farms, which belong to the cultivator. It is true, some few, appertaining to the church, are let; but always on a lease for life, generally renewed in favour of the eldest son, who has this advantage, as well as a right to a double portion of the property. But the value of the farm is estimated; and after his portion is assigned to him, he must be answerable for the residue to the remaining part of the family.

Every farmer, for ten years, is obliged to attend annually about twelve days, to learn the military exercise; but it is always at a small distance from his dwelling, and does not lead him into any new habits of life.

There are about six thousand regulars also, garrisoned at Christiania and Fredericshall,* which are equally reserved, with the militia, for the defence of their own country. So that when the Prince Royal* passed into Sweden, in 1788, he was obliged to request, not command, them to accompany him on this expedition.

These corps are mostly composed of the sons of the cottagers, who being labourers on the farms, are allowed a few acres to cultivate for themselves. These men voluntarily enlist; but it is only for a limited period, (six years) at the expiration of which they have the liberty of retiring. The pay is only two-pence a day, and bread; still, considering the cheapness of the country, it is more than sixpence in England.

The distribution of landed property into small farms, produces a degree of equality which I have seldom seen elsewhere; and the rich being all merchants, who are obliged to divide their personal fortune amongst their children, the boys always receiving twice as much as the girls, property has not a chance of accumulating till overgrown wealth destroys the balance of liberty.

You will be surprised to hear me talk of liberty; yet the Norwegians appear to me to be the most free community I have ever observed.

The mayor of each town or district, and the judges in the country, exercise an authority almost patriarchal. They can do much good, but little harm, as every individual can appeal from their judgment: and as they may always be forced to give a reason for their conduct, it is generally regulated by prudence. 'They have not time to learn to be tyrants,' said a gentleman to me, with whom I discussed the subject.

The farmers not fearing to be turned out of their farms, should they displease a man in power, and having no vote to be commanded at an election for a mock representative, are a manly race; for not being obliged to submit to any debasing tenure, in order to live, or advance themselves in the world, they act with an independent spirit. I never yet have heard of anything like domineering, or oppression, excepting such as has arisen from natural causes. The freedom the people enjoy may, perhaps, render them a little litigious, and subject them to the impositions of cunning practitioners of the law; but the authority of office is bounded, and the emoluments of it do not destroy its utility.

Last year a man, who had abused his power, was cashiered, on the representation of the people to the bailiff of the district.

There are four in Norway, who might with propriety be termed sheriffs; and, from their sentence, an appeal, by either party, may be made to Copenhagen.*

Near most of the towns are commons,* on which the cows of all the inhabitants, indiscriminately, are allowed to graze.

The poor, to whom a cow is necessary, are almost supported by it. Besides, to render living more easy, they all go out to fish in their own boats; and fish is their principal food.

The lower class of people in the towns are in general sailors; and the industrious have usually little ventures of their own that serve to render the winter comfortable.

With respect to the country at large, the importation is considerably in favour of Norway.

They are forbidden, at present, to export corn or rye,* on account of the advanced price.

The restriction which most resembles the painful subordination of Ireland, is that vessels, trading to the West Indies,* are obliged to pass by their own ports, and unload their cargoes at Copenhagen, which they afterwards re-ship. The duty is indeed inconsiderable; but the navigation being dangerous, they run a double risk.

There is an excise on all articles of consumption brought to the towns; but the officers are not strict; and it would be reckoned invidious to enter a house to search, as in England.

The Norwegians appear to me a sensible, shrewd people, with little scientific knowledge, and still less taste for literature: but they are arriving at the epoch which precedes the introduction of the arts and sciences.

Most of the towns are sea-ports, and sea-ports are not favourable to improvement. The captains acquire a little superficial knowledge by travelling, which their indefatigable attention to the making of money prevents their digesting; and the fortune that they thus laboriously acquire, is spent, as it usually is in towns of this description, in shew and good living. They love their country, but have not much public spirit.[1] Their exertions are, generally speaking, only for their families; which I conceive will always be the case, till politics, becoming a subject of discussion, enlarges the heart by opening the understanding. The French revolution will have this effect.* They sing

[1] The grand virtues of the heart, particularly the enlarged humanity which extends to the whole human race, depend more on the understanding, I believe, than is generally imagined.

at present, with great glee, many republican songs, and seem earnestly to wish that the republic may stand; yet they appear very much attached to their Prince Royal; and, as far as rumour can give an idea of a character, he appears to merit their attachment. When I am at Copenhagen, I shall be able to ascertain on what foundation their good opinion is built; at present I am only the echo of it.

In the year 1788 he travelled through Norway;* and acts of mercy gave dignity to the parade, and interest to the joy, his presence inspired. At this town he pardoned a girl condemned to die for murdering an illegitimate child, a crime seldom committed in this country. She is since married, and become the careful mother of a family. This might be given as an instance, that a desperate act is not always a proof of an incorrigible depravity of character; the only plausible excuse that has been brought forward to justify the infliction of capital punishments.

I will relate two or three other anecdotes to you; for the truth of which I will not vouch, because the facts were not of sufficient consequence for me to take much pains to ascertain them; and, true or false, they evince that the people like to make a kind of mistress of their prince.

An officer, mortally wounded at the ill-advised battle of Quistram, desired to speak with the prince; and, with his dying breath, earnestly recommended to his care a young woman of Christiania, to whom he was engaged. When the prince returned there, a ball was given by the chief inhabitants. He inquired whether this unfortunate girl was invited, and requested that she might, though of the second class. The girl came; she was pretty; and finding herself amongst her superiors, bashfully sat down as near the door as possible, nobody taking notice of her. Shortly after, the prince entering, immediately inquired for her, and asked her to dance, to the mortification of the rich dames. After it was over he handed her to the top of the room, and placing himself by her, spoke of the loss she had sustained, with tenderness, promising to provide for any one she should marry,—as the story goes. She is since married, and he has not forgotten his promise.

A little girl, during the same expedition, in Sweden, who informed him that the logs of a bridge were cut underneath, was taken by his orders to Christiania, and put to school at his expence.

Before I retail other beneficial effects of his journey, it is necessary to inform you that the laws here are mild, and do not punish capitally for any crime but murder, which seldom occurs. Every other offence merely subjects the delinquent to imprisonment and labour in the castle, or rather arsenal,* at Christiania, and the fortress at Fredericshall. The first and second conviction produces a sentence for a limited number of years,—two, three, five, or seven, proportioned to the atrocity of the crime. After the third he is whipped, branded in the forehead, and condemned to perpetual slavery. This is the ordinary march of justice. For some flagrant breaches of trust, or acts of wanton cruelty, criminals have been condemned to slavery for life, the first time of conviction, but not frequently. The number of these slaves do not, I am informed, amount to more than an hundred, which is not considerable, compared with the population, upwards of eight hundred thousand.* Should I pass through Christiania, on my return to Gothenburg, I shall probably have an opportunity of learning other particulars.

There is also a house of correction at Christiania for trifling misdemeanors, where the women are confined to labour and imprisonment even for life. The state of the prisoners was represented to the prince; in consequence of which, he visited the arsenal and house of correction. The slaves at the arsenal were loaded with irons of a great weight; he ordered them to be lightened as much as possible.

The people in the house of correction were commanded not to speak to him; but four women, condemned to remain there for life, got into the passage, and fell at his feet. He granted them a pardon; and inquiring respecting the treatment of the prisoners, he was informed that they were frequently whipt going in, and coming out; and for any fault, at the discretion of the inspectors. This custom he humanely abolished; though some of the principal inhabitants, whose situation in life had raised them above the temptation of stealing, were of opinion that these chastisements were necessary and wholesome.

In short, every thing seems to announce that the prince really cherishes the laudable ambition of fulfilling the duties of his station. This ambition is cherished and directed by the count Bernstorff,* the prime minister of Denmark, who is universally celebrated for his abilities and virtue. The happiness of the people is a substantial eulogium; and, from all I can gather, the inhabitants of Denmark and Norway are the least oppressed people of Europe. The press is free. They translate any of the French publications of the day, deliver their opinion on the subject, and discuss those it leads to with great freedom, and without fearing to displease the government.

On the subject of religion they are likewise becoming tolerant, at least, and perhaps have advanced a step further in freethinking.* One writer has ventured to deny the divinity of Jesus Christ, and to question the necessity or utility of the Christian system, without being considered universally as a monster, which would have been the case a few years ago. They have translated many German works on education;* and though they have not adopted any of their plans, it is become a subject of discussion. There are some grammar and free schools; but, from what I hear, not very good ones. All the children learn to read, write, and cast accounts for the purposes of common life. They have no university;* and nothing that deserves the name of science is taught; nor do individuals, by pursuing any branch of knowledge, excite a degree of curiosity which is the forerunner of improvement. Knowledge is not absolutely necessary to enable a considerable portion of the community to live; and, till it is, I fear, it never becomes general.

In this country, where minerals abound, there is not one collection: and, in all probability, I venture a conjecture, the want of mechanical and chemical knowledge renders the silver mines unproductive; for the quantity of silver obtained every year is not sufficient to defray the expences. It has been urged, that the employment of such a number of hands is very beneficial. But a positive loss is never to be done away; and the men, thus employed, would naturally find some other means of living, instead of being thus a dead weight on government, or rather on the community from whom its revenue is drawn.

About three English miles from Tonsberg there is a salt work,* belonging, like all their establishments, to government, in which they employ above an hundred and fifty men, and maintain nearly five hundred people, who earn their living. The clear profit, an increasing one, amounts to two thousand pounds sterling. And as the eldest son of the inspector, an ingenious young man, has been sent by the government to travel, and acquire some mathematical and chemical knowledge in Germany, it has a chance of being improved. He is the only person I have met with here, who appears to have a scientific turn of mind. I do not mean to assert that I have not met with others, who have a spirit of inquiry.

The salt-works at St. Ubes are basons* in the sand, and the sun produces the evaporation: but here there is no beach. Besides, the heat of summer is so short-lived, that it would be idle to contrive machines for such an inconsiderable portion of the year. They therefore always use fires; and the whole establishment appears to be regulated with judgment.

The situation is well chosen and beautiful. I do not find, from the observation of a person who has resided here for forty years, that the sea advances or recedes on this coast.

I have already remarked, that little attention is paid to education, excepting reading, writing and the rudiments of arithmetic; I ought to have added, that a catechism is carefully taught, and the children obliged to read in the churches, before the congregation, to prove that they are not neglected.

Degrees, to enable any one to practise any profession, must be taken at Copenhagen; and the people of this country, having the good sense to perceive that men who are to live in a community should at least acquire the elements of their knowledge, and form their youthful attachments there, are seriously endeavouring to establish an university in Norway. And Tonsberg, as a centrical place in the best part of the country, had the most suffrages; for, experiencing the bad effects of a metropolis, they have determined not to have it in or near Christiania. Should such an establishment take place, it will promote inquiry throughout the country, and give a new face to society. Premiums have been offered, and prize questions written, which I am told have merit. The building college-halls, and other appendages of the seat of science, might enable Tonsberg to recover its pristine consequence; for it is one of the most ancient towns of Norway, and once contained nine churches. At present there are only two. One is a very old structure, and has a gothic respectability about it, which scarcely amounts to grandeur, because, to render a gothic pile grand, it must have a huge unwieldiness of appearance. The chapel of Windsor may be an exception to this rule; I mean before it was in its present *nice, clean* state.* When I first saw it, the pillars within had acquired, by time, a sombre hue, which accorded with the architecture; and the gloom increased its dimensions to the eye by hiding its parts; but now it all bursts on the view at once; and the sublimity has vanished before the brush and broom; for it has been white-washed and scraped till it is become as bright and neat as the pots and pans in a notable house-wife's kitchen—yes; the very spurs on the recumbent knights were deprived of their venerable rust, to give a striking proof that a love of order in trifles, and taste for proportion and arrangement, are very distinct. The glare of light thus introduced, entirely destroys the sentiment these piles are calculated to inspire; so that, when I heard something like a jig from the organ-loft, I thought it an excellent hall for dancing or feasting. The measured pace of thought with which I had entered the cathedral, changed into a trip; and I bounded on the terrace, to see the royal family, with a number of ridiculous images in my head, that I shall not now recall.

The Norwegians are fond of music; and every little church has an organ. In the church I have mentioned, there is an inscription importing that a king,[1] James the sixth, of Scotland, and first of

[1] 'Anno 1589, St. Martin's Daÿ, which was the 11th Day of November, on a Tuesday, came the high-born Prince and Lord Jacob Stuart, King in Scotland, to this Town, and the 25th Sunday after Trinity (Sundaÿ) which was the 16th Day of November, stood his Grace in this Pew, and heard Scotch Preaching from the 23rd Psalm, "The Lord is my Shepherd," &c. which M. David Lentz, Preacher in Lith, then preached between 10 and 12.'
The above is an inscription which stands in St. Mary's church, in Tonsberg.

England,* who came with more than princely gallantry, to escort his bride home, stood there, and heard divine service.

There is a little recess full of coffins, which contains bodies embalmed long since—so long, that there is not even a tradition to lead to a guess at their names.

A desire of preserving the body seems to have prevailed in most countries of the world, futile as it is to term it a preservation, when the noblest parts are immediately sacrificed merely to save the muscles, skin and bone from rottenness. When I was shewn these human petrifactions, I shrunk back with disgust and horror. 'Ashes to ashes!' thought I—'Dust to dust!'*—If this be not dissolution, it is something worse than natural decay—It is treason against humanity, thus to lift up the awful veil which would fain hide its weakness. The grandeur of the active principle is never more strongly felt than at such a sight; for nothing is so ugly as the human form when deprived of life, and thus dried into stone, merely to preserve the most disgusting image of death. The contemplation of noble ruins produces a melancholy that exalts the mind.*—We take a retrospect of the exertions of man, the fate of empires and their rulers; and marking the grand destruction of ages, it seems the necessary change of time leading to improvement.—Our very soul expands, and we forget our littleness; how painfully brought to our recollection by such vain attempts to snatch from decay what is destined so soon to perish. Life, what art thou? Where goes this breath? this *I*, so much alive? In what element will it mix, giving or receiving fresh energy?—What will break the enchantment of animation?—For worlds, I would not see a form I loved—embalmed in my heart—thus sacrilegiously handled!—Pugh! my stomach turns.—Is this all the distinction of the rich in the grave?—They had better quietly allow the scythe of equality to mow them down with the common mass, than struggle to become a monument of the instability of human greatness.

It is known that king James the sixth went to Norway, to marry princess Anna, the daughter of Frederick the second, and sister to Christian the fourth; and that the wedding was performed at Opslo* (now Christiania), where the princess, by contrary winds, was detained; but that the king, during this voyage, was at Tonsberg, nobody would have known, if an inscription, in remembrance of it, had not been placed in this church.

The teeth, nails and skin were whole, without appearing black like the Egyptian mummies; and some silk, in which they had been wrapt, still preserved its colour, pink, with tolerable freshness.

I could not learn how long the bodies had been in this state, in which they bid fair to remain till the day of judgment, if there is to be such a day; and before that time, it will require some trouble to make them fit to appear in company with angels, without disgracing humanity.—God bless you! I feel a conviction that we have some perfectible principle in our present vestment, which will not be destroyed just as we begin to be sensible of improvement; and I care not what habit it next puts on, sure that it will be wisely formed to suit a higher state of existence. Thinking of death makes us tenderly cling to our affections—with more than usual tenderness, I therefore assure you that I am your's, wishing that the temporary death of absence may not endure longer than is absolutely necessary.

LETTER VIII

Tonsberg was formerly the residence of one of the little sovereigns* of Norway; and on an adjacent mountain the vestiges of a fort remain, which was battered down by the Swedes; the entrance of the bay lying close to it.

Here I have frequently strayed, sovereign of the waste, I seldom met any human creature; and sometimes, reclining on the mossy down, under the shelter of a rock, the prattling of the sea amongst the pebbles has lulled me to sleep—no fear of any rude satyr's approaching to interrupt my repose. Balmy were the slumbers, and soft the gales, that refreshed me, when I awoke to follow, with an eye vaguely curious, the white sails, as they turned the cliffs, or seemed to take shelter under the pines which covered the little islands that so gracefully rose to render the terrific ocean beautiful. The fishermen were calmly casting their nets; whilst the seagulls hovered over the unruffled deep. Every thing seemed to harmonize into tranquillity—even the mournful call of the bittern was in cadence with the tinkling bells on the necks of the cows, that, pacing slowly one after the other, along an inviting path in the vale below, were repairing to the cottages to be milked. With what ineffable pleasure have I not gazed—and gazed again, losing my breath through my eyes—my very soul diffused itself in the scene—and, seeming to become all senses, glided in the scarcely-agitated waves, melted in the freshening breeze, or, taking its flight with fairy wing, to the misty mountains which bounded the prospect, fancy tript over new lawns, more beautiful even than the lovely slopes on the winding shore before me.—I pause, again breathless, to trace, with renewed delight, sentiments which entranced me, when, turning my humid eyes from the expanse below to the vault above, my sight pierced the fleecy clouds that softened the azure brightness; and, imperceptibly recalling the reveries of childhood, I bowed before the awful throne of my Creator, whilst I rested on its footstool.*

You have sometimes wondered, my dear friend, at the extreme affection of my nature—But such is the temperature of my soul—It is not the vivacity of youth, the hey-day of existence. For years have I endeavoured to calm an impetuous tide—labouring to make my feelings take an orderly course.—It was striving against the stream.—I must love and admire with warmth, or I sink into sadness.* Tokens of love which I have received have rapt me in Elysium*—purifying the heart they enchanted.—My bosom still glows,—Do not saucily ask, repeating Sterne's question, 'Maria, is it still so warm?'* Sufficiently, O my God! has it been chilled by sorrow and unkindness—still nature will prevail—and if I blush at recollecting past enjoyment, it is the rosy hue of pleasure heightened by modesty; for the blush of modesty and shame are as distinct as the emotions by which they are produced.

I need scarcely inform you, after telling you of my walks, that my constitution has been renovated here; and that I have recovered my activity, even whilst attaining a little *embonpoint*.* My imprudence last winter, and some untoward accidents just at the time I was weaning my child, had reduced me to a state of weakness which I never before experienced. A slow fever preyed on me every night, during my residence in Sweden, and after I arrived at Tonsberg. By chance I found a fine rivulet filtered through the rocks, and confined in a bason for the cattle. It tasted to me like a chalybeat;* at any rate it was pure; and the good effect of the various waters which invalids are sent to drink, depends, I believe, more on the air, exercise and change of scene, than on their medicinal qualities. I therefore determined to turn my morning walks towards it, and seek for health from the nymph of the fountain; partaking of the beverage offered to the tenants of the shade.

Chance likewise led me to discover a new pleasure, equally beneficial to my health. I wished to avail myself of my vicinity to the sea, and bathe; but it was not possible near the town; there was no convenience. The young woman whom I mentioned to you, proposed rowing me across the water, amongst the rocks; but as she was pregnant, I insisted on taking one of the oars, and learning to row. It was not difficult; and I do not know a pleasanter exercise. I soon became expert, and my train of thinking kept time, as it were, with the oars, or I suffered the boat to be carried along by the current, indulging a pleasing forgetfulness, or fallacious hopes.—How fallacious! yet, without hope, what is to sustain life, but the fear of annihilation—the only thing of which I have ever felt a dread—I cannot bear to think of being no more—of losing myself—though existence is often but a painful consciousness of misery; nay, it appears to me impossible that I should cease to exist, or that this active, restless spirit, equally alive to joy and sorrow, should only be organized dust—ready to fly abroad the moment the spring snaps, or the spark goes out, which kept it together. Surely something resides in this heart that is not perishable—and life is more than a dream.*

Sometimes, to take up my oar, once more, when the sea was calm, I was amused by disturbing the innumerable young star fish* which floated just below the surface: I had never observed them before; for they have not a hard shell, like those which I have seen on the sea-shore. They look like thickened water, with a white edge; and four purple circles, of different forms, were in the middle, over an incredible number of fibres, or white lines. Touching them, the cloudy substance would turn or close, first on one side, then on the other, very gracefully; but when I took one of them up in the ladle with which I heaved the water out of the boat, it appeared only a colourless jelly.

I did not see any of the seals, numbers of which followed our boat when we landed in Sweden; for though I like to sport in the water, I should have had no desire to join in their gambols.

Enough, you will say, of inanimate nature, and of brutes, to use the lordly phrase of man; let me hear something of the inhabitants.

The gentleman with whom I had business, is the mayor of Tonsberg; he speaks English intelligibly; and, having a sound understanding, I was sorry that his numerous occupations prevented my gaining as much information from him as I could have drawn forth, had we frequently conversed. The people of the town, as far as I had an opportunity of knowing their sentiments, are extremely well satisfied with his manner of discharging his office. He has a degree of information and good sense which excites respect, whilst a chearfulness, almost amounting to gaiety, enables him to reconcile differences, and keep his neighbours in good humour.—'I lost my horse,' said a woman to me; 'but ever since, when I want to send to the mill, or go out, the mayor lends me one.—He scolds if I do not come for it.'

A criminal was branded, during my stay here, for the third offence; but the relief he received made him declare that the judge was one of the best men in the world.

I sent this wretch a trifle, at different times, to take with him into slavery. As it was more than he expected, he wished very much to see me; and this wish brought to my remembrance an anecdote I heard when I was in Lisbon.*

A wretch who had been imprisoned several years, during which period lamps had been put up, was at last condemned to a cruel death; yet, in his way to execution, he only wished for one night's respite, to see the city lighted.

Having dined in company at the mayor's, I was invited with his family to spend the day at one of the richest merchant's houses.—Though I could not speak Danish,* I knew that I could see a great deal: yes; I am persuaded that I have formed a very just opinion of the character of the Norwegians, without being able to hold converse with them.

I had expected to meet some company; yet was a little disconcerted at being ushered into an apartment full of well-dressed people; and, glancing my eyes round, they rested on several very pretty faces. Rosy cheeks, sparkling eyes, and light brown or golden locks; for I never saw so much hair with a yellow cast; and, with their fine complexions, it looked very becoming.

These women seem a mixture of indolence and vivacity; they scarcely ever walk out, and were astonished that I should, for pleasure; yet they are immoderately fond of dancing. Unaffected in their manners, if they have no pretensions to elegance, simplicity often produces a gracefulness of deportment, when they are animated by a particular desire to please—which was the case at present. The solitariness of my situation, which they thought terrible, interested them very much in my favour. They gathered round me—sung to me—and one of the prettiest, to whom I gave my hand, with some degree of cordiality, to meet the glance of her eyes, kissed me very affectionately.

At dinner, which was conducted with great hospitality, though we remained at table too long, they sung several songs, and, amongst the rest, translations of some patriotic French ones. As the evening advanced, they became playful, and we kept up a sort of conversation of gestures. As their minds were totally uncultivated, I did not lose much, perhaps gained, by not being able to understand them; for fancy probably filled up, more to their advantage, the void in the picture. Be that as it may, they excited my sympathy; and I was very much flattered when I was told, the next day, that they said it was a pleasure to look at me, I appeared so good-natured.

The men were generally captains of ships. Several spoke English very tolerably; but they were merely matter of fact men, confined to a very narrow circle of observation. I found it difficult to obtain from them any information respecting their own country, when the fumes of tobacco did not keep me at a distance.

I was invited to partake of some other feasts, and always had to complain of the quantity of provision, and the length of time taken to consume it; for it would not have been proper to have said devour, all went on so fair and softly. The servants wait as slowly as their mistresses carve.

The young women here, as well as in Sweden, have commonly bad teeth, which I attribute to the same causes. They are fond of finery, but do not pay the necessary attention to their persons, to render beauty less transient than a flower; and that interesting expression which sentiment and accomplishments give, seldom supplies its place.

The servants have likewise an inferior sort of food here; but their masters are not allowed to strike them with impunity. I might have added mistresses; for it was a complaint of this kind, brought before the mayor, which led me to a knowledge of the fact.

The wages are low, which is particularly unjust, because the price of clothes is much higher than provisions. A young woman, who is wet nurse to the mistress of the inn where I lodge, receives only twelve dollars a year, and pays ten for the nursing of her own child; the father had run away to get clear of the expence. There was something in this most painful state of widowhood which excited my compassion, and led me to reflections on the instability of the most flattering plans of happiness, that were painful in the extreme, till I was ready to ask whether this world was not created to exhibit every possible combination of wretchedness. I asked these questions of a heart writhing with anguish, whilst I listened to a melancholy ditty sung by this poor girl. It was too early for thee to be abandoned, thought I, and I hastened out of the house, to take my solitary evening's walk—And here I am again, to talk of any thing, but the pangs arising from the discovery of estranged affection, and the lonely sadness of a deserted heart.

The father and mother, if the father can be ascertained, are obliged to maintain an illegitimate child at their joint expence;* but, should the father disappear, go up the country or to sea, the mother must maintain it herself. However, accidents of this kind do not prevent their marrying; and then it is not unusual to take the child or children home; and they are brought up very amicably with the marriage progeny.

I took some pains to learn what books were written originally in their language; but for any certain information respecting the state of Danish literature, I must wait till I arrive at Copenhagen.*

The sound of the language is soft, a great proportion of the words ending in vowels; and there is a simplicity in the turn of some of the phrases which have been translated to me, that pleased and interested me. In the country, the farmers use the *thou* and *thee*;* and they do not acquire the polite plurals of the towns by meeting at market. The not having markets established in the large towns appears to me a great inconvenience. When the farmers have any thing to sell, they bring it to the neighbouring town, and take it from house to house. I am surprised that the inhabitants do not feel how very incommodious this usage is to both parties, and redress it. They indeed perceive it; for when I have introduced the subject, they acknowledged that they were often in want of necessaries, there being no butchers, and they were often obliged to buy what they did not want; yet it was the *custom*; and the changing of customs of a long standing* requires more energy than they yet possess. I received a similar reply, when I attempted to persuade the women that they injured their children by keeping them too warm. The only way of parrying off my reasoning was, that they must do as other people did. In short, reason on any subject of change, and they stop you by saying that 'the town would talk.' A person of sense, with a large fortune, to insure respect, might be very useful here, by inducing them to treat their children, and manage their sick properly, and eat food dressed in a simpler manner: the example, for instance, of a count's lady.

Reflecting on these prejudices made me revert to the wisdom of those legislators who established institutions for the good of the body, under the pretext of serving heaven for the salvation of the soul. These might with strict propriety be termed pious frauds; and I admire the Peruvian pair* for asserting that they came from the sun, when their conduct proved that they meant to enlighten a benighted country, whose obedience, or even attention, could only be secured by awe.

Thus much for conquering the *inertia* of reason; but, when it is once in motion, fables, once held sacred, may be ridiculed; and sacred they were, when useful to mankind.—Prometheus* alone stole fire to animate the first man; his posterity need not supernatural aid to preserve the species, though love is generally termed a flame; and it may not be necessary much longer to suppose men inspired by heaven to inculcate the duties which demand special grace, when reason convinces them that they are the happiest who are the most nobly employed.

In a few days I am to set out for the western part of Norway, and then shall return by land to Gothenburg. I cannot think of leaving this place without regret. I speak of the place before the inhabitants, though there is a tenderness in their artless kindness which attaches me to them; but it is an attachment that inspires a regret very different from that I felt at leaving Hull, in my way to Sweden. The domestic happiness, and good-humoured gaiety, of the amiable family where I and my Frances* were so hospitably received, would have been sufficient to insure the tenderest remembrance, without the recollection of the social evenings to stimulate it, when good-breeding gave dignity to sympathy, and wit, zest to reason.

Adieu!—I am just informed that my horse has been waiting this quarter of an hour. I now venture to ride out alone. The steeple serves as a land-mark. I once or twice lost my way, walking alone, without being able to inquire after a path. I was therefore obliged to make to the steeple, or wind-mill, over hedge and ditch.

Your's truly.

LETTER IX

I HAVE already informed you that there are only two noblemen who have estates of any magnitude in Norway. One of these has a house near Tonsberg, at which he has not resided for some years, having been at court, or on embassies. He is now the Danish ambassador in London.* The house is pleasantly situated, and the grounds about it fine; but their neglected appearance plainly tells that there is nobody at home.

A stupid kind of sadness, to my eye, always reigns in a huge habitation where only servants live to put cases on the furniture and open the windows. I enter as I would into the tomb of the Capulets,* to look at the family pictures that here frown in armour, or smile in ermine. The mildew respects not the lordly robe; and the worm riots unchecked on the cheek of beauty.

There was nothing in the architecture of the building, or the form of the furniture, to detain me from the avenue where the aged pines stretched along majestically. Time had given a greyish cast to their ever-green foliage; and they stood, like sires of the forest, sheltered on all sides by a rising progeny. I had not ever seen so many oaks together in Norway, as in these woods, nor such large aspens as here were agitated by the breeze, rendering the wind audible—nay, musical; for melody seemed on the wing around me. How different was the fresh odour that re-animated me in the avenue, from the damp chillness of the apartments; and as little did the gloomy thoughtfulness excited by the dusty hangings, and worm-eaten pictures, resemble the reveries inspired by the soothing melancholy of their shade. In the winter, these august pines, towering above the snow, must relieve the eye beyond measure, and give life to the white waste.

The continual recurrence of pine and fir groves, in the day, sometimes wearies the sight; but, in the evening, nothing can be more picturesque, or, more properly speaking, better calculated to produce poetical images. Passing through them, I have been struck with a mystic kind of reverence, and I did, as it were, homage to their venerable shadows. Not nymphs, but philosophers, seemed to inhabit them—ever musing; I could scarcely conceive that they were without some consciousness of existence—without a calm enjoyment of the pleasure they diffused.

How often do my feelings produce ideas that remind me of the origin of many poetical fictions. In solitude, the imagination bodies forth its conceptions unrestrained, and stops enraptured to adore the beings of its own creation. These are moments of bliss; and the memory recalls them with delight.

But I have almost forgotten the matters of fact I meant to relate, respecting the counts. They have the presentation of the livings on their estates, appoint the judges, and different civil officers, the crown reserving to itself the privilege of sanctioning them. But, though they appoint, they cannot dismiss. Their tenants* also occupy their farms for life, and are obliged to obey any summons to work on the part he reserves for himself; but they are paid for their labour. In short, I have seldom heard of any noblemen so innoxious.

Observing that the gardens round the count's estate were better cultivated than any I had before seen, I was led to reflect on the advantages which naturally accrue from the feudal tenures. The tenants of the count are obliged to work at a stated price, in his grounds and garden; and the instruction which they imperceptibly receive from the head gardener, tends to render them useful, and makes them, in the common course of things, better husbandmen and gardeners on their own little farms. Thus the great, who alone travel, in this period of society, for the observation of manners and customs made by sailors is very confined, bring home improvement to promote their own comfort, which is gradually spread abroad amongst the people, till they are stimulated to think for themselves.

The bishops have not large revenues; and the priests are appointed by the king before they come to them to be ordained. There is commonly some little farm annexed to the parsonage; and the inhabitants subscribe voluntarily, three times a year, in addition to the church fees, for the support of the clergyman. The church lands were seized when Lutheranism was introduced;* the desire of obtaining them being probably the real stimulus of reformation. The tithes, which are never required in kind, are divided into three parts; one to the king, another to the incumbent, and the third to repair the delapidations of the parsonage. They do not amount to much. And the stipend allowed to the different civil officers is also too small, scarcely deserving to be termed an independence; that of the custom-house officers is not sufficient to procure the necessaries of life—no wonder, then, if necessity leads them to knavery. Much public virtue cannot be expected till every employment, putting perquisites out of the question, has a salary sufficient to reward industry, whilst none are so great as to permit the possessor to remain idle. It is this want of proportion between profit and labour which debases men, producing the sycophantic appellations of patron and client; and that pernicious *esprit du corps*, proverbially vicious.

The farmers are hospitable, as well as independent. Offering once to pay for some coffee I drank when taking shelter from the rain, I was asked, rather angrily, if a little coffee was worth paying for. They smoke, and drink drams; but not so much as formerly. Drunkenness, often the attendant disgrace of hospitality, will here, as well as every where else, give place to gallantry and refinement of manners; but the change will not be suddenly produced.

The people of every class are constant in their attendance at church; they are very fond of dancing: and the Sunday evenings in Norway, as in Catholic countries, are spent in exercises which exhilerate the spirits, without vitiating the heart. The rest of labour ought to be gay; and the gladness I have felt in France on a Sunday, or decadi,* which I caught from the faces around me, was a sentiment more truly religious than all the stupid stillness which the streets of London ever inspired where the Sabbath is so decorously observed. I recollect, in the country parts of England the churchwardens used to go out, during the service, to see if they could catch any luckless wight playing at bowls or skittles; yet what could be more harmless? It would even, I think, be a great advantage to the English, if feats of activity, I do not include boxing matches, were encouraged on a Sunday, as it might stop the progress of Methodism,* and of that fanatical spirit which appears to be gaining ground. I was surprised when I visited Yorkshire, in my way to Sweden, to find that sullen narrowness of thinking had made such a progress since I was an inhabitant of the country. I could hardly have supposed that sixteen or seventeen years could have produced such an alteration for the worse in the morals of a place;* yes, I say morals; for observance of forms, and avoiding of practices, indifferent in themselves, often supplies the place of that regular attention to duties which are so natural, that they seldom are vauntingly exercised, though they are worth all the precepts of the law and the prophets. Besides, many of these deluded people, with the best meaning, actually lose their reason, and become miserable, the dread of damnation throwing them into a state which merits the term: and still more, in running after their preachers, expecting to promote their salvation, they disregard their welfare in this world, and neglect the interest and comfort of their families: so that in proportion as they attain a reputation for piety, they become idle.

Aristocracy and fanaticism seem equally to be gaining ground in England, particularly in the place I have mentioned: I saw very little of either in Norway. The people are regular in their attendance on public worship; but religion does not interfere with their employments.

As the farmers cut away the wood, they clear the ground. Every year, therefore, the country is becoming fitter to support the inhabitants. Half a century ago the Dutch, I am told, only paid for the cutting down of the wood, and the farmers were glad to get rid of it without giving themselves any trouble. At present they form a just estimate of its value; nay, I was surprised to find even fire wood so dear, when it appears to be in such plenty. The destruction, or gradual reduction, of their forests, will probably meliorate the climate; and their manners will naturally improve in the same ratio as industry requires ingenuity. It is very fortunate that men are, a long time, but just above the brute creation, or the greater part of the earth would never have been rendered habitable; because it is the patient labour of men, who are only seeking for a subsistence, which produces whatever embellishes existence, affording leisure for the cultivation of the arts and sciences, that lift man so far above his first state. I never, my friend, thought so deeply of the advantages obtained by human industry as since I have been in Norway. The world requires, I see, the hand of man to perfect it; and as this task naturally unfolds the faculties he exercises, it is physically impossible that he should have remained in Rousseau's golden age of stupidity.* And, considering the question of human happiness, where, oh! where does it reside?

Has it taken up its abode with unconscious ignorance, or with the high-wrought mind? Is it the offspring of thoughtless animal spirits, or the elve of fancy continually flitting round the expected pleasure?

The increasing population of the earth must necessarily tend to its improvement, as the means of existence are multiplied by invention.

You have probably made similar reflections in America,* where the face of the country, I suppose, resembles the wilds of Norway. I am delighted with the romantic views I daily contemplate, animated by the purest air; and I am interested by the simplicity of manners which reigns around me. Still nothing so soon wearies out the feelings as unmarked simplicity. I am, therefore, half convinced, that I could not live very comfortably exiled from the countries where mankind are so much further advanced in knowledge, imperfect as it is, and unsatisfactory to the thinking mind. Even now I begin to long to hear what you are doing in England and France. My thoughts fly from this wilderness to the polished circles of the world, till recollecting its vices and follies, I bury myself in the woods, but find it necessary to emerge again, that I may not lose sight of the wisdom and virtue which exalts my nature.

What a long time it requires to know ourselves; and yet almost every one has more of this knowledge than he is willing to own, even to himself. I cannot immediately determine whether I ought to rejoice at having turned over in this solitude a new page in the history of my own heart, though I may venture to assure you that a further acquaintance with mankind only tends to increase my respect for your judgment, and esteem for your character.

Farewell!

LETTER X

I HAVE once more, my friend, taken flight; for I left Tonsberg yesterday; but with an intention of returning, in my way back to Sweden.

The road to Laurvig is very fine, and the country the best cultivated in Norway. I never before admired the beech tree; and when I met stragglers here, they pleased me still less. Long and lank, they would have forced me to allow that the line of beauty requires some curves, if the stately pine, standing near, erect, throwing her vast arms around, had not looked beautiful, in opposition to such narrow rules.

In these respects my very reason obliges me to permit my feelings to be my criterion. Whatever excites emotion has charms for me; though I insist that the cultivation of the mind, by warming, nay almost creating the imagination, produces taste, and an immense variety of sensations and emotions, partaking of the exquisite pleasure inspired by beauty and sublimity. As I know of no end to them, the word infinite, so often misapplied, might, on this occasion, be introduced with something like propriety.

But I have rambled away again. I intended to have remarked to you the effect produced by a grove of towering beech. The airy lightness of their foliage admitting a degree of sunshine, which, giving a transparency to the leaves, exhibited an appearance of freshness and elegance that I had never before remarked, I thought of descriptions of Italian scenery. But these evanescent graces seemed the effect of enchantment; and I imperceptibly breathed softly, lest I should destroy what was real, yet looked so like the creation of fancy. Dryden's fable of the flower and the leaf* was not a more poetical reverie.

Adieu, however, to fancy, and to all the sentiments which ennoble our nature. I arrived at Laurvig, and found myself in the midst of a group of lawyers, of different descriptions. My head turned round, my heart grew sick, as I regarded visages deformed by vice; and listened to accounts of chicanery that were continually embroiling the ignorant. These locusts will probably diminish, as the people become more enlightened. In this period of social life the commonalty are always cunningly attentive to their own interest; but their faculties, confined to a few objects, are so narrowed, that they cannot discover it in the general good.* The profession of the law renders a set of men still shrewder and more selfish than the rest; and it is these men, whose wits have been sharpened by knavery, who here undermine morality, confounding right and wrong.

The count of Bernstorff, who really appears to me, from all I can gather, to have the good of the people at heart, aware of this, has lately sent to the mayor of each district to name, according to the size of the place, four or six of the best-informed inhabitants, not men of the law, out of which the citizens were to elect two, who are to be termed *mediators*.* Their office is to endeavour to prevent litigious suits, and conciliate differences. And no suit is to be commenced before the parties have discussed the dispute at their weekly meeting. If a reconciliation should, in consequence, take place, it is to be registered, and the parties are not allowed to retract.

By these means ignorant people will be prevented from applying for advice to men who may justly be termed stirrers-up of strife. They have, for a long time, to use a significant vulgarism, set the people by the ears, and lived by the spoil they caught up in the scramble. There is some reason to hope that this regulation will diminish their number, and restrain their mischievous activity. But till trials by jury* are established, little justice can be expected in Norway. Judges who cannot be bribed are often timid, and afraid of offending bold knaves, lest they should raise a set of hornets about themselves. The fear of censure undermines all energy of character; and, labouring to be prudent, they lose sight of rectitude. Besides, nothing is left to their conscience, or sagacity; they must be governed by evidence, though internally convinced that it is false.

There is a considerable iron manufactory at Laurvig, for coarse work, and a lake near the town supplies the water necessary for working several mills belonging to it.

This establishment belongs to the count of Laurvig.* Without a fortune, and influence equal to his, such a work could not have been set afloat; personal fortunes are not yet sufficient to support such undertakings; nevertheless the inhabitants of the town speak of the size of his estate as an evil, because it obstructs commerce. The occupiers of small farms are obliged to bring their wood to the neighbouring sea-ports, to be shipped; but he, wishing to increase the value of his, will not allow it to be thus gradually cut down; which turns the trade into another channel. Added to this, nature is against them, the bay being open and insecure. I could not help smiling when I was informed that in a hard gale a vessel had been wrecked in the main street. When there are such a number of excellent harbours on the coast, it is a pity that accident has made one of the largest towns grow up in a bad one.

The father of the present count was a distant relation of the family; he resided constantly in Denmark; and his son follows his example. They have not been in possession of the estate many years; and their predecessor lived near the town, introducing a degree of profligacy of manners which has been ruinous to the inhabitants in every respect, their fortunes not being equal to the prevailing extravagance.

What little I have seen of the manners of the people does not please me so well as those of Tonsberg. I am forewarned that I shall find them still more cunning and fraudulent as I advance towards the west-ward, in proportion as traffic takes place of agriculture; for their towns are built on naked rocks; the streets are narrow bridges; and the inhabitants are all seafaring men, or owners of ships, who keep shops.

The inn I was at in Laurvig, this journey, was not the same that I was at before. It is a good one; the people civil, and the accommodations decent. They seem to be better provided in Sweden; but in justice I ought to add, that they charge more extravagantly. My bill at Tonsberg was also much higher than I had paid in Sweden, and much higher than it ought to have been where provisions are so cheap. Indeed they seem to consider foreigners as strangers whom they should never see again, and might fairly pluck. And the inhabitants of the western coast, insulated, as it were, regard those of the east almost as strangers. Each town in that quarter seems to be a great family, suspicious of every other, allowing none to cheat them, but themselves; and, right or wrong, they support one another in the face of justice.

On this journey I was fortunate enough to have one companion with more enlarged views than the generality of his countrymen, who spoke English tolerably.

I was informed that we might still advance a mile and a quarter in our *cabrioles*; afterwards there was no choice, but of a single horse and wretched path, or a boat, the usual mode of travelling.

We therefore sent our baggage forward in the boat, and followed rather slowly, for the road was rocky and sandy. We passed, however, through several beech groves, which still delighted me by the freshness of their light green foliage, and the elegance of their assemblage, forming retreats to veil, without obscuring the sun.

I was surprised, at approaching the water, to find a little cluster of houses pleasantly situated, and an excellent inn. I could have wished to have remained there all night; but as the wind was fair, and the evening fine, I was afraid to trust to the wind, the uncertain wind of to-morrow. We therefore left Helgeraac* immediately, with the declining sun.

Though we were in the open sea, we sailed more amongst the rocks and islands than in my passage from Stromstad; and they often formed very picturesque combinations. Few of the high ridges were entirely bare; the seeds of some pines or firs had been wafted by the winds or waves, and they stood to brave the elements.

Sitting then in a little boat on the ocean, amidst strangers, with sorrow and care pressing hard on me,—buffeting me about from clime to clime,—I felt

> 'Like the lone shrub at random cast,
> That sighs and trembles at each blast!'*

On some of the largest rocks there were actually groves, the retreat of foxes and hares, which, I suppose, had tript over the ice during the winter, without thinking to regain the main land before the thaw.

Several of the islands were inhabited by pilots; and the Norwegian pilots are allowed to be the best in the world; perfectly acquainted with their coast, and ever at hand to observe the first signal or sail. They pay a small tax to the king, and to the regulating officer, and enjoy the fruit of their indefatigable industry.

One of the islands, called Virgin Land,* is a flat, with some depth of earth, extending for half a Norwegian mile, with three farms on it, tolerably well cultivated.

On some of the bare rocks I saw straggling houses; they rose above the denomination of huts inhabited by fishermen. My companions assured me that they were very comfortable dwellings, and that they have not only the necessaries, but even what might be reckoned the superfluities of life. It was too late for me to go on shore, if you will allow me to give that name to shivering rocks, to ascertain the fact.

But rain coming on, and the night growing dark, the pilot declared that it would be dangerous for us to attempt to go to the place of our destination, *East Riisoer*,* a Norwegian mile and a half further; and we determined to stop for the night at a little haven; some half dozen houses scattered under the curve of a rock. Though it became darker and darker, our pilot avoided the blind rocks with great dexterity.

It was about ten o'clock when we arrived; and the old hostess quickly prepared me a comfortable bed—a little too soft, or so; but I was weary; and opening the window to admit the sweetest of breezes to fan me to sleep, I sunk into the most luxurious rest: it was more than refreshing. The hospitable sprites of the grots surely hovered round my pillow; and if I woke, it was to listen to the melodious whispering of the wind amongst them, or to feel the mild breath of morn. Light slumbers produced dreams, where Paradise was before me. My little cherub was again hiding her face in my bosom. I heard her sweet cooing beat on my heart from the cliffs, and saw her tiny footsteps on the sands. New-born hopes seemed, like the rainbow, to appear in the clouds of sorrow, faint, yet sufficient to amuse away despair.

Some refreshing but heavy showers have detained us; and here I am writing quite alone—something more than gay, for which I want a name.

I could almost fancy myself in Nootka Sound,* or on some of the islands on the north west coast of America. We entered by a narrow pass through the rocks, which from this abode appear more romantic than you can well imagine; and seal-skins, hanging at the door to dry, add to the illusion.

It is indeed a corner of the world; but you would be surprised to see the cleanliness and comfort of the dwelling. The shelves are

not only shining with pewter and queen's ware,* but some articles
in silver, more ponderous, it is true, than elegant. The linen is
good, as well as white. All the females spin; and there is a loom in
the kitchen. A sort of individual taste appeared in the arrangement of the furniture, (this is not the place for imitation) and a
kindness in their desire to oblige—how superior to the apish
politeness of the towns! where the people, affecting to be well
bred, fatigue with their endless ceremony.

The mistress is a widow; her daughter is married to a pilot, and
has three cows. They have a little patch of land at about the
distance of two English miles, where they make hay for the winter, which they bring home in a boat. They live here very cheap,
getting money from the vessels which stress of weather, or other
causes, bring into their harbour. I suspect, by their furniture, that
they smuggle a little. I can now credit the account of the other
houses, which I last night thought exaggerated.

I have been conversing with one of my companions respecting
the laws and regulations of Norway. He is a man with a great portion
of common sense, and heart,—yes, a warm heart. This is not the
first time I have remarked heart without sentiment: they are distinct. The former depends on the rectitude of the feelings, on truth
of sympathy: these characters have more tenderness than passion;
the latter has a higher source; call it imagination, genius, or what you
will, it is something very different. I have been laughing with these
simple, worthy *folk*, to give you one of my half score Danish words,
and letting as much of my heart flow out in sympathy as they can
take. Adieu! I must trip up the rocks. The rain is over. Let me catch
pleasure on the wing—I may be melancholy to-morrow. Now all
my nerves keep time with the melody of nature. Ah! let me be
happy whilst I can. The tear starts as I think of it. I must fly from
thought, and find refuge from sorrow in a strong imagination—the
only solace for a feeling heart. Phantoms of bliss! ideal forms of
excellence! again inclose me in your magic circle, and wipe clear
from my remembrance the disappointments which render the sympathy painful, which experience rather increases than damps; by
giving the indulgence of feeling the sanction of reason.

Once more farewell!

LETTER XI

I LEFT Portoer,* the little haven I mentioned, soon after I finished my last letter. The sea was rough; and I perceived that our pilot was right not to venture farther during a hazy night. We had agreed to pay four dollars for a boat from Helgeraac. I mention the sum, because they would demand twice as much from a stranger. I was obliged to pay fifteen for the one I hired at Stromstad. When we were ready to set out, our boatman offered to return a dollar,* and let us go in one of the boats of the place, the pilot who lived there being better acquainted with the coast. He only demanded a dollar and half, which was reasonable. I found him a civil and rather intelligent man: he was in the American service several years, during the revolution.*

I soon perceived that an experienced mariner was necessary to guide us; for we were continually obliged to tack about, to avoid the rocks, which, scarcely reaching to the surface of the water, could only be discovered by the breaking of the waves over them.

The view of this wild coast, as we sailed along it, afforded me a continual subject for meditation. I anticipated the future improvement of the world, and observed how much man had still to do, to obtain of the earth all it could yield. I even carried my speculations so far as to advance a million or two of years to the moment when the earth would perhaps be so perfectly cultivated, and so completely peopled, as to render it necessary to inhabit every spot; yes; these bleak shores. Imagination went still farther, and pictured the state of man when the earth could no longer support him. Where was he to fly to from universal famine? Do not smile: I really became distressed for these fellow creatures, yet unborn. The images fastened on me, and the world appeared a vast prison. I was soon to be in a smaller one—for no other name can I give to Rusoer.* It would be difficult to form an idea of the place, if you have never seen one of these rocky coasts.

We were a considerable time entering amongst the islands, before we saw about two hundred houses crowded together, under a very high rock—still higher appearing above. Talk not of bastilles! To be born here, was to be bastilled by nature*—shut out from all that opens the understanding, or enlarges the heart. Huddled one behind another, not more than a quarter of the dwellings even had a prospect of the sea. A few planks formed passages from house to house, which you must often scale, mounting steps like a ladder, to enter.

The only road across the rocks leads to a habitation, sterile enough, you may suppose, when I tell you that the little earth on the adjacent ones was carried there by the late inhabitant. A path, almost impracticable for a horse, goes on to Arendall, still further to the westward.

I enquired for a walk, and mounting near two hundred steps made round a rock, walked up and down for about a hundred yards, viewing the sea, to which I quickly descended by steps that cheated the declivity. The ocean, and these tremendous bulwarks, enclosed me on every side. I felt the confinement, and wished for wings to reach still loftier cliffs, whose slippery sides no foot was so hardy as to tread; yet what was it to see?—only a boundless waste of water—not a glimpse of smiling nature—not a patch of lively green to relieve the aching sight, or vary the objects of meditation.

I felt my breath oppressed, though nothing could be clearer than the atmosphere. Wandering there alone, I found the solitude desirable; my mind was stored with ideas, which this new scene associated with astonishing rapidity. But I shuddered at the thought of receiving existence, and remaining here, in the solitude of ignorance, till forced to leave a world of which I had seen so little; for the character of the inhabitants is as uncultivated, if not as picturesquely wild, as their abode.

Having no employment but traffic, of which a contraband trade makes the basis of their profit, the coarsest feelings of honesty are quickly blunted. You may suppose that I speak in general terms; and that, with all the disadvantages of nature and circumstances, there are still some respectable exceptions, the more praise-worthy, as tricking is a very contagious mental disease that dries up all the generous juices of the heart.* Nothing genial, in fact, appears around this place, or within the circle of its rocks.

And, now I recollect, it seems to me that the most genial and humane characters I have met with in life, were most alive to the sentiments inspired by tranquil country scenes. What, indeed, is to humanise these beings, who rest shut up, for they seldom even open their windows, smoking, drinking brandy, and driving bargains? I have been almost stifled by these smoakers. They begin in the morning, and are rarely without their pipe till they go to bed. Nothing can be more disgusting than the rooms and men towards the evening: breath, teeth, clothes, and furniture, all are spoilt. It is well that the women are not very delicate, or they would only love their husbands because they were their husbands. Perhaps, you may add, that the remark need not be confined to so small a part of the world; and, *entre nous*, I am of the same opinion. You must not term this inuendo saucy, for it does not come home.

If I had not determined to write, I should have found my confinement here, even for three or four days, tedious. I have no books; and to pace up and down a small room, looking at tiles, overhung by rocks, soon becomes wearisome. I cannot mount two hundred steps, to walk a hundred yards, many times in the day. Besides, the rocks, retaining the heat of the sun, are intolerably warm. I am nevertheless very well; for though there is a shrewdness in the character of these people, depraved by a sordid love of money which repels me, still the comparisons they force me to make keep my heart calm, by exercising my understanding.

Every where wealth commands too much respect; but here, almost exclusively; and it is the only object pursued—not through brake and briar,* but over rocks and waves—yet of what use would riches be to me? I have sometimes asked myself, were I confined to live in such a spot. I could only relieve a few distressed objects, perhaps render them idle, and all the rest of life would be a blank.

My present journey has given fresh force to my opinion, that no place is so disagreeable and unimproving as a country town. I should like to divide my time between the town and country; in a lone house, with the business of farming and planting, where my mind would gain strength by solitary musing; and in a metropolis to rub off the rust of thought, and polish the taste which the contemplation of nature had rendered just. Thus do we wish as we float down the stream of life, whilst chance does more to gratify a desire of knowledge than our best-laid plans. A degree of exertion, produced by some want, more or less painful, is probably the price we must all pay for knowledge. How few authors or artists have arrived at eminence who have not lived by their employment?

I was interrupted yesterday by business, and was prevailed upon to dine with the English vice-consul. His house being open to the sea, I was more at large; and the hospitality of the table pleased me, though the bottle was rather too freely pushed about. Their manner of entertaining was such as I have frequently remarked when I have been thrown in the way of people without education, who have more money than wit, that is, than they know what to do with. The women were unaffected, but had not the natural grace which was often conspicuous at Tonsberg. There was even a striking difference in their dress; these having loaded themselves with finery, in the style of the sailors' girls of Hull or Portsmouth. Taste has not yet taught them to make any but an ostentatious display of wealth: yet I could perceive even here the first steps of the improvement which I am persuaded will make a very obvious progress in the course of half a century; and it ought not to be sooner, to keep pace with the cultivation of the earth. Improving manners will introduce finer moral feelings. They begin to read translations of some of the most useful German productions lately published;* and one of our party sung a song, ridiculing the powers coalesced against France, and the company drank confusion to those who had dismembered Poland.*

The evening was extremely calm and beautiful. Not being able to walk, I requested a boat, as the only means of enjoying free air.

The view of the town was now extremely fine. A huge rocky mountain stood up behind it; and a vast cliff stretched on each side, forming a semicircle. In a recess of the rocks was a clump of pines, amongst which a steeple rose picturesquely beautiful.

The church-yard is almost the only verdant spot in the place. Here, indeed, friendship extends beyond the grave; and, to grant a sod of earth, is to accord a favour. I should rather chuse, did it admit of a choice, to sleep in some of the caves of the rocks; for I am become better reconciled to them since I climbed their craggy sides, last night, listening to the finest echoes I ever heard. We had a French-horn with us; and there was an enchanting wildness in the dying away of the reverberation, that quickly transported me to Shakspeare's magic island.* Spirits unseen seemed to walk abroad, and flit from cliff to cliff, to sooth my soul to peace.

I reluctantly returned to supper, to be shut up in a warm room, only to view the vast shadows of the rocks extending on the slumbering waves. I stood at the window some time before a buzz filled the drawing-room; and now and then the dashing of a solitary oar rendered the scene still more solemn.

Before I came here, I could scarcely have imagined that a simple object, rocks, could have admitted of so many interesting combinations—always grand, and often sublime.

Good night! God bless you!

LETTER XII

I LEFT East Rusoer the day before yesterday. The weather was very fine; but so calm that we loitered on the water near fourteen hours, only to make about six and twenty miles.

It seemed to me a sort of emancipation when we landed at Helgeraac. The confinement which every where struck me whilst sojourning amongst the rocks, made me hail the earth as a land of promise; and the situation shone with fresh lustre from the contrast—from appearing to be a free abode. Here it was possible to travel by land—I never thought this a comfort before, and my eyes, fatigued by the sparkling of the sun on the water, now contentedly reposed on the green expanse, half persuaded that such verdant meads had never till then regaled them.

I rose early to pursue my journey to Tonsberg. The country still wore a face of joy—and my soul was alive to its charms. Leaving the most lofty, and romantic of the cliffs behind us, we were almost continually descending to Tonsberg, through Elysian scenes;* for not only the sea, but mountains, rivers, lakes, and groves, gave an almost endless variety to the prospect. The cottagers were still leading home the hay; and the cottages, on this road, looked very comfortable. Peace and plenty—I mean not abundance, seemed to reign around—still I grew sad as I drew near my old abode. I was sorry to see the sun so high; it was broad noon. Tonsberg was something like a home—yet I was to enter without lighting-up pleasure in any eye—I dreaded the solitariness of my apartment, and wished for night to hide the starting tears, or to shed them on my pillow, and close my eyes on a world where I was destined to wander alone. Why has nature so many charms for me—calling forth and cherishing refined sentiments, only to wound the breast that fosters them? How illusive, perhaps the most so, are the plans of happiness founded on virtue and principle;* what inlets of misery do they not open in a half civilized society? The satisfaction arising from conscious rectitude, will not calm an injured heart, when tenderness is ever finding excuses; and self-applause is a cold solitary feeling, that cannot supply the place of disappointed affection, without throwing a gloom over every prospect, which, banishing pleasure, does not exclude pain. I reasoned and reasoned; but my heart was too full to allow me to remain in the house, and I walked, till I was wearied out, to purchase rest—or rather forgetfulness.

Employment has beguiled this day, and tomorrow I set out for Moss,* in my way to Stromstad. At Gothenburg I shall embrace my *Fannikin*;* probably she will not know me again— and I shall be hurt if she do not. How childish is this! still it is a natural feeling. I would not permit myself to indulge the 'thick coming fears'* of fondness, whilst I was detained by business.—Yet I never saw a calf bounding in a meadow, that did not remind me of my little frolicker. A calf, you say. Yes; but a *capital** one, I own.

I cannot write composedly—I am every instant sinking into reveries—my heart flutters, I know not why. Fool! It is time thou wert at rest.

Friendship and domestic happiness are continually praised; yet how little is there of either in the world, because it requires more cultivation of mind to keep awake affection, even in our own hearts, than the common run of people suppose. Besides, few like to be seen as they really are; and a degree of simplicity, and of undisguised confidence, which, to uninterested observers, would almost border on weakness, is the charm, nay the essence of love or friendship: all the bewitching graces of childhood again appearing. As objects merely to exercise my taste, I therefore like to see people together who have an affection for each other; every turn of their features touches me, and remains pictured on my imagination in indelible characters. The zest of novelty is, however, necessary to rouse the languid sympathies which have been hacknied in the world; as is the factitious behaviour, falsely termed good-breeding, to amuse those, who, defective in taste, continually rely for pleasure on their animal spirits, which not being maintained by the imagination, are unavoidably sooner exhausted than the sentiments of the heart. Friendship is in general sincere at the commencement, and lasts whilst there is any thing to support it; but as a mixture of novelty and vanity is the usual prop, no wonder if it fall with the slender stay. The fop in the play,* payed a greater compliment than he was aware of, when he said to a person, whom he meant to flatter, 'I like you almost as well as a *new acquaintance*.' Why am I talking of friendship, after which I have had such a wild-goose chace.—I thought only of telling you that the crows, as well as wild-geese, are here birds of passage.

LETTER XIII

I LEFT Tonsberg yesterday, the 22d of August. It is only twelve or thirteen English miles to Moss, through a country, less wild than any tract I had hitherto passed over in Norway. It was often beautiful; but seldom afforded those grand views, which fill, rather than sooth the mind.

We glided along the meadows, and through the woods, with sun-beams playing around us; and though no castles adorned the prospects, a greater number of comfortable farms met my eyes, during this ride, than I have ever seen, in the same space, even in the most cultivated part of England. And the very appearance of the cottages of the labourers, sprinkled amidst them, excluded all those gloomy ideas inspired by the contemplation of poverty.

The hay was still bringing in; for one harvest in Norway, treads on the heels of the other. The woods were more variegated; interspersed with shrubs. We no longer passed through forests of vast pines, stretching along with savage magnificence. Forests that only exhibited the slow decay of time, or the devastation produced by warring elements. No; oaks, ashes, beech; and all the light and graceful tenants of our woods here sported luxuriantly. I had not observed many oaks before; for the greater part of the oak planks, I am informed, come from the westward.

In France the farmers generally live in villages, which is a great disadvantage to the country; but the Norwegian farmers, always owning their farms, or being tenants for life, reside in the midst of them; allowing some labourers a dwelling, rent free, who have a little land appertaining to the cottage, not only for a garden, but for crops of different kinds, such as rye, oats, buck-wheat, hemp, flax, beans, potatoes, and hay, which are sown in strips about it; reminding a stranger of the first attempts at culture, when every family was obliged to be an independent community.

These cottagers work at a certain price, ten-pence per day, for the farmers on whose ground they live; and they have spare time enough to cultivate their own land; and lay in a store of fish for the winter. The wives and daughters spin; and the husbands and sons weave: so that they may fairly be reckoned independent; having also a little money in hand to buy coffee, brandy, and some other superfluities.

The only thing I disliked was the military service, which trammels them more than I at first imagined. It is true that the militia is only called out once a year—yet, in case of war, they have no alternative, but must abandon their families. Even the manufacturers are not exempted, though the miners are, in order to encourage undertakings which require a capital at the commencement. And what appears more tyrannical, the inhabitants of certain districts are appointed for the land, others for the sea service. Consequently, a peasant, born a soldier, is not permitted to follow his inclination, should it lead him to go to sea: a natural desire near so many sea ports.

In these regulations the arbitrary government, the king of Denmark being the most absolute monarch in Europe, appears, which in other respects, seeks to hide itself in a lenity that almost renders the laws nullities. If any alteration of old customs is thought of, the opinion of the whole country is required, and maturely considered. I have several times had occasion to observe, that fearing to appear tyrannical, laws are allowed to become obsolete, which ought to be put in force, or better substituted in their stead; for this mistaken moderation, which borders on timidity, favours the least respectable part of the people.

I saw on my way not only good parsonage houses, but comfortable dwellings, with glebe land* for the clerk: always a consequential man in every country: a being proud of a little smattering of learning, to use the appropriate epithet, and vain of the stiff good-breeding reflected from the vicar; though the servility practised in his company gives it a peculiar cast.

The widow of the clergyman is allowed to receive the benefit of the living for a twelve-month, after the death of the incumbent.

Arriving at the ferry, the passage over to Moss is about six or eight English miles; I saw the most level shore I had yet seen in Norway. The appearance of the circumjacent country had been preparing me for the change of scene, which was to greet me, when I reached the coast. For the grand features of nature had been dwindling into prettiness as I advanced; yet the rocks, on smaller scale, were finely wooded to the water's edge. Little art appeared, yet sublimity every where gave place to elegance. The road had often assumed the appearance of a graveled one, made in pleasure grounds, whilst the trees excited only an idea of embellishment. Meadows, like lawns, in an endless variety, displayed

the careless graces of nature; and the ripening corn gave a richness to the landscape, analogous with the other objects.

Never was a southern sky more beautiful, nor more soft its
gales. Indeed, I am led to conclude, that the sweetest summer in
the world, is the northern one. The vegetation being quick and
luxuriant, the moment the earth is loosened from its icy fetters,
and the bound streams regain their wonted activity. The balance
of happiness, with respect to climate, may be more equal than I at
first imagined; for the inhabitants describe with warmth the
pleasures of a winter, at the thoughts of which I shudder. Not
only their parties of pleasure but of business are reserved for this
season, when they travel with astonishing rapidity, the most
direct way, skimming over hedge and ditch.

On entering Moss I was struck by the animation which seemed
to result from industry. The richest of the inhabitants keep shops,
resembling in their manners, and even the arrangement of their
houses, the tradespeople of Yorkshire; with an air of more independence, or rather consequence, from feeling themselves the
first people in the place. I had not time to see the iron works,
belonging to Mr. Anker, of Christiania, a man of fortune and
enterprise; and I was not very anxious to see them, after having
viewed those at Laurvig.

Here I met with an intelligent literary man, who was anxious to
gather information from me, relative to the past and present
situation of France. The newspapers printed at Copenhagen,* as
well as those in England, give the most exaggerated accounts of
their atrocities and distresses; but the former without any apparent comments or inferences. Still the Norwegians, though more
connected with the English, speaking their language, and copying
their manners, wish well to the republican cause; and follow,
with the most lively interest, the successes of the French arms.
So determined were they, in fact, to excuse every thing, disgracing the struggle of freedom, by admitting the tyrant's plea necessity,* that I could hardly persuade them that Robespierre was a
monster.*

The discussion of this subject is not so general as in England,
being confined to the few, the clergy and physician, with a small

portion of people who have a literary turn and leisure: the greater part of the inhabitants, having a variety of occupations, being owners of ships, shopkeepers and farmers, have employment enough at home. And their ambition to become rich may tend to cultivate the common sense, which characterizes and narrows both their hearts and views; confining the former to their families, taking the *handmaids* of it into the circle of pleasure, if not of interest; and the latter to the inspection of their workmen, including the noble science of bargain-making—that is getting every thing at the cheapest, and selling it at the dearest rate. I am now more than ever convinced, that it is an intercourse with men of science and artists, which not only diffuses taste, but gives that freedom to the understanding, without which I have seldom met with much benevolence of character, on a large scale.

Besides, though you do not hear of much pilfering and stealing in Norway, yet they will, with a quiet conscience, buy things at a price which must convince them they were stolen. I had an opportunity of knowing that two or three reputable people had purchased some articles of vagrants, who were detected. How much of the virtue, which appears in the world, is put on for the world! And how little dictated by self respect—so little, that I am ready to repeat the old question—and ask, where is truth or rather principle to be found? These are, perhaps, the vapourings of a heart ill at ease—the effusions of a sensibility wounded almost to madness.* But enough of this—we will discuss the subject in another state of existence—where truth and justice will reign. How cruel are the injuries which make us quarrel with human nature!—At present black melancholy hovers round my footsteps; and sorrow sheds a mildew over all the future prospects, which hope no longer gilds.

A rainy morning prevented my enjoying the pleasure the view of a picturesque country would have afforded me; for though this road passed through a country, a greater extent of which was under cultivation, than I had usually seen here, it nevertheless retained all the wild charms of Norway. Rocks still enclosed the valleys, whose grey sides enlivened their verdure. Lakes appeared like branches of the sea, and branches of the sea assumed the appearance of tranquil lakes; whilst streamlets prattled amongst the pebbles, and the broken mass of stone which had rolled into them; giving fantastic turns to the trees whose roots they bared.

It is not, in fact, surprising that the pine should be often undermined, it shoots its fibres in such an horizontal direction, merely on the surface of the earth, requiring only enough to cover those that cling to the craggs. Nothing proves to me, so clearly, that it is the air which principally nourishes trees and plants, as the flourishing appearance of these pines.——The firs demanding a deeper soil, are seldom seen in equal health, or so numerous on the barren cliffs. They take shelter in the crevices, or where, after some revolving ages, the pines have prepared them a footing.

Approaching, or rather descending, to Christiania, though the weather continued a little cloudy, my eyes were charmed with the view of an extensive undulated valley, stretching out under the shelter of a noble amphitheatre of pine-covered mountains. Farm houses scattered about animated, nay, graced a scene which still retained so much of its native wildness, that the art which appeared, seemed so necessary it was scarcely perceived. Cattle were grazing in the shaven meadows; and the lively green, on their swelling sides, contrasted with the ripening corn and rye. The corn that grew on the slopes, had not, indeed, the laughing luxuriance of plenty, which I have seen in more genial climes. A fresh breeze swept across the grain, parting its slender stalks; but the wheat did not wave its head with its wonted, careless dignity, as if nature had crowned it the king of plants.

The view, immediately on the left, as we drove down the mountain, was almost spoilt by the depredations committed on the rocks to make alum.* I do not know the process.——I only saw that the rocks looked red after they had been burnt; and regretted that the operation should leave a quantity of rubbish, to introduce an image of human industry in the shape of destruction. The situation of Christiania is certainly uncommonly fine; and I never saw a bay that so forcibly gave me an idea of a place of safety from the storms of the ocean—all the surrounding objects were beautiful, and even grand. But neither the rocky mountains, nor the woods that graced them, could be compared with the sublime prospects I had seen towards the westward; and as for the hills, 'capped with *eternal* snow,' Mr. Coxe's description* led me to look for them; but they had flown; for I looked vainly around for this noble back-ground.

A few months ago the people of Christiania, rose,* exasperated by the scarcity, and consequent high price of grain. The immediate cause was the shipping of some, said to be for Moss; but which they suspected was only a pretext to send it out of the country: and I am not sure that they were wrong in their conjecture.—Such are the tricks of trade! They threw stones at Mr. Anker, the owner of it, as he rode out of town to escape from their fury; they assembled about his house. And the people demanded afterwards, with so much impetuosity, the liberty of those who were taken up in consequence of the tumult, that the Grand Bailiff thought it prudent to release them without further altercation.

You may think me too severe on commerce; but from the manner it is at present carried on, little can be advanced in favour of a pursuit that wears out the most sacred principles of humanity and rectitude. What is speculation, but a species of gambling, I might have said fraud, in which address generally gains the prize? I was led into these reflections when I heard of some tricks practised by merchants, mis-called reputable, and certainly men of property, during the present war, in which common honesty was violated: damaged goods, and provisions, having been shipped for the express purpose of falling into the hands of the English, who had pledged themselves to reimburse neutral nations, for the cargoes they seized: cannon also, sent back as unfit for service, have been shipped as *a good speculation*; the captain receiving orders to cruize about till he fell in with an English frigate.* Many individuals, I believe, have suffered by the seizures of their vessels; still I am persuaded that the English government has been very much imposed upon in the charges made by merchants, who contrived to get their ships taken. This censure is not confined to the Danes. Adieu! For the present, I must take advantage of a moment of fine weather to walk out and see the town.

At Christiania I met with that polite reception, which rather characterises the progress of manners in the world, than of any particular portion of it. The first evening of my arrival I supped with some of the most fashionable people of the place; and almost imagined myself in a circle of English ladies, so much did they resemble them in manners, dress, and even in beauty; for the fairest of my countrywomen would not have been sorry to rank with the Grand Bailiff's lady.* There were several pretty girls present, but she outshone them all; and what interested me still more, I could not avoid observing that in acquiring the easy politeness which distinguishes people of quality, she had pre-served her Norwegian simplicity. There was, in fact, a graceful timidity in her address, inexpressibly charming. This surprised me a little, because her husband was quite a Frenchman of the *ancien régime*,* or rather a courtier, the same kind of animal in every country.

Here I saw the cloven foot of despotism. I boasted, to you, that they had no viceroy in Norway; but these grand bailiffs, particu-larly the superior one, who resides at Christiania, are political monsters of the same species. Needy sycophants are provided for by their relations and connexions at Copenhagen, as at other courts. And though the Norwegians are not in the abject state of the Irish,* yet this second-hand government is still felt by their being deprived of several natural advantages to benefit the domineering state.

The grand bailiffs are mostly noblemen from Copenhagen, who act as men of common minds will always act in such situations—aping a degree of courtly parade which clashes with the independent character of a magistrate. Besides, they have a degree of power over the country judges, which some of them who exercise a jurisdiction truly patriarchal, most painfully feel. I can scarcely say why, my friend, but in this city, thoughtfulness seemed to be sliding into melancholy, or rather dullness.—The fire of fancy, which had been kept alive in the country, was almost extinguished by reflections on the ills that harass such a large por-tion of mankind.—I felt like a bird fluttering on the ground unable to mount; yet unwilling to crawl tranquilly like a reptile, whilst still conscious it had wings.

I walked out, for the open air is always my remedy when an aching-head proceeds from an oppressed heart. Chance directed my steps towards the fortress, and the sight of the slaves, working with chains on their legs, only served to embitter me still more against the regulations of society, which treated knaves in such a different manner, especially as there was a degree of energy in some of their countenances which unavoidably excited my attention, and almost created respect.

I wished to have seen, through an iron grate, the face of a man who has been confined six years,* for having induced the farmers to revolt against some impositions of the government. I could not obtain a clear account of the affair; yet, as the complaint was against some farmers of taxes, I am inclined to believe, that it was not totally without foundation. He must have possessed some eloquence, or have had truth on his side; for the farmers rose by hundreds to support him, and were very much exasperated at his imprisonment; which will probably last for life, though he has sent several very spirited remonstrances to the upper court, which makes the judges so averse to giving a sentence which may be cavilled at, that they take advantage of the glorious uncertainty of the law, to protract a decision which is only to be regulated by reasons of state.

The greater number of the slaves, I saw here, were not confined for life. Their labour is not hard; and they work in the open air, which prevents their constitutions from suffering by imprisonment. Still as they are allowed to associate together, and boast of their dexterity, not only to each other but to the soldiers around them, in the garrison, they commonly, it is natural to conclude, go out more confirmed, and more expert knaves than when they entered.

It is not necessary to trace the origin of the association of ideas, which led me to think that the stars and gold keys, which surrounded me the evening before, disgraced the wearers, as much as the fetters I was viewing—perhaps more. I even began to investigate the reason which led me to suspect that the former produced the latter.

The Norwegians are extravagantly fond of courtly distinction, and of titles, though they have no immunities annexed to them, and are easily purchased. The proprietors of mines have many privileges: they are almost exempt from taxes, and the peasantry born on their estates, as well as those on the count's, are not born soldiers or sailors.

One distinction, or rather trophy of nobility, which might have occurred to the Hottentots,* amused me; it was a bunch of hog's bristles placed on the horses' heads; surmounting that part of the harness to which a round piece of brass often dangles, fatiguing the eye with its idle motion.

From the fortress I returned to my lodging, and quickly was taken out of town to be shewn a pretty villa, and English garden.* To a Norwegian both might have been objects of curiosity, and of use, by exciting to the comparison which leads to improvement. But whilst I gazed, I was employed in restoring the place to nature, or taste, by giving it the character of the surrounding scene. Serpentine walks, and flowering shrubs, looked trifling in a grand recess of the rocks, shaded by towering pines. Groves of lesser trees might have been sheltered under them, which would have melted into the landscape, displaying only the art which ought to point out the vicinity of a human abode, furnished with some elegance. But few people have sufficient taste to discern, that the art of embellishing, consists in interesting, not in astonishing.

Christiania is certainly very pleasantly situated; and the environs I passed through, during this ride, afforded many fine, and cultivated prospects; but, excepting the first view approaching to it, rarely present any combination of objects so strikingly new, or picturesque, as to command remembrance.

Adieu!

LETTER XIV

CHRISTIANIA is a clean, neat city; but it has none of the graces of architecture, which ought to keep pace with the refining manners of a people—or the outside of the house will disgrace the inside;

giving the beholder an idea of overgrown wealth devoid of taste. Large square wooden houses offend the eye, displaying more than gothic* barbarism. Huge gothic piles, indeed, exhibit a characteristic sublimity, and a wildness of fancy peculiar to the period when they were erected; but size, without grandeur or elegance, has an emphatical stamp of meanness, of poverty of conception, which only a commercial spirit could give.

The same thought has struck me, when I have entered the meeting-house of my respected friend, Dr. Price.* I am surprised that the dissenters, who have not laid aside all the pomps and vanities of life, should imagine a noble pillar, or arch, unhallowed. Whilst men have senses, whatever sooths them lends wings to devotion; else why do the beauties of nature, where all that charm them are spread around with a lavish hand, force even the sorrowing heart to acknowledge that existence is a blessing; and this acknowledgement is the most sublime homage we can pay to the Deity.

The argument of convenience is absurd. Who would labour for wealth, if it were to procure nothing but conveniencies? If we wish to render mankind moral from principle, we must, I am persuaded, give a greater scope to the enjoyments of the senses, by blending taste with them. This has frequently occurred to me since I have been in the north, and observed that there sanguine characters always take refuge in drunkenness after the fire of youth is spent.

But I have flown from Norway, to go back to the wooden houses. Farms constructed with logs, and even little villages, here erected in the same simple manner, have appeared to me very picturesque. In the more remote parts I had been particularly pleased with many cottages situated close to a brook, or bordering on a lake, with the whole farm contiguous. As the family increases, a little more land is cultivated: thus the country is obviously enriched by population. Formerly the farmers might more justly have been termed wood-cutters. But now they find it necessary to spare the woods a little; and this change will be universally beneficial; for whilst they lived entirely by selling the trees they felled, they did not pay sufficient attention to husbandry; consequently, advanced very slowly in agricultural knowledge. Necessity will in future more and more spur them on; for the ground, cleared of wood, must be cultivated, or the farm loses its value: there is no waiting for food till another generation of pines be grown to maturity.

The people of property are very careful of their timber; and, rambling through a forest near Tonsberg, belonging to the count, I have stopt to admire the appearance of some of the cottages inhabited by a woodman's family—a man employed to cut down the wood necessary for the houshold and the estate. A little lawn was cleared, on which several lofty trees were left which nature had grouped, whilst the encircling firs sported with wild grace. The dwelling was sheltered by the forest, noble pines spreading their branches over the roof; and before the door a cow, goat, nag, and children, seemed equally content with their lot; and if contentment be all we can attain, it is perhaps, best secured by ignorance.

As I have been most delighted with the country parts of Norway, I was sorry to leave Christiania, without going further to the north, though the advancing season admonished me to depart, as well as the calls of business and affection.

June and July are the months to make a tour through Norway; for then the evenings and nights are the finest I have ever seen; but towards the middle, or latter end of August, the clouds begin to gather, and summer disappears almost before it has ripened the fruit of autumn—even, as it were, slips from your embraces, whilst the satisfied senses seem to rest in enjoyment.

You will ask, perhaps, why I wished to go further northward. Why? not only because the country, from all I can gather, is most romantic, abounding in forests and lakes, and the air pure, but I have heard much of the intelligence of the inhabitants, substantial farmers, who have none of that cunning to contaminate their simplicity, which displeased me so much in the conduct of the people on the sea coast. A man, who has been detected in any dishonest act, can no longer live among them. He is universally shunned, and shame becomes the severest punishment. Such a contempt have they, in fact, for every species of fraud, that they will not allow the people on the western coast to be their country-men; so much do they despise the arts for which those traders who live on the rocks are notorious.

The description I received of them carried me back to the fables of the golden age: independence and virtue; affluence without vice; cultivation of mind, without depravity of heart; with 'ever smiling liberty;'* the nymph of the mountain*—I want faith! My imagination hurries me forward to seek an asylum in such a retreat from all the disappointments I am threatened with; but reason drags me back, whispering that the world is still the world, and man the same compound of weakness and folly, who must occasionally excite love and disgust, admiration and contempt. But this description, though it seems to have been sketched by a fairy pencil, was given me by a man of sound understanding, whose fancy seldom appears to run away with him.

A law in Norway, termed the *odels right*,* has lately been modified, and probably will be abolished as an impediment to commerce. The heir of an estate had the power of repurchasing it at the original purchase money, making allowance for such improvements as were absolutely necessary, during the space of twenty years. At present ten is the term allowed for after thought; and when the regulation was made, all the men of abilities were invited to give their opinion whether it were better to abrogate or modify it. It is certainly a convenient and safe way of mortgaging land; yet the most rational men, whom I conversed with on the subject, seemed convinced that the right was more injurious than beneficial to society; still if it contribute to keep the farms in the farmers' own hands, I should be sorry to hear that it were abolished.

The aristocracy in Norway, if we keep clear of Christiania, is far from being formidable; and it will require a long time to enable the merchants to attain a sufficient monied interest to induce them to reinforce the upper class, at the expence of the yeomanry, with whom they are usually connected.

England and America owe their liberty to commerce, which created a new species of power to undermine the feudal system.

But let them beware of the consequence; the tyranny of wealth is still more galling and debasing than that of rank.

Farewell! I must prepare for my departure.

LETTER XV

I LEFT Christiania yesterday. The weather was not very fine; and having been a little delayed on the road, I found that it was too late to go round, a couple of miles, to see the cascade near Fredericstadt, which I had determined to visit. Besides, as Fredericstadt is a fortress, it was necessary to arrive there before they shut the gate.

The road along the river is very romantic, though the views are not grand; and the riches of Norway, its timber, floats silently down the stream, often impeded in its course by islands and little cataracts, the offspring, as it were, of the great one I had frequently heard described.

I found an excellent inn at Fredericstadt, and was gratified by the kind attention of the hostess, who, perceiving that my clothes were wet, took great pains to procure me, as a stranger, every comfort for the night.

It had rained very hard; and we passed the ferry in the dark, without getting out of our carriage, which I think wrong, as the horses are sometimes unruly. Fatigue and melancholy, however, had made me regardless whether I went down or across the stream; and I did not know that I was wet before the hostess remarked it. My imagination has never yet severed me from my griefs—and my mind has seldom been so free as to allow my body to be delicate.[1]

How I am altered by disappointment!—When going to Lisbon, the elasticity of my mind was sufficient to ward off weariness, and my imagination still could dip her brush in the rainbow of fancy, and sketch futurity in glowing colours.* Now—but let me talk of something else—will you go with me to the cascade?

---

[1] 'When the mind's free,
The body's delicate.'*
Vid. King Lear.

The cross road to it was rugged and dreary; and though a considerable extent of land was cultivated on all sides, yet the rocks were entirely bare, which surprised me, as they were more on a level with the surface than any I had yet seen. On inquiry, however, I learnt that some years since a forest had been burnt. This appearance of desolation was beyond measure gloomy, inspiring emotions that sterility had never produced. Fires of this kind are occasioned by the wind suddenly rising when the farmers are burning roots of trees, stalks of beans, &c. with which they manure the ground. The devastation must, indeed, be terrible, when this, literally speaking, wild fire, runs along the forest, flying from top to top, and crackling amongst the branches. The soil, as well as the trees, is swept away by the destructive torrent; and the country, despoiled of beauty and riches, is left to mourn for ages.

Admiring, as I do, these noble forests, which seem to bid defiance to time, I looked with pain on the ridge of rocks that stretched far beyond my eye, formerly crowned with the most beautiful verdure.

I have often mentioned the grandeur, but I feel myself unequal to the task of conveying an idea of the beauty and elegance of the scene when the spiral tops of the pines are loaded with ripening seed, and the sun gives a glow to their light green tinge, which is changing into purple, one tree more or less advanced, contrasting with another. The profusion with which nature has decked them, with pendant honours, prevents all surprise at seeing, in every crevice, some sapling struggling for existence. Vast masses of stone are thus encircled; and roots, torn up by the storms, become a shelter for a young generation. The pine and fir woods, left entirely to nature, display an endless variety; and the paths in the wood are not entangled with fallen leaves, which are only interesting whilst they are fluttering between life and death. The grey cobweb-like appearance of the aged pines is a much finer image of decay; the fibres whitening as they lose their moisture, imprisoned life seems to be stealing away. I cannot tell why—but death, under every form, appears to me like something getting free—to expand in I know not what element; nay I feel that this conscious being must be as unfettered, have the wings of thought, before it can be happy.

Reaching the cascade, or rather cataract, the roaring of which had a long time announced its vicinity, my soul was hurried by the falls into a new train of reflections. The impetuous dashing of the rebounding torrent from the dark cavities which mocked the exploring eye, produced an equal activity in my mind: my thoughts darted from earth to heaven, and I asked myself why I was chained to life and its misery? Still the tumultuous emotions this sublime object excited, were pleasurable; and, viewing it, my soul rose, with renewed dignity, above its cares—grasping at immortality—it seemed as impossible to stop the current of my thoughts, as of the always varying, still the same, torrent before me—I stretched out my hand to eternity, bounding over the dark speck of life to come.

We turned with regret from the cascade.* On a little hill, which commands the best view of it, several obelisks are erected to commemorate the visits of different kings. The appearance of the river above and below the falls is very picturesque, the ruggedness of the scenery disappearing as the torrent subsides into a peaceful stream. But I did not like to see a number of saw-mills crowded together close to the cataracts; they destroyed the harmony of the prospect.

The sight of a bridge erected across a deep valley, at a little distance, inspired very dissimilar sensations. It was most ingeniously supported by mast-like trunks, just stript of their branches; and logs, placed one across the other, produced an appearance equally light and firm, seeming almost to be built in the air when we were below it; the height taking from the magnitude of the supporting trees give them a slender, graceful look.

There are two noble estates in this neighbourhood, the proprietors of which seem to have caught more than their portion of the enterprising spirit that is gone abroad. Many agricultural experiments have been made; and the country appears better enclosed and cultivated; yet the cottages had not the comfortable aspect of those I had observed near Moss, and to the westward. Man is always debased by servitude, of any description; and here the peasantry are not entirely free.

Adieu!

I almost forgot to tell you, that I did not leave Norway without making some inquiries after the monsters said to have been seen in the northern sea; but though I conversed with several captains, I could not meet with one who had ever heard any traditional description of them, much less had any ocular demonstration of their existence. Till the fact be better ascertained, I should think the account of them ought to be torn out of our Geographical Grammars.*

LETTER XVI

I SET out from Fredericstadt about three o'clock in the afternoon, and expected to reach Stromstad* before the night closed in; but the wind dying away, the weather became so calm, that we scarcely made any perceptible advances towards the opposite coast, though the men were fatigued with rowing.

Getting amongst the rocks and islands as the moon rose, and the stars darted forward out of the clear expanse, I forgot that the night stole on, whilst indulging affectionate reveries, the poetical fictions of sensibility; I was not, therefore, aware of the length of time we had been toiling to reach Stromstad. And when I began to look around, I did not perceive any thing to indicate that we were in its neighbourhood. So far from it, that when I inquired of the pilot, who spoke a little English, I found that he was only accustomed to coast along the Norwegian shore; and had been, only once, across to Stromstad. But he had brought with him a fellow better acquainted, he assured me, with the rocks by which they were to steer our course; for we had not a compass on board; yet, as he was half a fool, I had little confidence in his skill. There was then great reason to fear that we had lost our way, and were straying amidst a labyrinth of rocks, without a clue.

This was something like an adventure; but not of the most agreeable cast; besides, I was impatient to arrive at Stromstad, to be able to send forward, that night, a boy to order horses on the road to be ready; for I was unwilling to remain there a day, without having any thing to detain me from my little girl; and from the letters which I was impatient to get from you.

I began to expostulate, and even to scold the pilot, for not having informed me of his ignorance, previous to my departure. This made him row with more force; and we turned round one rock only to see another, equally destitute of the tokens we were in search of to tell us where we were. Entering also into creek after creek, which promised to be the entrance of the bay we were seeking, we advanced merely to find ourselves running aground.

The solitariness of the scene, as we glided under the dark shadows of the rocks, pleased me for a while; but the fear of passing the whole night thus wandering to and fro, and losing the next day, roused me. I begged the pilot to return to one of the largest islands, at the side of which we had seen a boat moored. As we drew nearer, a light, through a window on the summit, became our beacon; but we were farther off than I supposed.

With some difficulty the pilot got on shore, not distinguishing the landing place; and I remained in the boat, knowing that all the relief we could expect, was a man to direct us. After waiting some time, for there is an insensibility in the very movements of these people,[1] that would weary more than ordinary patience, he brought with him a man, who, assisting them to row, we landed at Stromstad a little after one in the morning.

It was too late to send off a boy; but I did not go to bed before I had made the arrangements necessary to enable me to set out as early as possible.

The sun rose with splendor. My mind was too active to allow me to loiter long in bed, though the horses did not arrive till between seven and eight. However, as I wished to let the boy, who went forward to order the horses, get considerably the start of me, I bridled-in my impatience.

This precaution was unavailing, for after the three first posts, I had to wait two hours, whilst the people at the post-house went,

---

[1] It is very possible that he staid to smoke a pipe, though I was waiting in the cold.

fair and softly, to the farm, to bid them bring up the horses, which were carrying in the first-fruits of the harvest. I discovered here that these sluggish peasants had their share of cunning. Though they had made me pay for a horse, the boy had gone on foot, and only arrived half an hour before me. This disconcerted the whole arrangement of the day; and being detained again three hours, I reluctantly determined to sleep at Quistram, two posts short of Uddervalla,* where I had hoped to have arrived that night.

But, when I reached Quistram, I found I could not approach the door of the inn, for men, horses, and carts, cows, and pigs huddled together. From the concourse of people, I had met on the road, I conjectured that there was a fair in the neighbourhood, this crowd convinced me that it was but too true. The boisterous merriment that almost every instant produced a quarrel or made me dread one, with the clouds of tobacco, and fumes of brandy, gave an infernal appearance to the scene. There was every thing to drive me back, nothing to excite sympathy in a rude tumult of the senses, which I foresaw would end in a gross debauch. What was to be done? No bed was to be had, or even a quiet corner to retire to for a moment—all was lost in noise, riot, and confusion.

After some debating they promised me horses, which were to go on to Uddervalla, two stages. I requested something to eat first, not having dined; and the hostess, whom I have mentioned to you before, as knowing how to take care of herself, brought me a plate of fish, for which she charged a rixdollar and a half. This was making hay whilst the sun shone. I was glad to get out of the uproar, though not disposed to travel in an incommodious open carriage all night, had I thought that there was any chance of getting horses.

Quitting Quistram, I met a number of joyous groups, and though the evening was fresh, many were stretched on the grass like weary cattle; and drunken men had fallen by the road side. On a rock, under the shade of lofty trees, a large party of men and women had lighted a fire, cutting down fuel around to keep it alive all night. They were drinking, smoking, and laughing, with all their might and main. I felt for the trees whose torn branches strewed the ground.—Hapless nymphs! thy haunts I fear were polluted by many an unhallowed flame; the casual burst of the moment!

The horses went on very well; but when we drew near the post-house, the postilion stopt short, and neither threats, nor promises, could prevail on him to go forward. He even began to howl and weep, when I insisted on his keeping his word. Nothing, indeed, can equal the stupid obstinacy of some of these half alive beings, who seem to have been made by Prometheus, when the fire he stole from Heaven was so exhausted, that he could only spare a spark to give life, not animation, to the inert clay.

It was some time before we could rouse any body; and, as I expected, horses we were told could not be had in less than four or five hours. I again attempted to bribe the churlish brute, who brought us there; but I discovered, that in spite of the courteous hostess's promise, he had received orders not to go any farther.

As there was no remedy I entered, and was almost driven back by the stench—a softer phrase would not have conveyed an idea of the hot vapour that issued from an apartment, in which some eight or ten people were sleeping, not to reckon the cats and dogs stretched on the floor. Two or three of the men or women were lying on the benches, others on old chests; and one figure started half out of a trunk to look at me, whom I might have taken for a ghost, had the *chemise* been white, to contrast with the sallow visage. But the *costume* of apparitions not being preserved I passed, nothing dreading, excepting the effluvia, warily amongst the pots, pans, milk-pails, and washing-tubs. After scaling a ruinous staircase, I was shewn a bed-chamber. The bed did not invite me to enter; opening, therefore, the window, and taking some clean towels out of my night-sack, I spread them over the coverlid, on which tired nature found repose, in spite of the previous disgust.

With the grey of the morn the birds awoke me; and descending to enquire for the horses, I hastened through the apartment, I have already described, not wishing to associate the idea of a pigstye with that of a human dwelling.

I do not now wonder that the girls lose their fine complexions at such an early age, or that love here is merely an appetite, to fulfil the main design of nature, never enlivened by either affection or sentiment.

For a few posts we found the horses waiting; but afterwards I was retarded, as before, by the peasants, who, taking advantage of my ignorance of the language, made me pay for the fourth horse, that ought to have gone forward to have the others in readiness, though it had never been sent. I was particularly impatient at the last post, as I longed to assure myself that my child was well.

My impatience, however, did not prevent my enjoying the journey. I had six weeks before passed over the same ground, still it had sufficient novelty to attract my attention, and beguile, if not banish, the sorrow that had taken up its abode in my heart. How interesting are the varied beauties of nature; and what peculiar charms characterize each season! The purple hue which the heath now assumed, gave it a degree of richness, that almost exceeded the lustre of the young green of spring—and harmonized exquisitely with the rays of the ripening corn. The weather was uninterruptedly fine, and the people busy in the fields cutting down the corn, or binding up the sheaves, continually varied the prospect. The rocks, it is true, were unusually rugged and dreary, yet as the road runs for a considerable way by the side of a fine river, with extended pastures on the other side, the image of sterility was not the predominant object, though the cottages looked still more miserable, after having seen the Norwegian farms. The trees, likewise, appeared of the growth of yesterday, compared with those Nestors* of the forest I have frequently mentioned. The women and children were cutting off branches from the beech, birch, oak, &c, and leaving them to dry—This way of helping out their fodder, injures the trees. But the winters are so long, that the poor cannot afford to lay in a sufficient stock of hay. By such means they just keep life in the poor cows, for little milk can be expected when they are so miserably fed.

It was Saturday, and the evening was uncommonly serene. In the villages I every where saw preparations for Sunday; and I passed by a little car loaded with rye, that presented, for the pencil and heart, the sweetest picture of a harvest home I had ever beheld. A little girl was mounted a straddle on a shaggy horse, brandishing a stick over its head; the father was walking at the side of the car with a child in his arms, who must have come to meet him with tottering steps, the little creature was stretching out its arms to cling round his neck; and a boy, just above petticoats, was labouring hard, with a fork, behind, to keep the sheaves from falling.

My eyes followed them to the cottage, and an involuntary sigh whispered to my heart, that I envied the mother, much as I dislike cooking, who was preparing their pottage. I was returning to my babe, who may never experience a father's care or tenderness. The bosom that nurtured her, heaved with a pang at the thought which only an unhappy mother could feel.

Adieu!

LETTER XVII

I WAS unwilling to leave Gothenburg, without visiting Trolhættæ.* I wished not only to see the cascade, but to observe the progress of the stupendous attempt to form a canal through the rocks, to the extent of an English mile and a half.

This work is carried on by a company who employ daily nine hundred men; five years was the time mentioned in the proposals, addressed to the public, as necessary for the completion. A much more considerable sum than the plan requires has been subscribed, for which there is every reason to suppose the promoters will receive ample interest.

The Danes survey the progress of this work with a jealous eye, as it is principally undertaken to get clear of the Sound duty.

Arrived at Trolhættæ, I must own that the first view of the cascade disappointed me: and the sight of the works, as they advanced, though a grand proof of human industry, was not calculated to warm the fancy. I, however, wandered about; and at last coming to the conflux of the various cataracts, rushing from different falls, struggling with the huge masses of rock, and rebounding from the profound cavities, I immediately retracted, acknowledging that it was indeed a grand object. A little island stood in the midst, covered with firs, which, by dividing the torrent, rendered it more picturesque; one half appearing to issue from a dark cavern, that fancy might easily imagine a vast fountain, throwing up its waters from the very centre of the earth.

I gazed I know not how long, stunned with the noise; and growing giddy with only looking at the never-ceasing tumultuous motion, I listened, scarcely conscious where I was, when I observed a boy, half obscured by the sparkling foam, fishing under the impending rock on the other side. How he had descended I could not perceive; nothing like human footsteps appeared; and the horrific craggs seemed to bid defiance even to the goat's activity. It looked like an abode only fit for the eagle, though in its crevices some pines darted up their spiral heads; but they only grew near the cascade; every where else sterility itself reigned with dreary grandeur; for the huge grey massy rocks which probably had been torn asunder by some dreadful convulsion of nature, had not even their first covering of a little cleaving moss. There were so many appearances to excite the idea of chaos, that, instead of admiring the canal and the works, great as they are termed, and little as they appear, I could not help regretting that such a noble scene had not been left in all its solitary sublimity. Amidst the awful roaring of the impetuous torrents, the noise of human instruments, and the bustle of workmen, even the blowing up of the rocks, when grand masses trembled in the darkened air—only resembled the insignificant sport of children.

One fall of water, partly made by art, when they were attempting to construct sluices, had an uncommonly grand effect; the water precipitated itself with immense velocity down a perpendicular, at least fifty or sixty yards, into a gulph, so concealed by the foam as to give full play to the fancy: there was a continual uproar: I stood on a rock to observe it, a kind of bridge formed by nature, nearly on a level with the commencement of the fall. After musing by it a long time, I turned towards the other side, and saw a gentle stream stray calmly out. I should have concluded that it had no communication with the torrent, had I not seen a huge log, that fell headlong down the cascade, steal peacefully into the purling stream.

I retired from these wild scenes with regret to a miserable inn, and next morning returned to Gothenburg, to prepare for my journey to Copenhagen.

I was sorry to leave Gothenburg, without travelling further into Sweden; yet I imagine I should only have seen a romantic country thinly inhabited, and these inhabitants struggling with poverty. The Norwegian peasantry, mostly independent, have a rough kind of frankness in their manner; but the Swedish, rendered more abject by misery, have a degree of politeness in their address, which, though it may sometimes border on insincerity, is oftener the effect of a broken spirit, rather softened than degraded by wretchedness.

In Norway there are no notes in circulation of less value than a Swedish rixdollar. A small silver coin, commonly not worth more than a penny, and never more than twopence, serves for change: but in Sweden they have notes as low as sixpence. I never saw any silver pieces there; and could not without difficulty, and giving a premium, obtain the value of a rixdollar, in a large copper coin, to give away on the road to the poor who open the gates.

As another proof of the poverty of Sweden, I ought to mention that foreign merchants, who have acquired a fortune there, are obliged to deposit the sixth part when they leave the kingdom. This law, you may suppose, is frequently evaded.

In fact, the laws here, as well as in Norway, are so relaxed, that they rather favour than restrain knavery.

Whilst I was at Gothenburg, a man who had been confined for breaking open his master's desk, and running away with five or six thousand rixdollars, was only sentenced to forty days confinement on bread and water; and this slight punishment his relations rendered nugatory by supplying him with more savoury food.

The Swedes are in general attached to their families; yet a divorce* may be obtained by either party, on proving the infidelity of the other, or acknowledging it themselves. The women do not often recur to this equal privilege; for they either retaliate on their husbands, by following their own devices, or sink into the

merest domestic drudges, worn down by tyranny to servile submission. Do not term me severe, if I add, that after youth is flown,
the husband becomes a sot; and the wife amuses herself by scold-
ing her servants. In fact, what is to be expected in any country
where taste and cultivation of mind do not supply the place of
youthful beauty and animal spirits? Affection requires a firmer
foundation than sympathy; and few people have a principle of
action sufficiently stable to produce rectitude of feeling; for, in
spite of all the arguments I have heard to justify deviations from
duty, I am persuaded that even the most spontaneous sensations
are more under the direction of principle than weak people are
willing to allow.

But adieu to moralizing. I have been writing these last sheets
at an inn in Elsineur, where I am waiting for horses; and as they
are not yet ready, I will give you a short account of my journey
from Gothenburg; for I set out the morning after I returned from
Trolhættæ.

The country, during the first day's journey, presented a most
barren appearance; as rocky, yet not so picturesque as Norway,
because on a diminutive scale. We stopt to sleep at a tolerable inn
in Falckersberg,* a decent little town.

The next day beeches and oaks began to grace the prospects,
the sea every now and then appearing to give them dignity.
I could not avoid observing also, that even in this part of Sweden,
one of the most sterile, as I was informed, there was more ground
under cultivation than in Norway. Plains of varied crops stretched
out to a considerable extent, and sloped down to the shore, no
longer terrific. And, as far as I could judge, from glancing my eye
over the country, as we drove along, agriculture was in a more
advanced state; though, in the habitations, a greater appearance of
poverty still remained. The cottages indeed often looked most
uncomfortable, but never so miserable as those I had remarked on
the road to Stromstad; and the towns were equal, if not superior
to many of the little towns in Wales,* or some I have passed
through in my way from Calais to Paris.

The inns, as we advanced, were not to be complained of, unless
I had always thought of England. The people were civil, and

much more moderate in their demands than the Norwegians, particularly to the westward, where they boldly charge for what you never had, and seem to consider you, as they do a wreck, if not as lawful prey, yet as a lucky chance, which they ought not to neglect to seize.

The prospect of Elsineur, as we passed the Sound, was pleasant. I gave three rixdollars for my boat, including something to drink. I mention the sum, because they impose on strangers.

Adieu! till I arrive at Copenhagen.

LETTER XVIII

COPENHAGEN

THE distance from Elsineur to Copenhagen is twenty-two miles; the road is very good, over a flat country diversified with wood, mostly beech, and decent mansions. There appeared to be a great quantity of corn land; and the soil looked much more fertile than it is in general so near the sea. The rising grounds indeed were very few; and around Copenhagen it is a perfect plain, of course has nothing to recommend it, but cultivation, not decorations. If I say that the houses did not disgust me, I tell you all I remember of them; for I cannot recollect any pleasurable sensations they excited; or that any object, produced by nature or art, took me out of myself. The view of the city, as we drew near, was rather grand, but without any striking feature to interest the imagination, excepting the trees which shade the foot-paths.

Just before I reached Copenhagen, I saw a number of tents on a wide plain, and supposed that the rage for encampments* had reached this city; but I soon discovered that they were the asylum of many of the poor families who had been driven out of their habitations by the late fire.*

Entering soon after, I passed amongst the dust and rubbish it had left, affrighted by viewing the extent of the devastation; for at least a quarter of the city had been destroyed. There was little in the appearance of fallen bricks and stacks of chimneys to allure the imagination into soothing melancholy reveries; nothing to attract the eye of taste, but much to afflict the benevolent heart. The depredations of time have always something in them to employ the fancy, or lead to musing on subjects which, withdrawing the mind from objects of sense, seem to give it new dignity: but here I was treading on live ashes. The sufferers were still under the pressure of the misery occasioned by this dreadful conflagration. I could not take refuge in the thought; *they suffered—but they are no more!* a reflection I frequently summon to calm my mind, when sympathy rises to anguish: I therefore desired the driver to hasten to the hotel recommended to me, that I might avert my eyes, and snap the train of thinking which had sent me into all the corners of the city, in search of houseless heads.

This morning I have been walking round the town, till I am weary of observing the ravages. I had often heard the Danes, even those who had seen Paris and London, speak of Copenhagen with rapture. Certainly I have seen it in a very disadvantageous light, some of the best streets having been burnt and the whole place thrown into confusion. Still the utmost that can, or could ever, I believe, have been said in its praise, might be comprised in a few words. The streets are open, and many of the houses large; but I saw nothing to rouse the idea of elegance or grandeur, if I except the circus where the king and Prince Royal reside.

The palace, which was consumed about two years ago, must have been a handsome spacious building: the stone-work is still standing; and a great number of the poor, during the late fire, took refuge in its ruins, till they could find some other abode. Beds were thrown on the landing places of the grand stair-case, where whole families crept from the cold, and every little nook is boarded up as a retreat for some poor creatures deprived of their home. At present a roof may be sufficient to shelter them from the night air; but as the season advances, the extent of the calamity will be more severely felt, I fear, though the exertions on the part of government are very considerable. Private charity has also, no doubt, done much to alleviate the misery which obtrudes itself at every turn; still public spirit appears to me to be hardly alive here.

Had it existed, the conflagration might have been smothered in the beginning, as it was at last, by tearing down several houses before the flames had reached them. To this the inhabitants would not consent; and the Prince Royal not having sufficient energy of character to know when he ought to be absolute, calmly let them pursue their own course, till the whole city seemed to be threatened with destruction. Adhering, with puerile scrupulosity, to the law, which he has imposed on himself, of acting exactly right, he did wrong by idly lamenting, whilst he marked the progress of a mischief that one decided step would have stopt.* He was afterwards obliged to resort to violent measures; but then—who could blame him? And, to avoid censure, what sacrifices are not made by weak minds!

A gentleman, who was a witness of the scene, assured me, likewise, that if the people of property had taken half as much pains to extinguish the fire, as to preserve their valuables and furniture, it would soon have been got under. But they who were not immediately in danger did not exert themselves sufficiently, till fear, like an electrical shock, roused all the inhabitants to a sense of the general evil. Even the fire engines were out of order, though the burning of the palace ought to have admonished them of the necessity of keeping them in constant repair. But this kind of indolence, respecting what does not immediately concern them, seems to characterize the Danes. A sluggish concentration in themselves makes them so careful to preserve their property, that they will not venture on any enterprise to increase it, in which there is a shadow of hazard.

Considering Copenhagen as the capital of Denmark and Norway, I was surprised not to see so much industry or taste as in Christiania. Indeed from every thing I have had an opportunity of observing, the Danes are the people who have made the fewest sacrifices to the graces.

The men of business are domestic tyrants,* coldly immersed in their own affairs, and so ignorant of the state of other countries, that they dogmatically assert that Denmark is the happiest country in the world; the Prince Royal the best of all possible princes; and count Bernstorff* the wisest of ministers.

As for the women, they are simply notable housewives; without accomplishments, or any of the charms that adorn more advanced social life. This total ignorance may enable them to save something in their kitchens; but it is far from rendering them better parents. On the contrary, the children are spoilt; as they usually are, when left to the care of weak, indulgent mothers, who having no principle of action to regulate their feelings become the slaves of infants, enfeebling both body and mind by false tenderness.

I am perhaps a little prejudiced, as I write from the impression of the moment; for I have been tormented to-day by the presence of unruly children, and made angry by some invectives thrown out against the maternal character of the unfortunate Matilda.* She was censured, with the most cruel insinuation, for her management of her son; though, from what I could gather, she gave proofs of good sense, as well as tenderness in her attention to him. She used to bathe him herself every morning; insisted on his being loosely clad; and would not permit his attendants to injure his digestion, by humouring his appetite. She was equally careful to prevent his acquiring haughty airs, and playing the tyrant in leading-strings. The queen dowager would not permit her to suckle him; but the next child being a daughter, and not the heir apparent of the crown, less opposition was made to her discharging the duty of a mother.

Poor Matilda! thou hast haunted me ever since my arrival; and the view I have had of the manners of the country, exciting my sympathy, has increased my respect for thy memory!

I am now fully convinced that she was the victim of the party she displaced, who would have overlooked, or encouraged, her attachment, had her lover not, aiming at being useful, attempted to overturn some established abuses before the people, ripe for the change, had sufficient spirit to support him when struggling in their behalf. Such indeed was the asperity sharpened against her, that I have heard her, even after so many years have elapsed, charged with licentiousness, not only for endeavouring to render the public amusements more elegant, but for her very charities, because she erected amongst other institutions, an hospital to receive foundlings. Disgusted with many customs which pass for virtues, though they are nothing more than observances of forms, often at the expence of truth, she probably ran into an error common to innovators, in wishing to do immediately what can only be done by time.

Many very cogent reasons have been urged by her friends to prove, that her affection for Struensee* was never carried to the length alledged against her, by those who feared her influence. Be that as it may, she certainly was not a woman of gallantry; and if she had an attachment for him, it did not disgrace her heart or understanding, the king being a notorious debauchee, and an idiot into the bargain. As the king's conduct had always been directed by some favourite, they also endeavoured to govern him, from a principle of self-preservation, as well as a laudable ambition; but, not aware of the prejudices they had to encounter, the system they adopted displayed more benevolence of heart than soundness of judgement. As to the charge, still believed, of their giving the king drugs to injure his faculties, it is too absurd to be refuted. Their oppressors had better have accused them of dabbling in the black art; for the potent spell still keeps his wits in bondage.

I cannot describe to you the effect it had on me to see this puppet of a monarch moved by the strings which count Bernstorff holds fast; sit, with vacant eye, erect, receiving the homage of courtiers, who mock him with a shew of respect. He is, in fact, merely a machine of state, to subscribe the name of a king to the acts of the government, which, to avoid danger, have no value, unless countersigned by the Prince Royal; for he is allowed to be absolutely an idiot, excepting that now and then an observation, or trick, escapes him, which looks more like madness than imbecility.

What a farce is life! This effigy of majesty is allowed to burn down to the socket, whilst the hapless Matilda was hurried into an untimely grave.

> 'As flies to wanton boys, are we to the gods;
> They kill us for their sport.'*

Adieu!

LETTER XIX

BUSINESS having obliged me to go a few miles out of town this morning, I was surprised at meeting a crowd of people of every description; and inquiring the cause, of a servant who spoke French, I was informed that a man had been executed two hours before, and the body afterwards burnt. I could not help looking with horror around—the fields lost their verdure—and I turned with disgust from the well-dressed women, who were returning with their children from this sight. What a spectacle for humanity! The seeing such a flock of idle gazers, plunged me into a train of reflections, on the pernicious effects produced by false notions of justice. And I am persuaded that till capital punishments be entirely abolished, executions ought to have every appearance of horrour given to them; instead of being, as they are now, a scene of amusement for the gaping crowd, where sympathy is quickly effaced by curiosity.

I have always been of opinion that the allowing actors to die, in the presence of the audience, has an immoral tendency; but trifling when compared with the ferocity acquired by viewing the reality as a show; for it seems to me, that in all countries the common people go to executions to see how the poor wretch plays his part, rather than to commiserate his fate, much less to think of the breach of morality which has brought him to such a deplorable end. Consequently executions, far from being useful examples to the survivors, have, I am persuaded, a quite contrary effect, by hardening the heart they ought to terrify.* Besides, the fear of an ignominious death, I believe, never deterred any one from the commission of a crime; because, in committing it, the mind is roused to activity about present circumstances. It is a game at hazard, at which all expect the turn of the die in their own favour; never reflecting on the chance of ruin, till it comes. In fact, from what I saw, in the fortresses of Norway, I am more and more convinced that the same energy of character, which renders a man a daring villain, would have rendered him useful to society, had that society been well organized. When a strong mind is not disciplined by cultivation, it is a sense of injustice that renders it unjust.*

Executions, however, occur very rarely at Copenhagen; for timidity, rather than clemency, palsies all the operations of the present government. The malefactor, who died this morning, would not, probably, have been punished with death at any other period; but an incendiary excites universal execration; and as the greater part of the inhabitants are still distressed by the late conflagration, an example was thought absolutely necessary; though, from what I can gather, the fire was accidental.

Not, but that I have very seriously been informed, that combustible materials were placed at proper distances, by the emissaries of Mr. Pitt;* and, to corroborate the fact, many people insist, that the flames burst out at once in different parts of the city; not allowing the wind to have any hand in it. So much for the plot. But the fabricators of plots in all countries build their conjectures on the 'baseless fabric of a vision;'* and, it seems even a sort of poetical justice, that whilst this minister is crushing at home, plots of his own conjuring up, that on the continent, and in the north, he should, with as little foundation, be accused of wishing to set the world on fire.

I forgot to mention, to you, that I was informed, by a man of veracity, that two persons came to the stake to drink a glass of the criminal's blood, as an infallible remedy for the apoplexy. And when I animadverted in the company, where it was mentioned, on such a horrible violation of nature, a Danish lady reproved me very severely, asking how I knew that it was not a cure for the disease? adding, that every attempt was justifiable in search of health. I did not, you may imagine, enter into an argument with a person the slave of such a gross prejudice. And I allude to it not only as a trait of the ignorance of the people, but to censure the government, for not preventing scenes that throw an odium on the human race.

Empiricism* is not peculiar to Denmark; and I know no way of rooting it out, though it be a remnant of exploded witchcraft, till the acquiring a general knowledge of the component parts of the human frame, become a part of public education.

Since the fire, the inhabitants have been very assiduously employed in searching for property secreted during the confusion; and it is astonishing how many people, formerly termed reputable, had availed themselves of the common calamity to purloin what the flames spared. Others, expert at making a distinction without a difference, concealed what they found, not troubling themselves to enquire for the owners, though they scrupled to search for plunder any where, but amongst the ruins.

To be honester than the laws require, is by most people thought a work of supererogation; and to slip through the grate of the law, has ever exercised the abilities of adventurers, who wish to get rich the shortest way. Knavery, without personal danger, is an art, brought to great perfection by the statesman and swindler; and meaner knaves are not tardy in following their footsteps.

It moves my gall to discover some of the commercial frauds practised during the present war. In short, under whatever point of view I consider society, it appears, to me, that an adoration of property is the root of all evil. Here it does not render the people enterprising, as in America, but thrifty and cautious. I never, therefore, was in a capital where there was so little appearance of active industry; and as for gaiety, I looked in vain for the sprightly gait of the Norwegians, who in every respect appear to me to have got the start of them. This difference I attribute to their having more liberty: a liberty which they think their right by inheritance, whilst the Danes, when they boast of their negative happiness, always mention it as the boon of the Prince Royal, under the superintending wisdom of count Bernstorff. Vassallage is nevertheless ceasing throughout the kingdom, and with it will pass away that sordid avarice which every modification of slavery is calculated to produce.

If the chief use of property be power, in the shape of the respect it procures, is it not among the inconsistencies of human nature most incomprehensible, that men should find a pleasure in hoarding up property which they steal from their necessities, even when they are convinced that it would be dangerous to display such an enviable superiority? Is not this the situation of serfs in every country; yet a rapacity to accumulate money seems to become stronger in proportion as it is allowed to be useless.

Wealth does not appear to be sought for, amongst the Danes, to obtain the elegant luxuries of life; for a want of taste is very conspicuous at Copenhagen; so much so, that I am not surprised to hear that poor Matilda offended the rigid Lutherans, by aiming to refine their pleasures. The elegance which she wished to introduce, was termed lasciviousness: yet I do not find that absence of gallantry renders the wives more chaste, or the husbands more constant. Love here seems to corrupt the morals, without polishing the manners, by banishing confidence and truth, the charm as well as cement of domestic life. A gentleman, who has resided in this city some time, assures me that he could not find language to give me an idea of the gross debaucheries into which the lower order of people fall; and the promiscuous amours of the men of the middling class with their female servants, debases both beyond measure, weakening every species of family affection.

I have every where been struck by one characteristic difference in the conduct of the two sexes; women, in general, are seduced by their superiors, and men jilted by their inferiors; rank and manners awe the one, and cunning and wantonness subjugate the other; ambition creeping into the woman's passion, and tyranny giving force to the man's; for most men treat their mistresses as kings do their favourites: *ergo* is not man then the tyrant of the creation?

Still harping on the same subject, you will exclaim—How can I avoid it, when most of the struggles of an eventful life have been occasioned by the oppressed state of my sex: we reason deeply, when we forcibly feel.

But to return to the straight road of observation. The sensuality so prevalent appears to me to arise rather from indolence of mind, and dull senses, than from an exuberance of life, which often fructifies the whole character when the vivacity of youthful spirits begins to subside into strength of mind.

I have before mentioned that the men are domestic tyrants, considering them as fathers, brothers, or husbands; but there is a kind of interregnum between the reign of the father and husband, which is the only period of freedom and pleasure that the women enjoy. Young people, who are attached to each other, with the consent of their friends, exchange rings, and are permitted to enjoy a degree of liberty together, which I have never noticed in any other country. The days of courtship are therefore prolonged, till it be perfectly convenient to marry: the intimacy often becomes very tender: and if the lover obtain the privilege of a husband, it can only be termed half by stealth, because the family is wilfully blind. It happens very rarely that these honorary engagements are dissolved or disregarded, a stigma being attached to a breach of faith, which is thought more disgraceful, if not so criminal, as the violation of the marriage vow.

Do not forget that, in my general observations, I do not pretend to sketch a national character;* but merely to note the present state of morals and manners, as I trace the progress of the world's improvement. Because, during my residence in different countries, my principal object has been to take such a dispassionate view of men as will lead me to form a just idea of the nature of man. And, to deal ingenuously with you, I believe I should have been less severe in the remarks I have made on the vanity and depravity of the French,[1]* had I travelled towards the north before I visited France.

The interesting picture frequently drawn of the virtues of a rising people has, I fear, been fallacious, excepting the accounts of the enthusiasm which various public struggles have produced. We talk of the depravity of the French, and lay a stress on the old age of the nation; yet where has more virtuous enthusiasm* been displayed than during the two last years, by the common people of France and in their armies? I am obliged sometimes to recollect the numberless instances which I have either witnessed, or heard well authenticated, to balance the account of horrours, alas! but too true. I am, therefore, inclined to believe that the gross vices which I have always seen allied with simplicity of manners, are the concomitants of ignorance.

What, for example, has piety, under the heathen or Christian system, been, but a blind faith in things contrary to the principles

[1] See Historical and Moral View of the French Revolution.

of reason? And could poor reason make considerable advances, when it was reckoned the highest degree of virtue to do violence to it's dictates? Lutherans preaching reformation, have built a reputation for sanctity on the same foundation as the Catholics; yet I do not perceive that a regular attendance on public worship, and their other observances, make them a whit more true in their affections, or honest in their private transactions. It seems, indeed, quite as easy to prevaricate with religious injunctions as human laws, when the exercise of their reason does not lead people to acquire principles for themselves to be the criterion of all those they receive from others.

If travelling, as the completion of a liberal education, were to be adopted on rational grounds, the northern states ought to be visited before the more polished parts of Europe, to serve as the elements even of the knowledge of manners, only to be acquired by tracing the various shades in different countries. But, when visiting distant climes, a momentary social sympathy should not be allowed to influence the conclusions of the understanding; for hospitality too frequently leads travellers, especially those who travel in search of pleasure, to make a false estimate of the virtues of a nation; which, I am now convinced, bear an exact proportion to their scientific improvements.

Adieu.

LETTER XX

I have formerly censured the French for their extreme attach-ment to theatrical exhibitions,* because I thought that they tended to render them vain and unnatural characters. But I must acknowledge, especially as women of the town never appear in the Parisian, as at our theatres, that the little saving of the week is more usefully expended there, every Sunday, than in porter or brandy, to intoxicate or stupify the mind. The common people of France have a great superiority over that class in every other country on this very score. It is merely the sobriety of the Parisians which renders their fêtes more interesting, their gaiety never becoming disgusting or dangerous; as is always the case when liquor circulates. Intoxication is the pleasure of savages, and of all those whose employments rather exhaust their animal spirits, than exercise their faculties. Is not this, in fact, the vice, both in England and the northern states of Europe, which appears to be the greatest impediment to general improvement? Drinking is here the principal relaxation of the men,* including smoking; but the women are very abstemious, though they have no public amusements as a substitute. I ought to except one theatre, which appears more than is necessary; for when I was there, it was not half full; and neither the ladies nor actresses displayed much fancy in their dress.

The play was founded on the story of the Mock Doctor;* and, from the gestures of the servants, who were the best actors, I should imagine contained some humour. The farce, termed ballat,* was a kind of pantomime, the childish incidents of which were sufficient to shew the state of the dramatic art in Denmark, and the gross taste of the audience. A magician, in the disguise of a tinker, enters a cottage where the women are all busy ironing, and rubs a dirty frying-pan against the linen. The women raise an hue-and-cry, and dance after him, rousing their husbands, who join in the dance, but get the start of them in the pursuit. The tinker, with the frying-pan for a shield, renders them immoveable, and blacks their cheeks. Each laughs at the other, unconscious of his own appearance; mean while the women enter to enjoy the sport, '*the rare fun*,' with other incidents of the same species.

The singing was much on a par with the dancing; the one as destitute of grace, as the other of expression; but the orchestra was well filled, the instrumental being far superior to the vocal music.

I have likewise visited the public library and museum, as well as the palace of Rosembourg.* This palace, now deserted, displays a gloomy kind of grandeur throughout; for the silence of spacious apartments always makes itself to be felt; I at least feel it; and I listen for the sound of my footsteps, as I have done at midnight to the ticking of the death-watch, encouraging a kind of fanciful superstition. Every object carried me back to past times, and impressed the manners of the age forcibly on my mind. In this point of view the preservation of old palaces, and their tarnished furniture, is useful; for they may be considered as historical documents.

The vacuum left by departed greatness was every where observable, whilst the battles and processions, pourtrayed on the walls, told you who had here excited revelry after retiring from slaughter; or dismissed pageantry in search of pleasure. It seemed a vast tomb, full of the shadowy phantoms of those who had played or toiled their hour out, and sunk behind the tapestry, which celebrated the conquests of love or war. Could they be no more—to whom my imagination thus gave life? Could the thoughts, of which there remained so many vestiges, have vanished quite away? And these beings, composed of such noble materials of thinking and feeling, have they only melted into the elements to keep in motion the grand mass of life? It cannot be!—As easily could I believe that the large silver lions, at the top of the banqueting room, thought and reasoned. But avaunt! ye waking dreams!—yet I cannot describe the curiosities to you.

There were cabinets full of baubles, and gems, and swords, which must have been wielded by giant's hand. The coronation ornaments wait quietly here till wanted; and the wardrobe exhibits the vestments which formerly graced these shews. It is a pity they do not lend them to the actors, instead of allowing them to perish ingloriously.

I have not visited any other palace, excepting Hirsholm;* the gardens of which are laid out with taste, and command the finest views the country affords. As they are in the modern and English style, I thought I was following the footsteps of Matilda, who wished to multiply around her the images of her beloved country. I was also gratified by the sight of a Norwegian landscape in miniature, which with great propriety makes a part of the Danish king's garden. The cottage is well imitated, and the whole has a pleasing effect, particularly so to me who love Norway—it's peaceful farms and spacious wilds.

The public library consists of a collection much larger than I expected to see; and it is well arranged. Of the value of the

Icelandic manuscripts* I could not form a judgment, though the alphabet of some of them amused me, by shewing what immense labour men will submit to, in order to transmit their ideas to posterity. I have sometimes thought it a great misfortune for individuals to acquire a certain delicacy of sentiment, which often makes them weary of the common occurrences of life; yet it is this very delicacy of feeling and thinking which probably has produced most of the performances that have benefited mankind. It might with propriety, perhaps, be termed the malady of genius; the cause of that characteristic melancholy which 'grows with its growth, and strengthens with its strength.'*

There are some good pictures in the royal museum—Do not start—I am not going to trouble you with a dull catalogue, or stupid criticisms on masters, to whom time has assigned their just niche in the temple of fame; had there been any by living artists of this country, I should have noticed them, as making a part of the sketches I am drawing of the present state of the place. The good pictures were mixed indiscriminately with the bad ones, in order to assort the frames. The same fault is conspicuous in the new splendid gallery forming at Paris; though it seems an obvious thought that a school for artists ought to be arranged in such a manner, as to shew the progressive discoveries and improvements in the art.*

A collection of the dresses, arms, and implements of the Laplanders* attracted my attention, displaying that first species of ingenuity which is rather a proof of patient perseverance, than comprehension of mind. The specimens of natural history, and curiosities of art, were likewise huddled together without that scientific order which alone renders them useful; but this may partly have been occasioned by the hasty manner in which they were removed from the palace, when in flames.

There are some respectable men of science here, but few literary characters, and fewer artists. They want encouragement, and will continue, I fear, from the present appearance of things, to languish unnoticed a long time; for neither the vanity of wealth, nor the enterprising spirit of commerce, has yet thrown a glance that way.

Besides, the Prince Royal, determined to be œconomical,*
almost descends to parsimony; and perhaps depresses his subjects, by labouring not to oppress them; for his intentions always
seem to be good—yet nothing can give a more forcible idea of
the dullness which eats away all activity of mind, than the insipid
routine of a court, without magnificence or elegance.

The prince, from what I can now collect, has very moderate
abilities; yet is so well disposed, that count Bernstorff finds him as
tractable as he could wish; for I consider the count as the real
sovereign, scarcely behind the curtain; the prince having none of
that obstinate self-sufficiency of youth, so often the fore-runner of
decision of character. He, and the princess his wife, dine every
day with the king, to save the expence of two tables. What a mum-
mery it must be to treat as a king a being who has lost the majesty
of man! But even count Bernstorff's morality submits to this
standing imposition; and he avails himself of it sometimes, to
soften a refusal of his own, by saying it is the *will* of the king, my
master, when every body knows that he has neither will nor
memory. Much the same use is made of him as, I have observed,
some termagant wives make of their husbands; they would dwell
on the necessity of obeying their husbands, poor passive souls,
who never were allowed *to will*, when they wanted to conceal their
own tyranny.

A story is told here of the king's formerly making a dog coun-
sellor of state, because when the dog, accustomed to eat at the
royal table, snatched a piece of meat off an old officer's plate, he
reproved him jocosely, saying that he, *monsieur le chien*,* had not
the privilege of dining with his majesty; a privilege annexed to
this distinction.

The burning of the palace was, in fact, a fortunate circum-
stance, as it afforded a pretext for reducing the establishment of
the household, which was far too great for the revenue of the
crown. The Prince Royal, at present, runs into the opposite
extreme; and the formality, if not the parsimony, of the court,
seems to extend to all the other branches of society, which I had
an opportunity of observing; though hospitality still characterizes
their intercourse with strangers.

But let me now stop; I may be a little partial, and view every thing with the jaundiced eye of melancholy——for I am sad——and have cause.

God bless you!

LETTER XXI

I HAVE seen count Bernstorff; and his conversation confirms me in the opinion I had previously formed of him;——I mean, since my arrival at Copenhagen. He is a worthy man, a little vain of his virtue *à la Necker*;* and more anxious not to do wrong, that is to avoid blame, than desirous of doing good; especially if any particular good demands a change. Prudence, in short, seems to be the basis of his character; and, from the tenour of the government, I should think inclining to that cautious circumspection which treads on the heels of timidity. He has considerable information, and some finesse; or he could not be a minister. Determined not to risk his popularity, for he is tenderly careful of his reputation, he will never gloriously fail like Struensee, or disturb, with the energy of genius, the stagnant state of the public mind.

I suppose that Lavater,* whom he invited to visit him two years ago, some say to fix the principles of the Christian religion firmly in the Prince Royal's mind, found lines in his face to prove him a statesman of the first order; because he has a knack at seeing a great character in the countenances of men in exalted stations, who have noticed him, or his works. Besides, the count's sentiments relative to the French revolution, agreeing with Lavater's, must have ensured his applause.

The Danes, in general, seem extremely averse to innovation, and, if happiness only consist in opinion, they are the happiest people in the world; for I never saw any so well satisfied with their own situation. Yet the climate appears to be very disagreeable; the weather being dry and sultry, or moist and cold; the atmosphere never having that sharp, bracing purity, which in Norway prepares you to brave its rigours. I do not then hear the inhabitants of this place talk with delight of the winter, which is the constant theme of the Norwegians, on the contrary they seem to dread its comfortless inclemency.

The ramparts are pleasant, and must have been much more so before the fire, the walkers not being annoyed by the clouds of dust, which, at present, the slightest wind wafts from the ruins. The wind-mills, and the comfortable houses contiguous, belonging to the millers, as well as the appearance of the spacious barracks for the soldiers and sailors, tend to render this walk more agreeable. The view of the country has not much to recommend it to notice, but its extent and cultivation: yet as the eye always delights to dwell on verdant plains, especially when we are resident in a great city, these shady walks should be reckoned amongst the advantages procured by the government for the inhabitants. I like them better than the royal gardens, also open to the public, because the latter seem sunk in the heart of the city, to concentrate its fogs.

The canals, which intersect the streets, are equally convenient and wholesome; but the view of the sea, commanded by the town, had little to interest me whilst the remembrance of the various bold and picturesque shores, I had seen, was fresh in my memory. Still the opulent inhabitants, who seldom go abroad, must find the spots where they fix their country seats much pleasanter on account of the vicinity of the ocean.

One of the best streets in Copenhagen is almost filled with hospitals, erected by the government; and, I am assured, as well regulated as institutions of this kind are in any country; but whether hospitals, or workhouses, are any where superintended with sufficient humanity, I have frequently had reason to doubt.

The autumn is so uncommonly fine, that I am unwilling to put off my journey to Hamburg* much longer, lest the weather should alter suddenly, and the chilly harbingers of winter catch me here, where I have nothing now to detain me but the hospitality of the families to whom I had recommendatory letters. I lodged at an hotel situated in a large open square, where the troops exercise, and the market is kept. My apartments were very good; and, on account of the fire, I was told that I should be charged very high; yet, paying my bill just now, I find the demands much lower in proportion than in Norway, though my dinners were in every respect better.

I have remained more at home, since I arrived at Copenhagen, than I ought to have done in a strange place; but the mind is not always equally active in search of information; and my oppressed heart too often sighs out,

> 'How dull, flat, and unprofitable
> Are to me all the usages of this world—
> That it should come to this!'—*

Farewell! Fare thee well, I say—if thou can'st, repeat the adieu in a different tone.

LETTER XXII

I ARRIVED at Corsoer the night after I quitted Copenhagen, purposing to take my passage across the Great Belt* the next morning, though the weather was rather boisterous. It is about four and twenty miles; but as neither I nor my little girl are ever attacked by sea sickness, though who can avoid *ennui*? I enter a boat with the same indifference as I change horses; and as for danger, come when it may, I dread it not sufficiently to have any anticipating fears.

The road from Copenhagen was very good, through an open, flat country, that had little to recommend it to notice excepting the cultivation, which gratified my heart more than my eye.

I took a barge with a German baron, who was hastening back from a tour into Denmark, alarmed by the intelligence of the French having passed the Rhine.* His conversation beguiled the time, and gave a sort of stimulus to my spirits, which had been growing more and more languid ever since my return to Gothenburg—you know why. I had often endeavoured to rouse myself to observation by reflecting that I was passing through scenes which I should probably never see again, and consequently ought not to omit observing; still I fell into reveries, thinking, by way of excuse, that enlargement of mind and refined feelings are of little use, but to barb the arrows of sorrow which waylay us every where, eluding the sagacity of wisdom, and rendering principles unavailing, if considered as a breast-work to secure our own hearts.

Though we had not a direct wind, we were not detained more than three hours and a half on the water, just long enough to give us an appetite for our dinner.

We travelled the remainder of the day, and the following night, in company with the same party, the German gentleman whom I have mentioned, his friend, and servant: the meetings, at the post-houses, were pleasant to me, who usually heard nothing but strange tongues around me. Marguerite and the child often fell asleep; and when they were awake, I might still reckon myself alone, as our train of thoughts had nothing in common. Marguerite, it is true, was much amused by the *costume* of the women; particularly by the *panier*[1]* which adorned both their heads and tails; and, with great glee, recounted to me the stories she had treasured up for her family, when once more within the barriers of dear Paris; not forgetting, with that arch, agreeable vanity peculiar to the French, which they exhibit whilst half ridiculing it, to remind me of the importance she should assume when she informed her friends of all her journeys by sea and land—shewing the pieces of money she had collected, and stammering out a few foreign phrases, which she repeated in a true Parisian accent. Happy thoughtlessness; aye, and enviable harmless vanity, which thus produced a *gaité du coeur** worth all my philosophy.

The man I had hired at Copenhagen advised me to go round, about twenty miles, to avoid passing the Little Belt,* excepting by a ferry, as the wind was contrary. But the gentlemen over-ruled his arguments, which we were all very sorry for afterwards, when we found ourselves becalmed on the Little Belt ten hours, tacking about, without ceasing, to gain on the shore.

An over-sight likewise made the passage appear much more tedious, nay almost insupportable. When I went on board at the

---

[1] This word in French means both basket and hoop.

Great Belt, I had provided refreshments in case of detention, which remaining untouched, I thought not then any such precaution necessary for the second passage, misled by the epithet of little, though I have since been informed that it is frequently the longest. This mistake occasioned much vexation; for the child, at last, began to cry so bitterly for bread, that fancy conjured up before me the wretched Ugolino,* with his famished children; and I, literally speaking, enveloped myself in sympathetic horrours, augmented by every tear my babe shed; from which I could not escape, till we landed, and a luncheon of bread, and bason of milk, routed the spectres of fancy.

I then supped with my companions, with whom I was soon after to part for ever—always a most melancholy, death-like idea—a sort of separation of soul; for all the regret which follows those from whom fate separates us, seems to be something torn from ourselves. These were strangers I remember; yet when there is any originality in a countenance, it takes its place in our memory; and we are sorry to lose an acquaintance the moment he begins to interest us, though picked up on the highway. There was, in fact, a degree of intelligence, and still more sensibility in the features and conversation of one of the gentlemen, that made me regret the loss of his society during the rest of the journey; for he was compelled to travel post, by his desire to reach his estate before the arrival of the French.

This was a comfortable inn, as were several others I stopt at; but the heavy sandy roads were very fatiguing, after the fine ones we had lately skimmed over both in Sweden and Denmark. The country resembled the most open part of England; laid out for corn, rather than grazing: it was pleasant; yet there was little in the prospects to awaken curiosity, by displaying the peculiar characteristics of a new country, which had so frequently stole me from myself in Norway. We often passed over large uninclosed tracts, not graced with trees, or at least very sparingly enlivened by them; and the half-formed roads seemed to demand the landmarks, set up in the waste, to prevent the traveller from straying far out of his way, and plodding through the wearisome sand.

The heaths were dreary, and had none of the wild charms of those of Sweden and Norway to cheat time; neither the terrific rocks, nor smiling herbage, grateful to the sight, and scented from afar, made us forget their length; still the country appeared much more populous; and the towns, if not the farm-houses, were superiour to those of Norway. I even thought that the inhabitants of the former had more intelligence, at least I am sure they had more vivacity in their countenances than I had seen during my northern tour: their senses seemed awake to business and pleasure. I was, therefore, gratified by hearing once more the busy hum of industrious men in the day, and the exhilarating sounds of joy in the evening; for as the weather was still fine, the women and children were amusing themselves at their doors, or walking under the trees, which in many places were planted in the streets; and as most of the towns of any note were situated on little bays, or branches, of the Baltic, their appearance, as we approached, was often very picturesque, and, when we entered, displayed the comfort and cleanliness of easy, if not the elegance of opulent, circumstances. But the chearfulness of the people in the streets was particularly grateful to me, after having been depressed by the deathlike silence of those of Denmark, where every house made me think of a tomb. The dress of the peasantry is suited to the climate; in short, none of that poverty and dirt appeared, at the sight of which the heart sickens.

As I only stopt to change horses, take refreshment, and sleep, I had not an opportunity of knowing more of the country than conclusions, which the information gathered by my eyes enabled me to draw; and that was sufficient to convince me that I should much rather have lived in some of the towns I now pass through, than in any I had seen in Sweden or Denmark. The people struck me, as having arrived at that period when the faculties will unfold themselves; in short, they look alive to improvement, neither congealed by indolence, nor bent down by wretchedness to servility.

From the previous impression, I scarcely can trace from whence I received it, I was agreeably surprised to perceive such an appearance of comfort in this part of Germany. I had formed a conception of the tyranny of the petty potentates that had thrown a gloomy veil over the face of the whole country, in my imagination, that cleared away like the darkness of night before the sun. As I saw the reality, I should probably have discovered much lurking misery, the consequence of ignorant oppression, no doubt, had I had time to inquire into particulars; but it did not stalk abroad, and infect the surface over which my eye glanced. Yes, I am persuaded that a considerable degree of general knowledge pervades this country; for it is only from the exercise of the mind that the body acquires the activity from which I drew these inferences. Indeed the king of Denmark's German dominions, Holstein, appeared to me far superiour to any other part of his kingdom which had fallen under my view; and the robust rustics to have their muscles braced, instead of the *as it were* lounge of the Danish peasantry.

Arriving at Sleswick,* the residence of prince Charles of Hesse-Cassel,* the sight of the soldiers recalled all the unpleasing ideas of German despotism,* which imperceptibly vanished as I advanced into the country. I viewed, with a mixture of pity and horrour, these beings training to be sold to slaughter, or be slaughtered, and fell into reflections, on an old opinion of mine, that it is the preservation of the species, not of individuals, which appears to be the design of the Deity throughout the whole of nature. Blossoms come forth only to be blighted; fish lay their spawn where it will be devoured: and what a large portion of the human race are born merely to be swept prematurely away. Does not this waste of budding life emphatically assert, that it is not men, but man, whose preservation is so necessary to the completion of the grand plan of the universe? Children peep into existence, suffer, and die; men play like moths about a candle, and sink into the flame: war, and 'the thousand ills which flesh is heir to,'* mow them down in shoals, whilst the more cruel prejudices of society palsies existence, introducing not less sure, though slower decay.

The castle was heavy and gloomy; yet the grounds about it were laid out with some taste; a walk, winding under the shade of lofty trees, led to a regularly built, and animated town.

I crossed the draw-bridge, and entered to see this shell of a court in miniature, mounting ponderous stairs, it would be a solecism to say a flight, up which a regiment of men might have marched, shouldering their firelocks, to exercise in vast galleries, where all the generations of the princes of Hesse-Cassel might have been mustered rank and file, though not the phantoms of all the wretched they had bartered to support their state, unless these airy substances could shrink and expand, like Milton's devils,* to suit the occasion.

The sight of the presence-chamber, and of the canopy to shade the *fauteuil*,* which aped a throne, made me smile. All the world is a stage,* thought I; and few are there in it who do not play the part they have learnt by rote; and those who do not, seem marks set up to be pelted at by fortune; or rather as sign-posts, which point out the road to others, whilst forced to stand still themselves amidst the mud and dust.

Waiting for our horses, we were amused by observing the dress of the women, which was very grotesque and unwieldy. The false notion of beauty which prevails here, as well as in Denmark, I should think very inconvenient in summer, as it consists in giving a rotundity to a certain part of the body, not the most slim, when nature has done her part. This Dutch prejudice often leads them to toil under the weight of some ten or a dozen petticoats, which, with an enormous basket, literally speaking, as a bonnet, or a straw hat of dimensions equally gigantic, almost completely concealing the human form, as well as face divine,* often worth shewing—still they looked clean, and tript along, as it were, before the wind, with a weight of tackle that I could scarcely have lifted. Many of the country girls, I met, appeared to me pretty, that is, to have fine complexions, sparkling eyes, and a kind of arch, hoyden playfulness which distinguishes the village coquette. The swains, in their Sunday trim, attended some of these fair ones, in a more slouching pace, though their dress was not so cumbersome. The women seem to take the lead in polishing the manners every where, that being the only way to better their condition.

From what I have seen throughout my journey, I do not think the situation of the poor in England is much, if at all superiour to that of the same class in different parts of the world; and in Ireland, I am sure, it is much inferiour. I allude to the former state of England; for at present the accumulation of national wealth only increases the cares of the poor, and hardens the hearts of the rich, in spite of the highly extolled rage for alms-giving.

You know that I have always been an enemy to what is termed charity,* because timid bigots endeavouring thus to cover their *sins*, do violence to justice, till, acting the demi-god, they forget that they are men. And there are others who do not even think of laying up a treasure in heaven,* whose benevolence is merely tyranny in disguise: they assist the most worthless, because the most servile, and term them helpless only in proportion to their fawning.

After leaving Sleswick, we passed through several pretty towns; Itzchol particularly pleased me: and the country still wearing the same aspect, was improved by the appearance of more trees and enclosures. But what gratified me most, was the population. I was weary of travelling four or five hours, never meeting a carriage, and scarcely a peasant—and then to stop at such wretched huts, as I had seen in Sweden, was surely sufficient to chill any heart, awake to sympathy, and throw a gloom over my favourite subject of contemplation, the future improvement of the world.

The farm-houses, likewise, with the huge stables, into which we drove, whilst the horses were putting to, or baiting, were very clean and commodious. The rooms, with a door into this hall-like stable and storehouse in one, were decent; and there was a compactness in the appearance of the whole family lying thus snugly together under the same roof, that carried my fancy back to the primitive times, which probably never existed with such a golden lustre as the animated imagination lends, when only able to seize the prominent features.

At one of them, a pretty young woman, with languishing eyes, of celestial blue, conducted us into a very neat parlour; and observing how loosely, and lightly, my little girl was clad, began to pity her in the sweetest accents, regardless of the rosy down of health on her cheeks. This same damsel was dressed, it was Sunday, with taste, and even coquetry, in a cotton jacket, ornamented with knots of blue ribbon, fancifully disposed to give life to her fine complexion. I loitered a little to admire her, for every gesture was graceful; and, amidst the other villagers, she looked like a garden lily suddenly rearing its head amongst grain, and corn-flowers. As the house was small, I gave her a piece of money, rather larger than it was my custom to give to the female waiters; for I could not prevail on her to sit down; which she received with a smile; yet took care to give it, in my presence, to a girl, who had brought the child a slice of bread; by which I perceived that she was the mistress, or daughter, of the house—and without doubt the *belle* of the village. There was, in short, an appearance of chearful industry, and of that degree of comfort which shut out misery, in all the little hamlets as I approached Hamburg, which agreeably surprised me.

The short jackets which the women wear here, as well as in France, are not only more becoming to the person, but much better calculated for women who have rustic or household employments, than the long gowns worn in England, dangling in the dirt.

All the inns on the road were better than I expected, though the softness of the beds still harassed me, and prevented my finding the rest I was frequently in want of, to enable me to bear the fatigue of the next day. The charges were moderate, and the people very civil, with a certain honest hilarity and independent spirit in their manner, which almost made me forget that they were inn-keepers, a set of men, waiters, hostesses, chamber-maids, &c. down to the ostler, whose cunning servility, in England, I think particularly disgusting.

The prospect of Hamburg, at a distance, as well as the fine road shaded with trees, led me to expect to see a much pleasanter city than I found.

I was aware of the difficulty of obtaining lodgings, even at the inns, on account of the concourse of strangers at present resorting to such a centrical situation, and determined to go to Altona* the next day to seek for an abode, wanting now only rest. But even for a single night we were sent from house to house, and found at last a vacant room to sleep in, which I should have turned from with disgust, had there been a choice.

I scarcely know any thing that produces more disagreeable sensations, I mean to speak of the passing cares, the recollection of which afterwards enlivens our enjoyments, than those excited by little disasters of this kind. After a long journey, with our eyes directed to some particular spot, to arrive and find nothing as it should be, is vexatious, and sinks the agitated spirits. But I, who received the cruelest of disappointments, last spring, in returning to my home, term such as these emphatically passing cares. Know you of what materials some hearts are made? I play the child, and weep at the recollection—for the grief is still fresh that stunned as well as wounded me—yet never did drops of anguish like these bedew the cheeks of infantine innocence—and why should they mine, that never were stained by a blush of guilt? Innocent and credulous as a child, why have I not the same happy thoughtlessness?

Adieu!

LETTER XXIII

I MIGHT have spared myself the disagreeable feelings I experienced the first night of my arrival at Hamburg, leaving the open air to be shut up in noise and dirt, had I gone immediately to Altona, where a lodging had been prepared for me by a gentleman from whom I received many civilities during my journey. I wished to have travelled in company with him from Copenhagen, because I found him intelligent and friendly; but business obliged him to hurry forward; and I wrote to him on the subject of accommodations, as soon as I was informed of the difficulties I might have to encounter to house myself and brat.

It is but a short and pleasant walk from Hamburg to Altona, under the shade of several rows of trees; and this walk is the more agreeable, after quitting the rough pavement of either place.

Hamburg is an ill, close-built town, swarming with inhabitants; and, from what I could learn, like all the other free towns,* governed in a manner which bears hard on the poor, whilst narrowing the minds of the rich, the character of the man is lost in the Hamburger. Always afraid of the encroachments of their Danish neighbours, that is, anxiously apprehensive of their sharing the golden harvest of commerce with them, or taking a little of the trade off their hands, though they have more than they know what to do with, they are ever on the watch, till their very eyes lose all expression, excepting the prying glance of suspicion.

The gates of Hamburg are shut at seven, in the winter, and nine in the summer, lest some strangers, who come to traffic in Hamburg, should prefer living, and consequently, so exactly do they calculate, spend their money out of the walls of the Hamburger's world. Immense fortunes have been acquired by the *per cents* arising from commissions, nominally only two and a half; but mounted to eight or ten at least, by the secret *manoeuvres* of trade, not to include the advantage of purchasing goods whole-sale, in common with contractors, and that of having so much money left in their hands—not to play with, I can assure you. Mushroom fortunes* have started up during the war; the men, indeed, seem of the species of the fungus; and the insolent vulgarity which a sudden influx of wealth usually produces in common minds, is here very conspicuous, which contrasts with the distresses of many of the emigrants, 'fallen—fallen from their high estate'*—such are the ups and downs of fortune's wheel! Many emigrants have met, with fortitude, such a total change of circumstances as scarcely can be paralleled, retiring from a palace, to an obscure lodging, with dignity; but the greater number glide about the ghosts of greatness, with the *croix de St. Louis** ostentatiously displayed, determined to hope, 'though heaven and earth their wishes crossed.'* Still good-breeding points out the gentleman; and sentiments of honour and delicacy appear the offspring of greatness of soul, when compared with the grovelling views of the sordid accumulators of *cent. per cent.*

Situation seems to be the mould in which men's characters are formed; so much so, inferring from what I have lately seen, that I mean not to be severe when I add, previously asking why priests are in general cunning, and statesmen false? that men entirely devoted to commerce never acquire, or lose, all taste and greatness of mind. An ostentatious display of wealth without elegance, and a greedy enjoyment of pleasure without sentiment, embrutes them till they term all virtue, of an heroic cast, romantic attempts at something above our nature; and anxiety about the welfare of others, a search after misery, in which we have no concern. But you will say that I am growing bitter, perhaps, personal. Ah! shall I whisper to you—that you—yourself, are strangely altered, since you have entered deeply into commerce—more than you are aware of—never allowing yourself to reflect, and keeping your mind, or rather passions, in a continual state of agitation—Nature has given you talents, which lie dormant, or are wasted in ignoble pursuits—You will rouse yourself, and shake off the vile dust that obscures you, or my understanding, as well as my heart, deceives me, egregiously—only tell me when? But to go farther a-field.

Madame La Fayette* left Altona the day I arrived, to endeavour, at Vienna, to obtain the enlargement of her husband, or permission to share his prison. She lived in a lodging up two pair of stairs, without a servant, her two daughters chearfully assisting; chusing, as well as herself, to descend to any thing before unnecessary obligations. During her prosperity, and consequent idleness, she did not, I am told, enjoy a good state of health, having a train of nervous complaints which, though they have not a name, unless the significant word *ennui* be borrowed, had an existence in the higher French circles; but adversity and virtuous exertions put these ills to flight, and dispossessed her of a devil, who deserves the appellation of legion.*

Madame Genlis,* also, resided at Altona some time, under an assumed name, with many other sufferers of less note, though higher rank. It is, in fact, scarcely possible to stir out without meeting interesting countenances, every lineament of which tells you that they have seen better days.

At Hamburg, I was informed, a duke had entered into partnership with his cook, who becoming a *traiteur*,* they were both comfortably supported by the profit arising from his industry.

Many noble instances of the attachment of servants to their unfortunate masters, have come to my knowledge both here and in France, and touched my heart, the greatest delight of which is to discover human virtue.

At Altona, a president of one of the *ci-devant** parliaments keeps an ordinary,* in the French style; and his wife, with chearful dignity, submits to her fate, though she is arrived at an age when people seldom relinquish their prejudices. A girl who waits there brought a dozen *double louis d'or** concealed in her clothes, at the risk of her life, from France; which she preserves, lest sickness, or any other distress, should overtake her mistress, 'who,' she observed, 'was not accustomed to hardships.' This house was particularly recommended to me by an acquaintance of your's, the author of the American Farmer's Letters.* I generally dine in company with him: and the gentleman whom I have already mentioned, is often diverted by our declamations against commerce, when we compare notes respecting the characteristics of the Hamburgers. 'Why, madam,' said he to me one day, 'you will not meet with a man who has any calf to his leg; body and soul, muscles and heart, are equally shrivelled up by a thirst of gain. There is nothing generous even in their youthful passions; profit is their only stimulus, and calculations the sole employment of their faculties; unless we except some gross animal gratifications which, snatched *at spare moments*, tend still more to debase the character, because, though touched by his tricking wand, they have all the arts, without the wit, of the wing-footed god.'*

Perhaps you may also think us too severe; but I must add, that the more I saw of the manners of Hamburg, the more was I confirmed in my opinion relative to the baleful effect of extensive speculations on the moral character. Men are strange machines; and their whole system of morality is in general held together by one grand principle, which loses its force the moment they allow themselves to break with impunity over the bounds which secured their self-respect. A man ceases to love humanity, and then individuals, as he advances in the chase after wealth; as one clashes with his interest, the other with his pleasures: to business, as it is termed, every thing must give way; nay, is sacrificed; and all the endearing charities of citizen, husband, father, brother, become empty names. But—but what? Why, to snap the chain of thought, I must say farewell. Cassandra* was not the only prophetess whose warning voice has been disregarded. How much easier it is to meet with love in the world, than affection!

Your's, sincerely.

LETTER XXIV

MY lodgings at Altona are tolerably comfortable, though not in any proportion to the price I pay; but, owing to the present circumstances, all the necessaries of life are here extravagantly dear. Considering it as a temporary residence, the chief inconvenience of which, I am inclined to complain, is the rough streets that must be passed before Marguerite and the child can reach a level road.

The views of the Elbe, in the vicinity of the town, are pleasant, particularly as the prospects here afford so little variety. I attempted to descend, and walk close to the water edge; but there was no path; and the smell of glue, hanging to dry, an extensive manufactory of which is carried on close to the beach, I found extremely disagreeable. But to commerce every thing must give way; profit and profit are the only speculations—'double—double, toil and trouble.'* I have seldom entered a shady walk without being soon obliged to turn aside to make room for the rope-makers; and the only tree, I have seen, that appeared to be planted by the hand of taste, is in the church-yard, to shade the tomb of the poet Klopstock's wife.*

Most of the merchants have country houses to retire to, during the summer; and many of them are situated on the banks of the Elbe, where they have the pleasure of seeing the packet-boats arrive, the periods of most consequence to divide their week.

The moving picture, consisting of large vessels and small-craft, which are continually changing their position with the tide, renders this noble river, the vital stream of Hamburg, very interesting; and the windings have sometimes a very fine effect, two or three turns being visible, at once, intersecting the flat meadows: a sudden bend often increasing the magnitude of the river; and the silvery expanse, scarcely gliding, though bearing on its bosom so much treasure, looks, for a moment, like a tranquil lake.

Nothing can be stronger than the contrast which this flat country and strand afford, compared with the mountains, and rocky coast, I have lately dwelt so much among. In fancy I return to a favourite spot, where I seemed to have retired from man and wretchedness; but the din of trade drags me back to all the care I left behind, when lost in sublime emotions. Rocks aspiring towards the heavens, and, as it were, shutting out sorrow, surrounded me, whilst peace appeared to steal along the lake to calm my bosom, modulating the wind that agitated the neighbouring poplars. Now I hear only an account of the tricks of trade, or listen to the distressful tale of some victim of ambition.

The hospitality of Hamburg is confined to Sunday invitations to the country houses I have mentioned, when dish after dish smoaks upon the board; and the conversation ever flowing in the muddy channel of business, it is not easy to obtain any appropriate information. Had I intended to remain here some time, or had my mind been more alive to general inquiries, I should have endeavoured to have been introduced to some characters, not so entirely immersed in commercial affairs; though, in this whirlpool of gain, it is not very easy to find any but the wretched or supercilious emigrants, who are not engaged in pursuits which, in my eyes, appear as dishonourable as gambling. The interests of nations are bartered by speculating merchants. My God! with what *sang froid* artful trains of corruption bring lucrative commissions into particular hands, disregarding the relative situation of different countries—and can much common honesty be expected in the discharge of trusts obtained by fraud? But this, *entre nous*.

During my present journey, and whilst residing in France, I have had an opportunity of peeping behind the scenes of what are vulgarly termed great affairs, only to discover the mean machinery which has directed many transactions of moment.

The sword has been merciful, compared with the depredations made on human life by contractors, and by the swarm of locusts who have battened on the pestilence they spread abroad. These men, like the owners of negro ships,* never smell on their money the blood by which it has been gained, but sleep quietly in their beds, terming such occupations *lawful callings*; yet the lightning marks not their roofs, to thunder conviction on them, 'and to justify the ways of God to man.'*

Why should I weep for myself?—'Take, O world! thy much indebted tear!'*

Adieu!

LETTER XXV

THERE is a pretty little French theatre at Altona; and the actors are much superiour to those I saw at Copenhagen. The theatres at Hamburg are not open yet, but will very shortly, when the shutting of the gates at seven o'clock forces the citizens to quit their country houses. But, respecting Hamburg, I shall not be able to obtain much more information, as I have determined to sail with the first fair wind for England.

The presence of the French army would have rendered my intended tour through Germany, in my way to Switzerland, almost impracticable, had not the advancing season obliged me to alter my plan. Besides, though Switzerland is the country which for several years I have been particularly desirous to visit, I do not feel inclined to ramble any farther this year; nay, I am weary of changing the scene, and quitting people and places the moment they begin to interest me.—This also is vanity!

DOVER

I left this letter unfinished, as I was hurried on board; and now I have only to tell you, that, at the sight of Dover cliffs, I wondered how any body could term them grand; they appear so insignificant to me, after those I had seen in Sweden and Norway.

Adieu! My spirit of observation seems to be fled—and I have been wandering round this dirty place, literally speaking, to kill time; though the thoughts, I would fain fly from, lie too close to my heart to be easily shook off, or even beguiled, by any employment, except that of preparing for my journey to London.—God bless you!

MARY—

APPENDIX

PRIVATE business and cares have frequently so absorbed me, as to prevent my obtaining all the information, during this journey, which the novelty of the scenes would have afforded, had my attention been continually awake to inquiry. This insensibility to present objects I have often had occasion to lament, since I have been preparing these letters for the press; but, as a person of any thought naturally considers the history of a strange country to contrast the former with the present state of its manners, a conviction of the increasing knowledge and happiness of the kingdoms I passed through, was perpetually the result of my comparative reflections.

The poverty of the poor, in Sweden, renders the civilization very partial; and slavery has retarded the improvement of every class in Denmark; yet both are advancing; and the gigantic evils of despotism and anarchy have in a great measure vanished before the meliorating manners of Europe. Innumerable evils still remain, it is true, to afflict the humane investigator, and hurry the benevolent reformer into a labyrinth of errour, who aims at destroying prejudices quickly which only time can root out, as the public opinion becomes subject to reason.

An ardent affection for the human race makes enthusiastic characters eager to produce alteration in laws and governments prematurely. To render them useful and permanent, they must be the growth of each particular soil, and the gradual fruit of the ripening understanding of the nation, matured by time, not forced by an unnatural fermentation. And, to convince me that such a change is gaining ground, with accelerating pace, the view I have had of society, during my northern journey, would have been sufficient, had I not previously considered the grand causes which combine to carry mankind forward, and diminish the sum of human misery.

NOTES

NOTE 1

NORWAY, according to geometrical measure, is 202 miles in length. In breadth it is very unequal. The common Norway mile contains about 24,000 yards, English measurement.

Norway is reckoned to contain 7558 quadrate miles: it is divided into four parts. There are four grand bailiffs, and four bishops. The four chief towns are Christiania, Thordheim, Bergen, and Christiansand. Its natural products are wood, silver, copper, and iron, a little gold has been found, fish, marble, and the skins of several animals. The exportation exceeds the importation. The balance in favour of Norway, in the year 1767, was about 476,085 rixdollars, 95,217l. sterling. It has been increasing ever since. The silver mines of Kongsberg yield silver to the amount of 350,000 rixdollars, 70,000l. sterling; but it is asserted, that this sum is not sufficient to defray the expences of working them. Kongsberg is the only inland town, and contains 10,000 souls.

The copper mines at Rorraas yield about 4000 ship-pound a year; a ship-pound is 320 pounds: the yearly profit amounts to 150,000 rixdollars, 30,000l. sterling. There are fifteen or sixteen iron works in Norway, which produce iron to the value of 400,000 rixdollars, 80,000l. per annum.

The exportation of salted and dried fish is very considerable. In the year 1786 the returns for its exportation amounted to 749,200 rixdollars, 169,840l.

There are four regiments of dragoons, each consisting of 108 men, officers included; two regiments of marching infantry, 1157 men each, with five companies in garrison, amounting to 3377 men; thirteen regiments of militia, 1916 men each, making 24,908 men; 960 men, light troops, who, in winter, whilst the snow is on the ground, run along on a kind of skates—a couple of long instruments made of wood.

NOTE 2

The taxes in Norway consist of

1. A land tax. Farms, worth from two to three thousand dollars, pay from fifteen to twenty dollars annually.

2. A duty on all articles of provision, and on all goods carried in or out.

3. A tax on rank and office.

4. A tax on pensions and salaries; two per cent on one hundred dollars, and in proportion to ten per cent.

5. A tax on money put out to interest, with security on land or houses, of a quarter per cent. And as the allowed interest is four per cent, the duty is one fourth of the interest.

APPENDIX 1

WOLLSTONECRAFT'S COMMISSION FROM IMLAY

May 19, 1795

KNOW all men by these presents that I Gilbert Imlay citizen of the United States of America residing at present in London do nominate constitute and appoint Mary Imlay my best friend and wife to take the sole management and direction of all my affairs and business which I had placed in the hands of Mr Elias Backman negotiant Gothenburg or in those of Messrs. Ryberg & co Copenhagen, desiring that she will manage and direct such concerns in such manner as she may deem most wise & prudent. For which this letter shall be a sufficient power enabling her to receive all the money or sums of money that may be recovered from Peter Ellefsen or his connections whenever the issue of the tryal now carrying on against him, instigated by Mr Elias Backman as my agent at my request for the violation of the trust which I had reposed in his integrity.

Considering the aggravated distresses, the accumulated losses, and damages sustained in consequence of this said Ellefsen's disobedience of my instructions I desire the said Mary Imlay will clearly ascertain the amount of such damages, taking first the advice of persons qualified to judge of the probab[il]ity of obtaining satisfaction or the means [of] said Ellefsen, or his connection, who may be proved to be implicated in his guilt, may have, or power of being able to make restitution and thus commence a new prosecution for the same accordingly.

Begging leave here only to observe to her that, her judgment will naturally point out the manner of employing the proper persons to make or form such estimate—the documents for which can readily be furnished by Mr. Backman.

Respecting the cargo or goods in the hands of Messrs Ryberg & Co, Mrs Imlay has only to consult the most experienced persons engaged in the disposition of such articles and then placing them at their disposal act as she may deem right and proper. Always I trust governing herself according to the best of her judgment in which I have no doubt but that the opinions of Messrs. Ryberg & Co will have a considerable and due influence.

Thus confiding in the talents zeal and earnestness of my dear beloved friend and companion[,] I submit the management of the affairs intirely and implicitly to her discretion—remaining most sincerity [*sic*] & affectionately yrs truly

May 19th 1795
G. Imlay
Witness J. Samoriel

Addressed crossways Mrs Mary Imlay

APPENDIX 2

WOLLSTONECRAFT'S LETTER TO THE DANISH PRIME MINISTER, COUNT BERNSTORFF

IMPRESSED with a respect for your character, I venture, Sir, to expostulate with you relative to an affair which Mr Wulfsberg has already in some measure explained to you, in the letter which accompanies this brief statement.

Previously allow me to introduce myself to you by [my] own name, Mary Wollstonecraft, and I think I may be permitted, in a strange country, without any breach of modesty, to assert that my character as a moral writer is too well established for any one to suspect that I would condescend to gloss over the truth, or to anything like subterfuge, even in my own cause.

Mr Imlay, my husband, being very much engaged in business could not, at this juncture, leave England to pursue, according to law, Peter Elefsen, who had fraudulently deprived him, and his Partner, of a considerable property. I, therefore, wishing to have an opportunity of writing an account of the present state of Sweden, Norway and Denmark, determined to undertake the business, being fully acquainted with all the circumstances.

Will you, Sir, spare a moment to peruse the following narrative.

In the spring of 94 Mr Imlay bought a ship of an American Captain, who had previously engaged Peter Elefsen to be his flag master. The transfer of the vessel deprived him of his employment, and his distress introduced him to our notice. For some time, without having any first plan of rendering him useful, Mr Imlay let him have the money necessary to support him—and at last sent him to Paris, two or three times, to bring down some silver to Havre de Grace. During the intervals between these journeys Mr Elefsen pointed out a vessel that could be bought cheap and Mr Imlay purchased it; and giving the command to Elefsen preparations were made for a voyage to Gothenburg. Mr Elefsen mean time lodged in the house of a merchant at Havre[,] Mr Imlay paying for it, as well as supplying his other wants. In his room the silver

Danish State Archives, Copenhagen: The Department of Foreign Affairs 1770–1848/ 893: 1795 (Miscellanea, letter I): Madame Imlays sag 1795–96.

was deposited. I saw it there and the mate, Thomas Coleman, an American, assisted Elefsen to carry it on board the ship.

Previous to his sailing he signed a bill of parcels, in which the articles he took were not specified, as well as a receipt for the silver, both of which Mr Wheatcroft and I read over, Mr Wheatcroft (a merchant at Havre) witnessing that Elefsen signed them. The receipt was enclosed in a letter to Mr Backman of Gothenburg with other instructions for clearing and loading the vessel.

I, Sir, gave Elefsen his last orders[,] Mr Imlay having set out for Paris the day before.

I have now to inform you that Elefsen took the silver privately on shore at Arendall, as the mate, Thos. Coleman, [h]as fully proved, and opened the letter addressed to Mr Backman taking out the receipt. The cover of the letter has been brought into court. Many corroborating testimonies have supported the evidence of the mate to the conviction of the judges and every impartial person, still the atrocities carried on during the time the trial has been pending to retard the march of justice have even been more flagrant than the breach of trust. Many of the inhabitants, particularly the post master, who has but one character in the country, having shared in the spoil, bribery has produced prevarication and perjury. His father-in-law, a major in the army, offered five hundred dollars to the wife of the first judge. When I arrived at East Risoer Elefsen waited on me and, as we were alone, behaved in the humblest manner, wished that the affair had never happened, though he assured me that I never should be able to bring the proofs forward sufficient to convict him. He enlarged on the expense we must run into—appealed to my humanity and assured me that he could not now return the money. Willing to settle the business I desired him to inquire of his relations, who are people of property, what they would advance, and come to me in the evening when I would endeavour to compromise the matter.—He came and was almost impertinent. He had been spurred on by his attorneys, the pest of the country. Their plan, I plainly perceive, was to weary us out by procrastination. The suit has already been pending a twelvemonth, and the want of such a considerable sum in trade, as well as the expenses incurred by the detention of the vessel, which it has been proved he endeavoured to sink, is a very serious injury to us, not to dwell on the vexatious circumstances attending the failure of a commercial plan. I am very well convinced that an English jury would long ago have decided in our favour not suffering justice to be insulted in the manner it has been with impunity; but the judges are timid.

To you, Sir, as a known lover of justice, I appeal, and I am supported by the most worthy Norwegians, who wished by the respect they paid me to disavow the conduct of their countryman.

I am Sir yours
Respectfully
Mary Wollstonecraft
femme Imlay

Copenhagen
Sepr 5th 1795

APPENDIX 3

WOLLSTONECRAFT'S LETTERS TO IMLAY

[The letters were edited by Godwin for the *Posthumous Works*. Additions in square brackets are by the present editors.]

June 27, Saturday

I ARRIVED in [Gothenburg] this afternoon, after vainly attempting to land at [Arendal]. I have now but a moment, before the post goes out, to inform you we have got here; though not without considerable difficulty, for we were set ashore in a boat above twenty miles below.

What I suffered in the vessel I will not now descant upon—nor mention the pleasure I received from the sight of the rocky coast.—This morning however, walking to join the carriage that was to transport us to this place, I fell, without any previous warning, senseless on the rocks—and how I escaped with life I can scarcely guess. I was in a stupour for a quarter of an hour; the suffusion of blood at last restored me to my senses—the contusion is great, and my brain confused. The child is well.

Twenty miles ride in the rain, after my accident, has sufficiently deranged me—and here I could not get a fire to warm me, or any thing warm to eat; the inns are mere stables—I must nevertheless go to bed. For God's sake, let me hear from you immediately, my friend! I am not well, and yet you see I cannot die.

Yours sincerely

****

June 29.

I WROTE to you by the last post, to inform you of my arrival; and I believe I alluded to the extreme fatigue I endured on ship-board, owing to [probably Marguerite]'s illness, and the roughness of the weather—I likewise mentioned to you my fall, the effects of which I still feel, though I do not think it will have any serious consequences.

From *Posthumous Works of the Author of A Vindication of the Rights of Woman*, 4 vols. (1798), vols. iii and iv.

[Backman] will go with me, if I find it necessary to go to [Copenhagen]. The inns here are so bad, I was forced to accept of an apartment in his house. I am overwhelmed with civilities on all sides, and fatigued with the endeavours to amuse me, from which I cannot escape.

My friend—my friend, I am not well—a deadly weight of sorrow lies heavily on my heart. I am again tossed on the troubled billows of life; and obliged to cope with difficulties, without being buoyed up by the hopes that alone render them bearable. 'How flat, dull, and unprofitable,' appears to me all the bustle into which I see people here so eagerly enter! I long every night to go to bed, to hide my melancholy face in my pillow; but there is a canker-worm in my bosom that never sleeps.

****

July 1.

I LABOUR in vain to calm my mind—my soul has been overwhelmed by sorrow and disappointment. Every thing fatigues me—this is a life that cannot last long. It is you who must determine with respect to futurity—and, when you have, I will act accordingly—I mean, we must either resolve to live together, or part for ever, I cannot bear these continual struggles—But I wish you to examine carefully your own heart and mind; and, if you perceive the least chance of being happier without me than with me, or if your inclination leans capriciously to that side, do not dissemble; but tell me frankly that you will never see me more. I will then adopt the plan I mentioned to you—for we must either live together, or I will be entirely independent.

My heart is so oppressed, I cannot write with precision—You know however that what I so imperfectly express, are not the crude sentiments of the moment—You can only contribute to my comfort (it is the consolation I am in need of) by being with me—and, if the tenderest friendship is of any value, why will you not look to me for a degree of satisfaction that heartless affections cannot bestow?

Tell me then, will you determine to meet me at Basle?—I shall, I should imagine, be at [Hamburg?] before the close of August; and after you settle your affairs at Paris, could we not meet there?

God bless you!

Yours truly

****

Poor [Fanny] has suffered during the journey with her teeth.

July 3.

THERE was a gloominess diffused through your last letter, the impression of which still rests on my mind—though, recollecting how quickly you throw off the forcible feelings of the moment, I flatter myself it has long since given place to your usual cheerfulness.

Believe me (and my eyes fill with tears of tenderness as I assure you) there is nothing I would not endure in the way of privation, rather than disturb your tranquility.—If I am fated to be unhappy, I will labour to hide my sorrows in my own bosom; and you shall always find me a faithful, affectionate friend.

I grow more and more attached to my little girl—and I cherish this affection without fear, because it must be a long time before it can become bitterness of soul.—She is an interesting creature.—On ship-board, how often as I gazed at the sea, have I longed to bury my troubled bosom in the less troubled deep; asserting with Brutus, 'that the virtue I had followed too far, was merely an empty name!' and nothing but the sight of her—her playful smiles, which seemed to cling and twine round my heart—could have stopped me.

What peculiar misery has fallen to my share! To act up to my principles, I have laid the strictest restraint on my very thoughts—yes; not to sully the delicacy of my feelings, I have reined in my imagination; and started with affright from every sensation, (I allude to——) that stealing with balmy sweetness into my soul, led me to scent from afar the fragrance of reviving nature.

My friend, I have dearly paid for one conviction.—Love, in some minds, is an affair of sentiment, arising from the same delicacy of perception (or taste) as renders them alive to the beauties of nature, poetry, &c, alive to the charms of those evanescent graces that are, as it were, impalpable—they must be felt, they cannot be described.

Love is a want of my heart. I have examined myself lately with more care than formerly, and find, that to deaden is not to calm the mind—Aiming at tranquillity, I have almost destroyed all the energy of my soul—almost rooted out what renders it estimable—Yes, I have damped that enthusiasm of character, which converts the grossest materials into a fuel, that imperceptibly feeds hopes, which aspire above common enjoyment. Despair, since the birth of my child, has rendered me stupid—soul and body seemed to be fading away before the withering touch of disappointment.

I am now endeavouring to recover myself—and such is the elasticity of my constitution, and the purity of the atmosphere here, that health unsought for, begins to reanimate my countenance.

I have the sincerest esteem and affection for you—but the desire of regaining peace, (do you understand me?) has made me forget the respect due to my own emotions—sacred emotions, that are the sure harbingers of the delights I was formed to enjoy—and shall enjoy, for nothing can extinguish the heavenly spark.

Still, when we meet again, I will not torment you, I promise you. I blush when I recollect my former conduct—and will not in future confound myself with the beings whom I feel to be my inferiors.—I will listen to delicacy, or pride.

July 4.

I HOPE to hear from you by to-morrow's mail. My dearest friend! I cannot tear my affections from you—and, though every remembrance stings me to the soul, I think of you, till I make allowance for the very defects of character, that have given such a cruel stab to my peace.

Still however I am more alive, than you have seen me for a long, long time. I have a degree of vivacity, even in my grief, which is preferable to the benumbing stupour that, for the last year, has frozen up all my faculties.—Perhaps this change is more owing to returning health, than to the vigour of my reason—for, in spite of sadness (and surely I have had my share), the purity of this air, and the being continually out in it, for I sleep in the country every night, has made an alteration in my appearance that really surprises me.—The rosy fingers of health already streak my cheeks—and I have seen a *physical* life in my eyes, after I have been climbing the rocks, that resembled the fond, credulous hopes of youth.

With what a cruel sigh have I recollected that I had forgotten to hope!—Reason, or rather experience, does not thus cruelly damp poor [Fanny]'s pleasures; she plays all day in the garden with [Backman]'s children, and makes friends for herself.

Do not tell me, that you are happier without us—Will you not come to us in Switzerland? Ah, why do not you love us with more sentiment?—why are you a creature of such sympathy, that the warmth of your feelings, or rather quickness of your senses, hardens your heart? It is my misfortune, that my imagination is perpetually shading your defects, and lending you charms, whilst the grossness of your senses makes you (call me not vain) overlook graces in me, that only dignity of mind, and the sensibility of an expanded heart can give.—God bless you! Adieu.

July 7.

I COULD not help feeling extremely mortified last post, at not receiving a letter from you. My being at [Strömstad] was but a chance, and you might have hazarded it; and would a year ago.

I shall not however complain—There are misfortunes so great, as to silence the usual expressions of sorrow—Believe me, there is such a thing as a broken heart! There are characters whose very energy preys upon them; and who, ever inclined to cherish by reflection some passion, cannot rest satisfied with the common comforts of life. I have endeavoured to fly from myself, and launched into all the dissipation possible here, only to feel keener anguish, when alone with my child.

Still, could any thing please me—had not disappointment cut me off from life, this romantic country, these fine evenings, would interest me.—My God! can any thing? and am I ever to feel alive only to painful sensations?—But it cannot—it shall not last long.

The post is again arrived; I have sent to seek for letters, only to be wounded to the soul by a negative.—My brain seems on fire. I must go into the air.

****

July 14.

I AM now on my journey to [Tønsberg]. I felt more at leaving my child, than I thought I should—and, whilst at night I imagined every instant that I heard the half-formed sounds of her voice,—I asked myself how I could think of parting with her for ever, of leaving her thus helpless?

Poor lamb! It may run very well in a tale, that 'God will temper the winds to the shorn lamb!' but how can I expect that she will be shielded, when my naked bosom has had to brave continually the pitiless storm? Yes; I could add, with poor Lear—What is the war of elements to the pangs of disappointed affection, and the horror arising from a discovery of a breach of confidence, that snaps every social tie!

All is not right somewhere!—When you first knew me, I was not thus lost. I could still confide—for I opened my heart to you—of this only comfort you have deprived me, whilst my happiness, you tell me, was your first object. Strange want of judgment!

I will not complain; but, from the soundness of your understanding, I am convinced, if you give yourself leave to reflect, you will also feel, that your conduct to me, so far from being generous, has not been just.—I mean not to allude to factitious principles of morality; but to the simple basis of all rectitude.—However I did not intend to argue—Your not writing is cruel—and my reason is perhaps disturbed by constant wretchedness.

Poor [Marguerite] would fain have accompanied me, out of tenderness; for my fainting, or rather convulsion, when I landed, and my sudden changes of countenance since, have alarmed her so much, that she is perpetually afraid of some accident—But it would have injured the child this warm season, as she is cutting her teeth.

I hear not of your having written to me at [Gothenburg?]. Very well! Act as you please—there is nothing I fear or care for! When I see whether I can, or cannot obtain the money I am come here about, I will not trouble you with letters to which you do not reply.

July 18.

I am here in [Tønsberg], separated from my child—and here I must remain a month at least, or I might as well never have come.

[In *PW* Godwin indicates several omitted lines.]

I have begun [probably *A Short Residence*] which will, I hope, discharge all my obligations of a pecuniary kind.—I am lowered in my own eyes, on account of my not having done it sooner.

I shall make no further comments on your silence. God bless you!

****

July 30.

I have just received two of your letters, dated the 26th and 30th of June; and you must have received several from me, informing you of my detention, and how much I was hurt by your silence.

[In *PW* Godwin indicates several omitted lines.]

Write to me then, my friend, and write explicitly. I have suffered, God knows, since I left you. Ah! you have never felt this kind of sickness of heart!—My mind however is at present painfully active, and the sympathy I feel almost rises to agony. But this is not a subject of complaint, it has afforded me pleasure,—and reflected pleasure is all I have to hope for—if a spark of hope be yet alive in my forlorn bosom.

I will try to write with a degree of composure. I wish for us to live together, because I want you to acquire an habitual tenderness for my poor girl. I cannot bear to think of leaving her alone in the world, or that she should only be protected by your sense of duty. Next to preserving her, my most earnest wish is not to disturb your peace. I have nothing to expect, and little to fear, in life—There are wounds that can never be healed—but they may be allowed to fester in silence without wincing.

When we meet again, you shall be convinced that I have more resolution than you give me credit for. I will not torment you. If I am destined always to be disappointed and unhappy, I will conceal the anguish I cannot dissipate; and the tightened cord of life or reason will at last snap, and set me free.

Yes; I shall be happy—This heart is worthy of the bliss its feelings anticipate—and I cannot even persuade myself, wretched as they have made me, that my principles and sentiments are not founded in nature and truth. But to have done with these subjects.

[In *PW* Godwin indicates several omitted lines.]

I have been seriously employed in this way since I came to [Tønsberg]; yet I never was so much in the air.—I walk, I ride on horseback—row, bathe, and even sleep in the fields; my health is consequently improved. The child, [Marguerite, or perhaps Backman] informs me, is well. I long to be with her.

Write to me immediately—were I only to think of myself, I could wish you to return to me, poor, with the simplicity of character, part of which you seem lately to have lost, that first attached to you.

Yours most affectionately

**** *****

[Mary Imlay]

I have been subscribing other letters—so I mechanically did the same to yours.

August 5.

EMPLOYMENT and exercise have been of great service to me; and I have entirely recovered the strength and activity I lost during the time of my nursing. I have seldom been in better health; and my mind, though trembling to the touch of anguish, is calmer—yet still the same.—I have, it is true, enjoyed some tranquillity, and more happiness here, than for a long—long time past.—(I say happiness, for I can give no other appellation to the exquisite delight this wild country and fine summer have afforded me.)—Still, on examining my heart, I find that it is so constituted, I cannot live without some particular affection—I am afraid not without a passion—and I feel the want of it more in society, than in solitude.—

[In *PW* Godwin indicates several omitted lines.]

Writing to you, whenever an affectionate epithet occurs—my eyes fill with tears, and my trembling hand stops—you may then depend on my resolution, when with you. If I am doomed to be unhappy, I will confine my anguish in my own bosom—tenderness, rather than passion, has made me sometimes overlook delicacy—the same tenderness will in future restrain me.
God bless you!

August 7.

AIR, exercise, and bathing, have restored me to health, braced my muscles, and covered my ribs, even whilst I have recovered my former activity.—I cannot tell you that my mind is calm, though I have snatched some moments of exquisite delight, wandering through the woods, and resting on the rocks.

This state of suspense, my friend, is intolerable; we must determine on something—and soon;—we must meet shortly, or part for ever. I am sensible that I acted foolishly—but I was wretched—when we were together—Expecting too much, I let the pleasure I might have caught, slip from me. I cannot live with you—I ought not—if you form another attachment. But I promise you, mine shall not be intruded on you. Little reason have I to expect a shadow of happiness, after the cruel disappointments that have rent my heart; but that of my child seems to depend on our being together. Still I do not wish you to sacrifice a chance of enjoyment for an uncertain good. I feel a conviction, that I can provide for her, and it shall be my object—if we are indeed to part to meet no more. Her affection must not be divided. She must be a comfort to me—if I am to have no other—and only know me as her support. I feel that I cannot endure the anguish of corresponding with you—if we are only to correspond.—No; if you seek for happiness elsewhere, my letters shall not interrupt your repose. I will be dead to you. I cannot express to you what pain it gives me to write about an eternal separation.—You must determine—examine yourself—But, for God's sake! spare me the anxiety of uncertainty!—I may sink under the trial; but I will not complain.

Adieu! If I had any thing more to say to you, it is all flown, and absorbed by the most tormenting apprehensions; yet I scarcely know what new form of misery I have to dread.

I ought to beg your pardon for having sometimes written peevishly; but you will impute it to affection, if you understand any thing of the heart of

Yours truly
****

August 9.

FIVE of your letters have been sent after me from [probably Gothenburg]. One, dated the 14th of July, was written in a style which I may have merited, but did not expect from you. However this is not a time to reply to it, except to assure you that you shall not be tormented with any more complaints. I am disgusted with myself for having so long importuned you with my affection.—

My child is very well. We shall soon meet, to part no more, I hope— I mean, I and my girl.—I shall wait with some degree of anxiety till I am informed how your affairs terminate.

Yours sincerely
****

August 26.

I ARRIVED here last night, and with the most exquisite delight, once more pressed my babe to my heart. We shall part no more. You perhaps cannot conceive the pleasure it gave me, to see her run about, and play alone. Her increasing intelligence attaches me more and more to her. I have promised her that I will fulfil my duty to her; and nothing in future shall make me forget it. I will also exert myself to obtain an independence for her; but I will not be too anxious on this head.

I have already told you, that I have recovered my health. Vigour, and even vivacity of mind, have returned with a renovated constitution. As for peace, we will not talk of it. I was not made, perhaps, to enjoy the calm contentment so termed.—

[In *PW* Godwin indicates several omitted lines.]

You tell me that my letters torture you; I will not describe the effect yours have on me. I received three this morning, the last dated the 7th of this month. I mean not to give vent to the emotions they produced.—Certainly you are right; our minds are not congenial. I have lived in an ideal world, and fostered sentiments that you do not comprehend—or you would not treat me thus. I am not, I will not be, merely an object of compassion—a clog, however light, to teize you. Forget that I exist: I will never remind you. Something emphatical whispers me to put an end to these struggles. Be free—I will not torment, when I cannot please. I can take care of my child; you need not continually tell me that our fortune is inseparable, *that you will try to cherish tenderness* for me. Do no violence to yourself! When we are separated, our interest, since you give so much weight to pecuniary considerations, will be entirely divided. I want not protection without affection; and support I need not, whilst my faculties are undisturbed. I had a dislike to living in England; but painful feelings must give way to superior considerations. I may not be able to acquire the sum necessary to maintain my child and self elsewhere. It is too late to go to Switzerland. I shall not remain at [London?], living expensively. But be not alarmed! I shall not force myself on you any more.

Adieu! I am agitated—my whole frame is convulsed—my lips tremble, as if shook by cold, though fire seems to be circulating in my veins.

God bless you.

****

September 6.

I RECEIVED just now your letter of the 20th. I had written you a letter last night, into which imperceptibly slipt some of my bitterness of soul. I will copy the part relative to business. I am not sufficiently vain to imagine that I can, for more than a moment, cloud your enjoyment of life—to prevent even that, you had better never hear from me—and repose on the idea that I am happy.

Gracious God! It is impossible for me to stifle something like resentment, when I receive fresh proofs of your indifference. What I have suffered this last year, is not to be forgotten! I have not that happy substitute for wisdom, insensibility—and the lively sympathies which bind me to my fellow-creatures, are all of a painful kind.—They are the agonies of a broken heart—pleasure and I have shaken hands.

I see here nothing but heaps of ruins, and only converse with people immersed in trade and sensuality.

I am weary of travelling—yet seem to have no home—no resting place to look to.—I am strangely cast off.—How often, passing through the rocks, I have thought, 'But for this child, I would lay my head on one of them, and never open my eyes again!' With a heart feelingly alive to all the affections of my nature—I have never met with one, softer than the stone that I would fain take for my last pillow. I once thought I had, but it was all a delusion. I meet with families continually, who are bound together by affection or principle—and, when I am conscious that I have fulfilled the duties of my station, almost to a forgetfulness of myself, I am ready to demand, in a murmuring tone, of Heaven, 'Why am I thus abandoned?'

You say now

[In *PW* Godwin indicates several omitted lines.]

I do not understand you. It is necessary for you to write more explicitly—and determine on some mode of conduct.—I cannot endure this suspense—Decide—Do you fear to strike another blow? We live together, or eternally part!—I shall not write to you again, till I receive an answer to this. I must compose my tortured soul, before I write on indifferent subjects.

[In *PW* Godwin indicates several omitted lines.]

I do not know whether I write intelligibly, for my head is disturbed. —But this you ought to pardon—for it is with difficulty frequently that I make out what you mean to say—You write, I suppose, at Mr. ——'s after dinner, when your head is not the clearest—and as for your heart, if you have one, I see nothing like the dictates of affection, unless a glimpse when you mention the child.—Adieu!

September 25.

I HAVE just finished a letter, to be given in charge to captain ——. In that I complained of your silence, and expressed my surprise that three mails should have arrived without bringing a line for me. Since I closed it, I hear of another, and still no letter.—I am labouring to write calmly—this silence is a refinement on cruelty. Had captain —— remained a few days longer, I would have returned with him to England. What have I to do here? I have repeatedly written to you fully.

Do you do the same—and quickly. Do not leave me in suspense. I have not deserved this of you. I cannot write, my mind is so distressed. Adieu!

****

[The remaining letters come from vol. iv of *Posthumous Works*]

September 27.

WHEN you receive this, I shall either have landed, or be hovering on the British coast—your letter of the 18th decided me.

By what criterion of principle or affection, you term my questions extraordinary and unnecessary, I cannot determine.—You desire me to decide—I had decided. You must have had long ago two letters of mine, from ——, to the same purport, to consider.—In these, God knows! there was but too much affection, and the agonies of a distracted mind were but too faithfully pourtrayed!—What more then had I to say?—The negative was to come from you.—You had perpetually recurred to your promise of meeting me in the autumn—Was it extraordinary that I should demand a yes, or no?—Your letter is written with extreme harshness, coldness I am accustomed to, in it I find not a trace of the tenderness of humanity, much less of friendship.—I only see a desire to heave a load off your shoulders.

I am above disputing about words.—It matters not in what terms you decide.

The tremendous power who formed this heart, must have foreseen that, in a world in which self-interest, in various shapes, is the principal mobile, I had little chance of escaping misery.—To the fiat of fate I submit.—I am content to be wretched; but I will not be contemptible. —Of me you have no cause to complain, but for having had too much regard for you—for having expected a degree of permanent happiness, when you only sought for a momentary gratification.

I am strangely deficient in sagacity.—Uniting myself to you, your tenderness seemed to make me amends for all my former misfortunes. —On this tenderness and affection with what confidence did I rest! —but I leaned on a spear, that has pierced me to the heart.—You have thrown off a faithful friend, to pursue the caprices of the moment.—We certainly are differently organized; for even now, when conviction has been stamped on my soul by sorrow, I can scarcely believe it possible.

It depends at present on you, whether you will see me or not.—I shall take no step, till I see or hear from you.

Preparing myself for the worst—I have determined, if your next letter be like the last, to write to Mr. [Johnson?] to procure me an obscure lodging, and not to inform any body of my arrival.—There I will endeavour in a few months to obtain the sum necessary to take me to France—from you I will not receive any more.—I am not yet sufficiently humbled to depend on your beneficence.

Some people, whom my unhappiness has interested, though they know not the extent of it, will assist me to attain the object I have in view, the independence of my child. Should a peace take place, ready money will go a great way in France—and I will borrow a sum, which my industry *shall* enable me to pay at my leisure, to purchase a small estate for my girl.—The assistance I shall find necessary to complete her education, I can get at an easy rate at Paris—I can introduce her to such society as she will like—and thus, securing for her all the chance for happiness, which depends on me, I shall die in peace, persuaded that the felicity which has hitherto cheated my expectation, will not always elude my grasp. No poor tempest-tossed mariner ever more earnestly longed to arrive at his port.

****

I shall not come up in the vessel all the way, because I have no place to go to. Captain —— will inform you where I am. It is needless to add, that I am not in a state of mind to bear suspense—and that I wish to see you, though it be for the last time.

October 4.

I WROTE to you by the packet, to inform you, that your letter of the 18th of last month, had determined me to set out with captain ——; but, as we sailed very quick, I take it for granted, that you have not yet received it.

You say, I must decide for myself.—I had decided, that it was most for the interest of my little girl, and for my own comfort, little as I expect, for us to live together; and I even thought that you would be glad, some years hence, when the tumult of business was over, to repose in the society of an affectionate friend, and mark the progress of our interesting child, whilst endeavouring to be of use in the circle you at last resolved to rest in; for you cannot run about for ever.

From the tenour of your last letter however, I am led to imagine, that you have formed some new attachment.—If it be so, let me earnestly request you to see me once more, and immediately. This is the only proof I require of the friendship you profess for me. I will then decide, since you boggle about a mere form.

I am labouring to write with calmness—but the extreme anguish I feel, at landing without having any friend to receive me, and even to be conscious that the friend whom I most wish to see, will feel a disagreeable sensation at being informed of my arrival, does not come under the description of common misery. Every emotion yields to an overwhelming flood of sorrow—and the playfulness of my child distresses me.—On her account, I wished to remain a few days here, comfortless as is my situation.—Besides, I did not wish to surprise you. You have told me, that you would make any sacrifice to promote my happiness—and, even in your last unkind letter, you talk of the ties which bind you to me and my child.—Tell me, that you wish it, and I will cut this Gordian knot.

I now most earnestly intreat you to write to me, without fail, by the return of the post. Direct your letter to be left at the post-office, and tell me whether you will come to me here, or where you will meet me. I can receive your letter on Wednesday morning.

Do not keep me in suspense.—I expect nothing from you, or any human being: my die is cast!—I have fortitude enough to determine to do my duty; yet I cannot raise my depressed spirits, or calm my trembling heart.—That being who moulded it thus, knows that I am unable to tear up by the roots the propensity to affection which has been the torment of my life—but life will have an end!

Should you come here (a few months ago I could not have doubted it) you will find me at ——. If you prefer meeting me on the road, tell me where.

Yours affectionately

****

APPENDIX 4

FROM WILLIAM GODWIN, *MEMOIRS OF THE AUTHOR OF A VINDICATION OF THE RIGHTS OF WOMAN*

CHAPTER VIII
1795, 1796

IN April 1795, Mary returned once more to London, being requested to do so by Mr. Imlay, who even sent a servant to Paris to wait upon her in the journey, before she could complete the necessary arrangements for her departure. But, notwithstanding these favourable appearances, she came to England with a heavy heart, not daring, after all the uncertainties and anguish she had endured, to trust to the suggestions of hope.

The gloomy forebodings of her mind, were but too faithfully verified. Mr. Imlay had already formed another connection; as it is said, with a young actress from a strolling company of players. His attentions therefore to Mary were formal and constrained, and she probably had but little of his society. This alteration could not escape her penetrating glance. He ascribed it to pressure of business, and some pecuniary embarrassments which, at that time, occurred to him; it was of little consequence to Mary what was the cause. She saw, but too well, though she strove not to see, that his affections were lost to her for ever.

It is impossible to imagine a period of greater pain and mortification than Mary passed, for about seven weeks, from the sixteenth of April to the sixth of June, in a furnished house that Mr. Imlay had provided for her. She had come over to England, a country for which she, at this time, expressed 'a repugnance, that almost amounted to horror,' in search of happiness. She feared that that happiness had altogether escaped her; but she was encouraged by the eagerness and impatience which Mr. Imlay at length seemed to manifest for her arrival. When she saw him, all her fears were confirmed. What a picture was she capable of forming to herself, of the overflowing kindness of a meeting, after an interval of so much anguish and apprehension! A thousand images of this sort were present to her burning imagination. It is in

Memoirs of the Author of A Vindication of the Rights of Woman (London, 1798), 123–31.

vain, on such occasions, for reserve and reproach to endeavour to curb in the emotions of an affectionate heart. But the hopes she nourished were speedily blasted. Her reception by Mr. Imlay, was cold and embarrassed. Discussions ('explanations' they were called) followed; cruel explanations, that only added to the anguish of a heart already overwhelmed in grief! They had small pretensions indeed to explicitness; but they sufficiently told, that the case admitted not of remedy.

Mary was incapable of sustaining her equanimity in this pressing emergency. 'Love, dear, delusive love!' as she expressed herself to a friend some time afterwards, 'rigorous reason had forced her to resign; and now her rational prospects were blasted, just as she had learned to be contented with rational enjoyments.' Thus situated, life became an intolerable burthen. While she was absent from Mr. Imlay, she could talk of purposes of separation and independence. But, now that they were in the same house, she could not withhold herself from endeavours to revive their mutual cordiality; and unsuccessful endeavours continually added fuel to the fire that destroyed her. She formed a desperate purpose to die.

This part of the story of Mary is involved in considerable obscurity. I only know, that Mr. Imlay became acquainted with her purpose, at a moment when he was uncertain whether or no it were already executed, and that his feelings were roused by the intelligence. It was perhaps owing to his activity and representations, that her life was, at this time, saved. She determined to continue to exist. Actuated by this purpose, she took a resolution worthy both of the strength and affectionateness of her mind. Mr. Imlay was involved in a question of considerable difficulty, respecting a mercantile adventure in Norway. It seemed to require the presence of some very judicious agent, to conduct the business to its desired termination. Mary determined to make the voyage, and take the business into her own hands. Such a voyage seemed the most desireable thing to recruit her health, and, if possible, her spirits, in the present crisis. It was also gratifying to her feelings, to be employed in promoting the interest of a man, from whom she had experienced such severe unkindness, but to whom she ardently desired to be reconciled. The moment of desperation I have mentioned, occurred in the close of May, and, in about a week after, she set out upon this new expedition.

The narrative of this voyage is before the world, and perhaps a book of travels that so irresistibly seizes on the heart, never, in any other instance, found its way from the press. The occasional harshness and ruggedness of character, that diversify her Vindication of the Rights of Woman, here totally disappear. If ever there was a book calculated to make a man in love with its author, this appears to me to be the book. She speaks of her sorrows, in a way that fills us with melancholy, and dissolves us in tenderness, at the same time that she displays a genius which commands all our admiration. Affliction had tempered her heart to a softness almost more than human; and the gentleness of her spirit seems precisely to accord with all the romance of unbounded attachment.

Thus softened and improved, thus fraught with imagination and sensibility, with all, and more than all, 'that youthful poets fancy, when they love,' she returned to England, and, if he had so pleased, to the arms of her former lover. Her return was hastened by the ambiguity, to her apprehension, of Mr. Imlay's conduct. He had promised to meet her upon her return from Norway, probably at Hamburgh; and they were then to pass some time in Switzerland. The style however of his letters to her during her tour, was not such as to inspire confidence; and she wrote to him very urgently, to explain himself, relative to the footing upon which they were hereafter to stand to each other. In his answer, which reached her at Hamburgh, he treated her questions as 'extraordinary and unnecessary,' and desired her to be at the pains to decide for herself. Feeling herself unable to accept this as an explanation, she instantly determined to sail for London by the very first opportunity, that she might thus bring to a termination the suspense that preyed upon her soul.

APPENDIX 5

CONTEMPORARY REVIEWS

REPRINTED below are excerpts from contemporary reviews and a letter to the *Monthly Magazine* on the treatment of religion in Wollstonecraft's book. Nearly all the excisions are copious quotations from *A Short Residence* typical of reviews in the period.

Analytical Review, 23 (1796), 229–38

A vigorous and cultivated intellect easily accommodates itself to new occupations. The notion, that individual genius can only excel in one thing, is a vulgar error. A mind endued by nature with strong powers and quick sensibility, and by culture furnished in an uncommon degree with habits of attention and reflection, wherever it is placed, will find itself employments, and whatever it undertakes, will execute it well. After the repeated proofs, which the ingenious and justly admired writer of these letters has given the public, that her talents are far above the ordinary level, it will not be thought surprising, that she should excel in different kinds of writing; that the qualifications, which have enabled her to instruct young people by moral lessons and tales, and to furnish the philosopher with original and important speculations, should also empower her to entertain and interest the public, in a manner peculiarly her own, by writing a book of travels.

We have no hesitation in ensuring our readers, that Mrs. W. has done this in the present volume. Her active mind has, throughout her tour, been awake to every object and occurrence. She has been at no loss to find in every new situation something interesting to describe, or some occasion for just reflection. The letters are evidently not the effect of elaborate study: but from a mind so well stored, and exercised, as this writer's, the easy unsolicited effusions of the moment, in a work of this kind, are preferable to artificial arrangements. 'In order to avoid becoming stiff and affected, I determined,' says Mrs. W., 'to let my remarks and reflections flow unrestrained, as I perceived that I could not give a just description of what I saw, but by relating the effect different objects had produced on my mind and feelings, whilst the impression was still fresh.' Her plan, as stated by herself, was 'simply to endeavour to give a just view of the present state of the countries she has passed through, as far as she could obtain information during so short a residence; avoiding those details, which, without being very useful to travellers who follow the same route, appear very insipid to those who only accompany you in their chair.'

The descriptions of nature in these letters are rather bold sketches, than finished paintings: and for this the writer assigns a good reason: P. 43: 'Only the grand features of a country admit of description. There is an individuality in every prospect, which remains in the memory as forcibly depicted as the particular features that have arrested our attention; yet we cannot find words to discriminate that individuality so as to enable a stranger to say, this is the face, that the view. We may amuse by setting the imagination to work; but we cannot store the memory with a fact.' Some of the grand outlines by which our female traveller sets her reader's imagination at work, are, however, highly picturesque. . . .

On the debasing influence of commerce upon the human mind our philosophical traveller makes some poignant, but perhaps too just remarks, in the account of Hamburgh, with which she closes her tour: but for these, with many other ingenious and important reflections, we must refer our readers to the volume itself.

We are sorry to add, that these letters, while they afford many proofs, that the writer is not more distinguished by strength of understanding than by delicacy of sensibility, also discover, that her feeling heart has suffered deeply from some recent affliction.

. . .

British Critic, 7 (June 1796), 'Preface' pp. x–xi and 602–10

['Preface', 7: pp. x–xi]

Mrs. Wollstonecraft, with much inflated affectation of fine writing, and much idle pretence to philosophy, has mixed in her *Letters from Sweden*, many particulars that are agreeable and some that are interesting. Had she been fortunate enough to escape the philosophical infection, she might have been a good writer, as well as a more useful member of society; but there is as much bad taste as bad morality, in the philosophy of French Deists, by which her mind has been perverted.

[From the review of the book, 7: 602–10]

That Mrs. Wollstonecraft possesses extensive information and considerable powers of reasoning, the public has been already apprized.

It remained for her to show that she is capable of joining to a *masculine* understanding, the finer sensibilities of a female. An heart exquisitely alive to the beauties of nature, and keenly susceptible of every soft impression, every tender emotion. It may, perhaps, not be difficult to account for her displaying now, and not till now, that delicacy and liveliness of feeling which is the peculiar characteristic of the sex. We are informed by report, and indeed we collect from the book before us, that she has lately been placed in situations where sentiments and emotions have been produced, unfelt and uncaused before. In exchange for the still calm of a single state, she has experienced alternately the endearments and the afflictions of a married life. The thrilling sensation of maternal tenderness has been excited towards an infant; and the pang of misplaced affection inflicted by a husband. We must not wonder then to see occasionally in the book before us the painful expression of wounded sensibility, and the glowing effusion of maternal rapture.

These letters will not be expected to set forth a dry and regular detail of incidents, or a methodical account of countries. The historian will find little that can swell his annals, and the connoisseur nothing to gratify his peculiar taste; but the lovers of nature will often feel their hearts beat in unison with that of the writer, in tracing the scenes she has past, and the emotions they have excited. The politician and the moralist will each find many a reflection addrest to their attention. Would we could say, in every instance, entitled to their approbation! But the peculiarity of Mrs. Wollstonecraft's sentiments on many important subjects, seems not to have been diminished, by a more extensive intercourse with mankind. We shall, however, as distinctly as we are able, place before our readers what we approve, and what, however reluctantly, we condemn, of this publication: and to begin with the more agreeable part, we must not fail to mark with our approbation the happy talent for animated description which this writer possesses, which does ample justice to her genuine relish of the beauties of nature.

It is probably unnecessary, after these quotations, to remark how greatly Mrs. Wollstonecraft has improved in her style of writing. Now and then we meet with turgid or obscure expressions and passages; but, upon the whole, a very great superiority is visible, in this respect, over her former publications. Indeed we barely do justice to the language, in pronouncing it entitled to praise for elegance and energy.

. . .

If the faults in the work before us were confined to blemishes of style, or to mere peculiarity of sentiment, we could pass them over as compensated by superior beauties, or we should take a pleasure in the exercise of that critical gallantry which may properly be extended to the *foibles* of a lady. We could allow Mrs. Wollstonecraft to stand forward the champion and defender of her sex, from the ruthless oppression of ours, and we could smile at an error which is so little likely to gain converts. But when a woman so far outsteps her proper sphere, as to deride facts which she cannot disprove, and avow opinions which it is dangerous to disseminate, we cannot consistently with our duty, permit her to pursue triumphantly her Phaeton-like career.

But upon subjects where errors in opinion must be danger in practice, we are bound to censure the presumption which formed, and the folly which publishes them. Has Mrs. Wollstonecraft sufficiently considered the complicated and extensive chain of evidence of reasoning by which revelation is supported, to enable her confidently to oppose her judgment to the acquiescence of the wisest, and to the decision of ages? Has she maturely weighed the analogy which subsists between the book of nature and the word of God? Has she diligently explored those fountains of knowledge, through which alone the proofs of revelation can be properly and accurately estimated? And can she securely bid defiance to that mass of moral probabilities which has assured to the most learned, and the most thinking men, the credibility of the Christian religion? We are convinced she has not done this; nor can we compliment her very much upon her powers of discernment, if she can suppose Paganism and Christianity supported by the same evidence, or entitled to the same respect.

If Mrs. W. could consider candidly and seriously the merits and the evidence of that system, which strengthen the obligations, and confirms the hopes, of natural religion, and at the same time adds superior motives for action, and ensures brighter prospects, she would not find her head so often sicken with anxiety, tremble with apprehension, and feel palsied with despair. She would find *refuge from sorrow*, in feelings and in hopes, prompted by something better than a *strong imagination*, *the only solace* she now *knows for a bleeding heart*.

We have been rather full in our account of a work not very extensive, because it appears to us to contain great merits and great defects;

and we are desirous of discriminating between the one and the other with accuracy and candour, that we may not be supposed incapable of relishing beauties with which blemishes are intermixed, and that our readers may not incur the greater hazard of being dazzled by erroneous opinions, amidst the splendor of animated descriptions and just sentiments, with which they are surrounded.

Letter to the *Monthly Magazine*, 1 (May 1796), 278–80

To the Editor of the Monthly Magazine.

SIR, *March 22d*, 1796.

Permit an admirer of the plan of your new Magazine, to send you a few strictures on a work lately published, replete with acuteness of observation and poignancy of feeling and which will not cease to be admired, as long as delicacy of sentiment and the amiable charities of the human heart are held in estimation. After this preamble, it will hardly be necessary to say, that the work I refer to is the Letters of Mrs. Wollstonecraft, during a short residence in Sweden, Norway, and Denmark.

I have not the pleasure of being acquainted with this lady; but as I think her one of the distinguished few whose writings may contribute towards dispelling the mists of prejudice and error, I regret the more, that want of sufficient attention, should, in some instances, have given rise to an inaccuracy of expression, which may tend to mislead, rather than instruct. Of this nature, I apprehend, is the following passage, page 217: 'What, for example, has piety under the Heathen or Christian system been, but a blind faith in things contrary to the principles of reason? And could poor reason make considerable advances, when it was reckoned the highest degree of virtue to do violence to its dictates?' From this statement, the inference might be, and to some minds the inference actually would be, that the piety of Heathenism, and of Christianity, had been alike inimical to the progress of reason, and degrading to human nature. Now, piety being an affection of the heart, and not a matter of speculative opinion, it may, perhaps, be a question how far it is really hurtful, even where the objects of its awe, fear, and love, producing reverence, humility, gratitude, trust, and confidence, have no real existence. But be this as it may, surely no one will affirm, that where the supreme object of adoration is the great Author of the Universe, and is considered as a being of spotless purity,

and of infinite goodness as well as power (and such is the God of the
rational Christian) these affections can have any tendency to *debase* the
human character; rather, on the contrary, would they lead the humble
worshipper to aspire after the imitation of these divine perfections, and
according to the emphatic language of Scripture, to become holy as
God is holy, righteous as he is righteous, and merciful as he is merciful.
Piety like this, far from debasing reason, is her noblest auxiliary,
animates her every generous exertion, is the truest refiner of the human
soul, and the only unfailing support of weak and erring creatures, in
the dangers, the difficulties, and calamities of life. But to return;—if a
slight alteration had been made in the construction of the sentence, and
if, instead of *piety*, Mrs. Wollstonecraft has used the term *religion*, she
would then merely have asserted what no rational Christian will deny,
namely, that a miserable superstition, enforcing many express
contradictions to reason, and very debasing to the human mind, has too
often in Christian as well as Heathen countries, been mistaken for
religion; and that, bound in such fetters, it was not possible for reason
to make considerable progress. . . .

April 19, 1796.   CHRISTIANA.

Monthly Mirror, 1 (March 1796), 285–9

The extraordinary avidity with which books of travels have been read
and received by the public, has induced many respectable characters
to quit their native country, in order to procure that fame and profit by
an account of their peregrinations which have been seldom withheld
from an ingenious and accurate tourist. The applause so unsparingly
bestowed on writers who have exposed themselves to every difficulty
and danger in this pursuit, has had an effect in many instances totally
opposite to that which was intended; for some have, in consequence,
described countries through which they never *passed*, and written about
curiosities they never *saw*.

The views, however, of such as write travels are so various and
distinct, that it is become necessary for readers to receive with caution
the accounts of different persons, and to weigh well the observations
made by each, before they subscribe to his opinions. The traveller, like
the historian, should be free from the trammels of party, otherwise his
statements will probably be erroneous, his sentiments narrowed by
prejudice, and his conclusions unfair. The political *quixotism* of modern
times has carried authors into foreign countries, to answer no other

purpose, it should seem, but to tell the world, through the medium of a few letters, that every king is a despot, every lord an oppressor, and every subject a slave. We are sorry to find a great similarity between Mrs. W. and some of her contemporaries in this respect. This lady is, indeed, a *political* traveller, and though she professes to have made but a *short residence* in Sweden, Norway, and Denmark, she has found very ample opportunities of finding fault with the laws and government of the three countries.

To such as have read Mr. Coxe's work, this volume will convey little information; the examination of Mrs. W. has been merely cursory; she tells scarcely any thing that was not known before, excluding, perhaps, some few circumstances relative to the conflagration at Copenhagen, and the Canal near Gothenburg. What, however, is wanting in information, is made up in descriptions of scenery, and in glowing sentiment, such as a mind rich and enthusiastic, as Mrs. W's would be supposed to indulge.

. . . it is evident that the mind of the fair author is not in that state of enviable tranquillity, which philosophy is said to bestow. The melancholy which seems to have taken strong hold of her, will probably excite that interest in the mind of the reader which her letters, considered as a source of topographical, historical, and political information, we fear will fail of producing. Mrs. W. perhaps, will thank us little for our compassion; we cannot, however, be charged with intrusion on her private sorrows, since her work was designed for publication before it was penned. It appears, indeed, to have been intended as an appeal to our feelings, and surely no object can be more interesting than that of an unhappy mother, wandering through foreign countries with her helpless infant, enduring all the fatigue and inconvenience of incessant traveling, bad accommodations, and occasional insult.

But neither our pity for Mrs. W's misfortunes, our admiration of her talents, or esteem for her virtues, can suffer us to pass unnoticed the spirit of scepticism, not to say infidelity, discoverable in some of her opinions. She not only directs her attack against some of the grand articles of the christian faith, but openly and without palliation, recommends the public breach of the sabbath. . . .

The style of these letters is extremely unequal, and there are many inaccuracies of expression which may probably be the effect of haste, such as 'There was a solemn silence in this scene which *made itself be felt*,' p. 5. 'for the putrifying herrings, which they use as manure, after the oil has been extracted, spread o'er the patches of earth, claimed by cultivation, destroyed *every other*,' Quere, What? p. 46. again, in the very next sentence, '*It* was intolerable.' *What* was intolerable? And in the next page, 'When a country arrives at a certain state of perfection, it looks as if it were made *so*.' Q. Made what? Many other passages equally objectionable might be produced.

Errors of this kind are only excuseable when letters written in the familiarity and confidence of private friendship, are placed by the injudicious partiality of their admirers, before the eye of the public; but as these letters were designed, *ab origine*, for publication, Mrs. W. is of course answerable for all the imperfections of her work.

Monthly Review, 20 (July 1796), 251–7

We have on several former occasions paid our willing tribute of respect to the strong—or, if the fair traveller will accept the epithet as a compliment, the *masculine*—mind of this female philosopher; and these Letters furnish us with new inducements to repeat it. The production before us is not, indeed, written with laboured accuracy: the thoughts are neither artfully arranged, nor expressed with studied elegance; and every sentiment appears to have been dictated by the present object, or the present occurrence, with no other care than to express it faithfully and forcibly: but if by fastidious delicacy this should be thought a defect, it is amply compensated by the undistinguished disclosure of an enlightened and contemplative mind, and still more by the natural and energetic expression of feelings which do credit to the writer's heart, and will not fail to touch that of the reader.

As a description of the country through which the author travelled, the publication is valuable; for it contains bold and picturesque delineations of natural scenery, and places the character and manners of the inhabitants in a striking, and in some respects a new, point of light:—but its chief value arises from the variety of just observations and interesting reflections which are dispersed through the work. To a mind inured to speculation, few occurrences can be so trivial as not to furnish matter for ingenious remark; and that this writer possesses such a mind, no one who has perused her former productions will doubt. She claims the traveller's privilege of speaking frequently of herself, but she uses it in a manner which always interests her readers: who may sometimes regret the circumstances which excite the writer's emotions, but will seldom see reason to censure her feelings, and will never be inclined to withhold their sympathy.

We occasionally remark, in these letters, such anomalies in expression as are common with writers of brilliant fancy. Of this kind are the following: men who remain near the brute creation have little or no imagination, to call forth the *curiosity* necessary to *fructify* the faint *glimmerings* of mind:—*imagination* dips her brush in the rainbow of *fancy: effigy* allowed to burn down to the *socket*. In two or three instances, we think that the opinions here advanced are not quite consistent with sound philosophy. We cannot agree with the fair writer in admiring pious frauds; nor in thinking that it may have been necessary for legislators to conquer the *inertia* of reason by fictions, which, though at first deemed sacred, may afterward be ridiculed. True philosophy knows no other path of utility than the straight road of truth. Nor can we, by any means, admit that 'the plans of happiness founded on virtue and principle are illusive, and open inlets to misery in a half-civilized society.' This last reflection, however, with others of a similar cast, we impute to the agitated state of mind under which the letters appear to have been written, rather than to the author's cool and settled judgment. Notwithstanding a few occasional blemishes, the work has uncommon merit, and will not fail to be admired for the happy union which it presents of refined sense, vigorous fancy, and lively sensibility.

EXPLANATORY NOTES

Barton   H. Arnold Barton, *Scandinavia in the Revolutionary Era 1760–1815* (Minneapolis, 1986).

Clarke   Edward Daniel Clarke, *Travels in Various Countries of Europe Asia and Africa*, part the third, Scandinavia, sections one and two (London, 1823).

Coxe (1784) William Coxe, *Travels into Poland, Russia, Sweden, and Denmark* (London, 1784), vol. ii.

Coxe (1790) *Travels into Poland, Russia, Sweden, and Denmark* (London, 1790), vol. iii.

Danielsen Rolf Danielsen, Ståle Dyrvik, Tore Grønlie, Knut Helle, and Edgar Hovland, *Norway: A History from the Vikings to our Own Times*, trans. Michael Drake (Oslo, 2002).

Dyrvik   Ståle Dyrvik, *Norsk Historie, 1625–1814* (Oslo, 1999).

Emigrants *The Emigrants*, ed. with introd. and notes W. M. Verhoeven and Amanda Gilroy (Harmondsworth, 1998).

Gordon   Lyndall Gordon, *Vindication: A Life of Mary Wollstonecraft* (London, 2005).

Guest   Harriet Guest, *Small Change: Women, Learning, Patriotism, 1750–1810* (Chicago, 2000).

Holmes   Mary Wollstonecraft and William Godwin, *A Short Residence in Sweden and Memoirs of the Author of 'The Rights of Woman'*, ed. with introd. Richard Holmes (Harmondsworth, 1987).

Leask   Nigel Leask, *Curiosity and the Aesthetic of Travel Writing 1770–1840* (Oxford, 2002).

Letters   Mary Wollstonecraft, *The Collected Letters*, ed. Janet Todd (Harmondsworth, 2003).

Malthus *The Travel Diaries of Thomas Robert Malthus*, ed. Patricia James (Cambridge, 1966).

Molden   Gunnar Molden, 'Sølvbriggen Maria Margrete: ut av historiens mørke', *Norsk Sjøfartsmuseum: Årsberetning. 1995* (Oslo, 1996), 139–54.

Nyström   Per Nyström, *Mary Wollstonecraft's Scandinavian Journey*, Acts of the Royal Society of Arts and Letters of Gothenburg, Humaniora 17 (Gothenburg, 1980).

Todd/Butler *The Works of Mary Wollstonecraft*, ed. Janet Todd and Marilyn Butler, 7 vols. (London, 1989).

Verhoeven Wil Verhoeven, *Gilbert Imlay: Citizen of the World* (London, 2008).

ADVERTISEMENT

3 In Laurence Sterne's *A Sentimental Journey* (1768) the narrator, Mr Yorick, categorizes different types of travellers, describing himself as a Sentimental Traveller: 'What a large volume of adventures may be grasped within this little span of life by him who interests his heart in every thing' (i. 86–9). The model of a sentimental traveller is important in Wollstonecraft's *Letters*, but many late eighteenth-century travel narratives adopted a style of 'affective realism' (Leask, 42). Possibly Wollstonecraft was directly influenced in this regard by George Forster's *A Voyage Round the World* (1777), which declares: 'I have sometimes obeyed the powerful dictates of my heart, and given voice to my feelings; for, as I do not pretend to be free from the weaknesses common to my fellow creatures, it was necessary for every reader to know the colour of the glass through which I looked' (i, pp xii–xiii). Wollstonecraft seems to have reviewed several such travel narratives for the *Analytical*, including Hester Lynch Piozzi's *Observations and Reflections, made in the course of a Journey through France, Italy, and Germany* (1792): see Introduction, p. xviii.

the little hero of each tale: Edward Young, *The Universal Passion. Satire I, to His Grace the Duke of Dorset* (1725), l. 120.

LETTER I

5 *Arendall . . . Gothenburg . . . Elsineur*: modern-day Arendal, Gothenburg, and Helsingør. Arendal in Norway was the centre of the Ellefsen family's commercial interests and the harbour close to where Peder was alleged to have unloaded the cargo of the silver ship. Wollstonecraft was to go there to find out more about what had happened to the ship and to assess the wealth of the Ellefsen family. For Gothenburg, see notes to Letter II. Elsinore or Helsingør is the setting of Shakespeare's *Hamlet*, which Wollstonecraft refers to in Letters II (p. 16), XXI (p. 116), and XXII (p. 120).

light-house: Nyström, 6, identifies this as the famous double beacon lighthouse in Nidingen, located south of Gothenburg. It had been established in 1624 to help guide ships safely through the dangerous Niding reef. See Wollstonecraft's letter to Imlay, Appendix 3, p. 140: 'we have got here; though not without considerable difficulty, for we were set ashore in a boat about twenty miles below.'

Despotism . . . cramped the industry of man: Wollstonecraft interprets the behaviour of the pilots as confirmation of her view of the Swedish political system as more oppressive and feudal than that of the other Scandinavian countries, especially Norway. See for instance her comment on their treatment of female servants, which she believes 'shews how far the Swedes are from having a just conception of rational equality' (Letter III, p. 17).

6 *Marguerite*: the French nurse who looked after Wollstonecraft's daughter Fanny between 1795 and 1797. Wollstonecraft's representation of her delicacy is often used as a contrast to her own hardiness.

Scarcely human in their appearance: according to Nyström, 6 n. 3, the two old men were peasants on duty at the coal-fired beacons and probably covered in coal dust.

7 *picturesque bay*: an aesthetic category associated with William Gilpin's influential *Observations of the River Wye* (1782). Gilpin provided travellers with means to appreciate landscapes and scenery, offering a middle way between the sublime and the beautiful (see note to p. 10 below). Wollstonecraft seems to have reviewed a new edition of Gilpin's text for the *Analytical Review* in 1789, as well as other essays by him on the topic: see Todd/Butler, vii. 161, 196, 38, and 455. An important development of Gilpin's ideas was published soon after Wollstonecraft's book by Uvedale Price in *An Essay on the Picturesque* (1796). The emphasis was on variety and the incorporation of elements of irregularity and ruggedness and the curiosity this diversity aroused in the viewer (Leask, 42).

8 *other evil*: Wollstonecraft euphemistically suggests rape.

excellent coffee . . . prohibited: coffee was among the most significant imported luxury goods in Sweden in the eighteenth century. Because it was expensive, importation potentially threatened the balance of trade. The Swedish government feared that coffee would become an object of speculation and provoke a financial crisis. Between 1756 and 1822 several bans were imposed on import and consumption, which led to widespread smuggling. As in Britain, consumption of coffee was associated with the emergence of a new bourgeois public sphere.

golden age: in Greek mythology, the ideal state of society which subsequently degenerated into the silver, bronze, and iron ages. The prelapsarian golden age was often regarded as a utopia in which humans lived in primitive harmony with nature and each other, without crime or injustice. Eighteenth-century *philosophes* frequently referred to the concept and Enlightenment historians applied the label to what they perceived as ages of celebrated liberty or progress. See Wollstonecraft's further use of the idea in Letters IX and XIV below.

9 *the person appointed to guard wrecks*: Nyström, 8–9 and n. 4, suggests that Wollstonecraft landed on the Onsala peninsula and that the officer with whom she stayed before continuing her journey to Gothenburg was district pilot inspector of Malösund.

perquisites: casual sources of income attached to a position. Middle-class radicals such as Wollstonecraft tended to see them as a sign of the corruption and inefficiency of the old feudal order.

letter: Wollstonecraft is probably referring to a letter written by Gilbert Imlay. Imlay returned the letters Mary had written to him when she asked for them to help her work on *A Short Residence*. See Appendix 3.

maidens call love in idleness: wild pansies or heartsease. In *A Midsummer Night's Dream*, II. i. 168, Oberon explains how a bolt from Cupid stained this formerly white flower with purple.

10 *horrors I had witnessed in France*: Wollstonecraft was appalled by the excesses of the Revolution in France, many of which she had witnessed directly during her sojourn there over 1792–5, but her *Historical and Moral View of the Origin and Progress of the French Revolution* (1794), p. vii, continued to see hope in 'the uncontaminated mass of the French nation, whose minds begin to grasp the sentiments of freedom' and urged against 'the erroneous inferences of sensibility' hinted at here.

sublime . . . beautiful: Wollstonecraft refers to the major aesthetic categories of the late eighteenth century, which were often identified with Edmund Burke's *Philosophical Enquiry into the Origin of our Ideas of the Sublime and the Beautiful* (1757). See Introduction, pp. xviii–xx.

11 *men's questions*: that is factual questions about social, political, and economic matters that were presumed to be beyond the ken of a woman.

car with post-horses: a carriage pulled by hired horses which were kept at post-houses or inns.

active principle: this phrase may reflect an awareness of debates around 'vitalism' and the question of whether life had its origins in some super-added principle or arose innately from the organization of matter. The latter position was favoured in the radical John Thelwall's *An Essay Towards a Definition of Animal Vitality* (1793). The vitalism debate intensified after Wollstonecraft's death and was an important influence on her daughter's novel *Frankenstein* (1818).

12 *sympathetic emotion . . . attraction of adhesion*: the language of the associationist psychology of David Hartley, influential in the London dissenting community in which Wollstonecraft moved, is evident in this and the previous paragraph, which may in their turn have influenced Coleridge's 'Frost at Midnight': see Introduction, pp. xxv–xxvi.

unprovided with a passport: until the mid-nineteenth century, travellers in Sweden, as in most of Europe at the time, were required to carry passports on domestic journeys. These passports were not books, but documents most often issued by a town's magistrate specifying the duration and purpose of the trip.

13 *one of my recommendatory letters, and the gentleman, to whom it was addressed*: in her private letters Wollstonecraft repeatedly complains about the quality of the inns in Sweden, which she characterizes as 'mere stables' (Appendix 3, p. 140). In Gothenburg Wollstonecraft stayed with Imlay's business associate Elias Backman, who had moved to Gothenburg in 1794: '[Backman] will go with me, if I find it necessary to go to [Copenhagen]. The inns here are so bad, I was forced to accept of an apartment in his house' (Appendix 3, p. 141).

LETTER II

13 *built by the Dutch, has canals running through each street*: the Swedish king
Gustav Adolf II hired Dutch engineers in 1621 to solve the problem of
the marshy areas that surrounded the city by constructing canals mod-
elled on those in Amsterdam.

several rich commercial houses: Gothenburg's location made it Sweden's
most important port for trade towards the west, a position reinforced by
the establishment of the Swedish East India Company in 1731. This
company was partially funded by a Scotsman, the merchant Colin
Campbell, and attracted both Scottish and British merchants who were
excluded from the British East India Company. With the city of
Marstrand, Gothenburg was one of only two cities on the west coast
allowed to trade with foreign merchants.

since the war: during the first war of the allied coalition (England, Austria,
Prussia) against revolutionary France, the Scandinavian countries
officially subscribed to a policy of neutrality. The Danish Prime Minister
A. P. Bernstorff (see note to p. 45, below) was, however, keen to retain
good relations with France, maintaining diplomatic connections, and
allowing for the export of great quantities of grain to the new republic. As
during the American War of Independence (1776–83), the Scandinavian
countries exploited the neutral status of their ships to evade the British
naval blockade of France, resulting in a booming trade in raw materials.
Gilbert Imlay and Elias Backman were involved in a scheme of this
nature.

14 *nothing new under the sun!*: Ecclesiastes 1: 9. This book is traditionally
attributed to Solomon.

equally applicable to Dublin: in 1786–7 Wollstonecraft had worked in
Dublin as a governess for the aristocratic Kingsborough family.

16 *but a to-morrow and a to-morrow*: Wollstonecraft alludes to *Macbeth*,
V. v. 18.

witching time of night: see *Hamlet*, II. ii. 377.

more than mortal music: William Cowper, 'Table Talk', l. 737, in *Poems*
(1782).

spirits of peace: see *Henry VIII*, IV. ii. 83.

airy stuff that dreams are made of: see *The Tempest*, IV. i. 156–7.

LETTER III

17 *population of Sweden*: Coxe (1784), 385, estimates the Swedish population
in 1781 as about 2,767,000. Clarke, section 2, 108, refers to a similar
number, 'two million and a half—not more than double the population of
London', but comments, as Wollstonecraft does, on the small number of
inhabitants and lack of cultivated land, '[t]he population is everywhere

small, because the whole country is covered in wood'. Owing to the fact
that the Swedes began officially collecting statistics for mortality as early
as 1749, the numbers referred to by Coxe and Clarke were quite accurate
and similar to the estimates by modern historians (Dyrvik, 90).

churlish pleasure of drinking drams: see pp. 70 and 110. Wollstonecraft's
distaste for drinking would have been strengthened by childhood experiences of her father's drunken violence.

oppressing the women: the first of several explicit comments in *A Short
Residence* that show the continuity of Wollstonecraft's concerns about the
condition of women from her *Vindication of the Rights of Woman*.

18 *footpads*: highwaymen who carried out robberies on foot.

brandy . . . not allowed to be privately distilled: as part of his reform
programme after the new constitution of 1772, Gustavus III attempted to
limit the production of spirits to a crown monopoly, a move strongly
opposed, particularly by the peasantry. Gustavus offered to allow household distillation, however, in trade for taxation. The opposition then
responded by claiming that the household distillation constituted a basic
property right (Barton, 103, 134, 139). For the prohibition of coffee, see
note to Letter I, p. 8.

wars carried on by the late king . . . increase the revenue, and retain the specie:
Gustavus III (1746–92), King of Sweden 1771–92. Through a coup in
1772, Gustavus III imposed a new constitution, introducing a version of
absolute monarchy. Coxe (1784), 330, describes the King's reforms from
1772 in great detail, comparing the pomp of his court to France under the
Bourbons. To help restore the Swedish currency and finance the war with
Russia (1788–90), Gustavus also introduced a series of economic reforms.
On 16 March 1792 he was assassinated at a masked ball after a conspiracy
by aristocratic opponents of the strengthening of royal power (Barton,
173–81, 200–3). The assassination was widely debated in the European
press; French Jacobins welcomed it, while others viewed it as an example
of the contagious potential of the French Revolution. See for example
James Gillray's caricature *Taking Physick: or The News of Shooting the
King of Sweden!* (11 April 1792, H. Humphrey). For Clarke's views, see
section 1, 157–62.

Charles the twelfth: Charles XII, King of Sweden 1697–1718. Known as
'the Lion of the North', Charles became a legendary warrior king, distinguishing himself in the Great Nordic War (1700–21). In 1716 he invaded
Norway, and besieged the Akershus fortress, but was defeated by
Tordenskjold at Dynekielen. Two years later he again invaded Norway,
this time the fortress of Fredriksten in Fredrikshald (today the town of
Halden). On 11 December 1718, he was shot while inspecting the tren-
ches and later died. Rumours abounded that he was assassinated by
Swedes rather than killed by Norwegian gunfire. Voltaire's famous account
the *History of Charles XII, King of Sweden* was published in 1731.

19 *taxes . . . exportation*: in order to integrate the different economies, the
Norwegian–Danish 'twin-state' had established a grain monopoly in 1735.
Typical of Scandinavian protectionist policies of the early eighteenth
century, this monopoly sought to ensure income generated by Norwegian
exports was spent on importing surplus Danish grain. Norwegians
resented the policy, claiming they were forced to buy costly, poor-quality
Danish grain. Following poor harvests, a peasant uprising in 1787, and a
change in economic thinking, the grain monopoly was abolished in 1788.
The speculative trade mentioned by Wollstonecraft combined with poor
harvests in 1794 resulted in scarcity and high prices (see note to p. 13).
There were riots in Christiania. The restrictions on the import of silver
and gold to Denmark-Norway had also been lifted as part of the liberal
reforms. The unpopularity of the monopolies may explain the relatively
early influx of liberal economic theories in Scandinavia, and particularly
Norway at this time, typified by the rapid translation into Danish of
Adam Smith's *An Inquiry into the Nature and Causes of the Wealth of
Nations* (1776). Clarke notes the enthusiasm of the Ankers in 1799 for
British commercialism.

the regent: Charles, Duke of Sødermanland (1748–1818), the future
Charles XIII, and regent of Sweden from 1792 to 1796.

severe restraints on the article of dress: Wollstonecraft could be referring to
the national dress designed by Gustavus III in 1778 for the nobility and
middle classes. The argument for this restriction of dress was similar to
that which prohibited coffee: a domestically produced costume would
help balance the trade deficit by reducing luxury imports. Coxe (1784),
328–30, gives a detailed description.

French revolution . . . more cautious: see note to p. 13 above.

20 *sensible writer*: Thomas Cooper (1759–1839), author of *Some Information
Respecting America* (1794), also brought out by Wollstonecraft's friend
and publisher Joseph Johnson. Born in London, Cooper was trained as a
lawyer and was a scientific, humanitarian, and radical writer. In spring
1792, he was in France on business, and established contact with revolutionary societies on behalf of the Manchester Constitutional Society.
Cooper had recommended Imlay to Brissot. He emigrated to Pennsylvania
with Joseph Priestley in 1794. The passage Wollstonecraft remembers
is from *Some Information*, 64: 'Literature in America is an amusement
only . . . In Europe it is a trade—a means of livelihood. No wonder therefore it is better done in Europe than in America; or that with their
usual good sense the Americans permit you [the Europeans] to be their
manufacturers of literature, as well as of crockery or calicoes.'

narrows the mind: in *Thoughts on the Education of Daughters* (1787), 100,
Wollstonecraft noted that 'being obliged to struggle with the world'
strengthens mental faculties. Being married, however, means that a
woman's 'sphere of action is not large, and if she is not taught to look

into her heart, how trivial are her occupations and pursuits! What little arts engross and narrow her mind!' Later in her career, she attacked Rousseau's reduction of women to creatures of sensibility, exhorting women to 'let the practice of every duty be subordinate to the grand one of improving our minds, and preparing our affections for a more exalted state!' (*Vindication of the Rights of Woman*, 204).

21 *I visited, near Gothenburg, a house*: Gunnebo, near Gothenburg, was the country house of the wealthy Scottish merchant John Hall. It was a wooden Italian villa in the Palladian style. See Nyström, 35–6.

LETTER IV

22 *the children . . . neither the graces nor charms of their age*: Wollstonecraft had been both a governess and teacher, and retained an interest in raising and educating children throughout her life. In *Thoughts on the Education of Daughters* (1787), she expresses disapproval of the use of wet nurses. After Fanny was born in 1794, Wollstonecraft refused to swaddle her daughter and dressed her in loose clothing.

23 *their stars . . . lead frail women astray*: Wollstonecraft alludes to Matthew Prior, 'Hans Carvell', ll. 9–12, lines which she slightly misquotes from memory in chapter 2 of *A Vindication of the Rights of Woman*.

> She made it plain, that Human Passion
> Was order'd by Predestination,
> That, if weak women went astray,
> Their Stars were more in fault than They.

The Swedish ladies . . . their ruby lips: in his *Promenade d'un Français en Suède et en Norvège* (1801), the French anti–Jacobin travel writer Bernard de La Tocnaye suggested that in these and other criticisms Wollstonecraft offended the women of Gothenburg and Sweden.

manners of Stockholm are refined: in a passage from *Reflections on the Revolution in France* (1790), 113–14, which was attacked by many radicals, Edmund Burke defended chivalry for its historical role in the evolution of European civilization and softening of authority through the influence of refined manners. In *Vindication of the Rights of Woman*, 26–7, Wollstonecraft attacks aristocratic gallantry, but her work was not hostile to 'refinement' as such, nor did she necessarily see progress in manners purely as a product of the chivalric tradition venerated by Burke. In *An Historical and Moral View of the Origin and Progress of the French Revolution*, 3–4, she attributed the 'gradual softening of manners' in European societies to the increased communication between nations generated by 'the friction of arts and commerce'. In some parts of *A Short Residence* she represents a degree of refinement as a necessary condition to prevent women becoming mere drudges or confining their minds to 'a narrow range' (p. 24): see Introduction.

24 *human face divine*: John Milton, *Paradise Lost*, III. 44, part of Satan's lament over his fallen state.

> Thus with the Year
> Seasons return, but not to me returns
> Day, or the sweet approach of Ev'n or Morn,
> Or sight of vernal bloom, or Summers Rose,
> Or flocks, or heards, or human face divine;
> But cloud in stead, and ever-during dark
> Surrounds me, from the cheerful wayes of men
> Cut off. (ll. 40–7)

The phrase 'Human form divine' appears in William Blake's 'The Divine Image' in *Songs of Innocence* (1789), a copy of which Wollstonecraft could conceivably have seen on display at Joseph Johnson's shop.

LETTER V

25 *allow the difference of climate to have its natural effect*: Charles-Louis de Secondat, Baron de Montesquieu, gave an account of the role of climate in determining national character in his enormously influential *The Spirit of the Laws* (1748). Wollstonecraft is generally sceptical about the idea of deriving national character on such grounds; see, for instance, pp. 33, 108.

my affairs called me to Stromstad: Wollstonecraft probably went here to meet A. J. Unger, the district judge of Norrviken, and the merchant Christoffer Nordberg, who on Imlay's behalf had been investigating the whereabouts of *Maria and Margaretha*. See Nyström, 23.

in company with two gentlemen: the post-station book at Eigst for July 1795 shows that Wollstonecraft was accompanied by Elias Backman, who went with her as far as Strömstad; see Nyström, 9 and 25.

I left my little girl behind me: while Wollstonecraft travelled into Norway, Fanny remained with Marguerite at the Backman family house in Gothenburg.

26 *avant courier . . . requisition horses*: an *avant courier* would be sent in advance of a person or group to notify others of their approach and to make food, accommodation, and travel arrangements. Horses were often requisitioned from private citizens by the government and army for official purposes.

Quistram: Kvistrum.

27 *botanist and natural historian*: Carl von Linné, Linnaeus (1707–78), a Swede, was the century's most important botanist; his system of taxonomy still provides the basis of plant classification today. In the 1790s, partly because of the example of Erasmus Darwin's *Loves of the Plants* (1790), another Joseph Johnson publication, botanizing was often identified with inappropriate interest in sexual matters and female independence (it had become a popular pastime among educated women).

28 *The last battle . . . fought at this place in 1788*: a reference to the Russo-Swedish war of 1788–90, in which Denmark-Norway became involved under its treaty obligations with Russia. At the battle of Kvistrum Bridge an invading Norwegian army defeated the Swedes.

30 *first dwelling of man . . . adore a sun so seldom seen*: Wollstonecraft's comments reflect the precedence attached to sun-worship in numerous eighteenth-century histories of religion, although most of these, including Volney's *Ruins of Empire* (see note to p. 48 below), assumed a southern origin—usually Egypt—contrary to Wollstonecraft's speculations here about the emergence of religion from the darkness of the north.

Dr. Johnson . . . where they never grew before: actually Jonathan Swift in part II, chapter 7 of *Gulliver's Travels* (1726). The King of Brobdingnag tells Gulliver that 'whoever could make two Ears of Corn, or two Blades of Grass, to grow on a Spot of Ground where only one grew before, would deserve better of Mankind, and do more essential Service to his Country than the whole race of Politicians put together'. In chapter 3 of *Memoirs of the Author of a Vindication of the Rights of Woman* (1798), Godwin describes Wollstonecraft meeting Samuel Johnson.

Swift's 'Dearly beloved Roger': an anecdote related in John Boyle, Earl of Orrery's *Remarks on the Life and Writings of Dr. Jonathan Swift* (1751). Whilst rector in Laracor, a small village in Ireland, Swift on one occasion found his congregation to consist solely of his clerk Roger. He began his sermon 'Dearly beloved Roger, the Scripture moveth you and me in sundry places' before completing the whole service.

31 *fine and numerous family*: Christoffer Nordberg's family; see Nyström, 9.

Fredericshall: modern-day Halden. Like most other tourists to Scandinavia at the time, Wollstonecraft was intrigued by the idea of seeing the place where Charles XII met his death. See note to p. 18 above.

32 *Switzerland . . . equal to the wild grandeur of these views*: Switzerland, partly because of the influence of Rousseau, a native of Geneva, was usually the prime model of the sublime landscape in the period. Wollstonecraft and Imlay spoke of meeting there after the Scandinavian journey, but the idea had been abandoned by the time she left Sweden: see the letter to Imlay in Appendix 3, p. 149.

33 *writers who have considered the history of man*: presumably these writers include Montesquieu, who gave such weight to climatic matters (see note to p. 25). Wollstonecraft's point of view concurs with that of other radicals, including William Godwin in *Political Justice* (1793), by emphasizing the role of 'government, including religion'.

34 *Alexander*: Alexander the Great of Macedon (356–323 BC) was a focus in the eighteenth century for moral debates concerning the heroic values of classical culture and their relevance for eighteenth-century societies. In Godwin's *Caleb Williams* (1794), II. i. 13–21, Caleb argues with his master Falkland over the extent to which Alexander deserves the epithet

'great'. Perhaps more significantly, given the sequence of Wollstonecraft's argument on this page, Montesquieu follows his discussion of Charles XII in *The Spirit of the Laws* with one about the merits of Alexander, whom he rates more highly.

noon of night: this phrase features in Dryden's *Aeneid*, IV. 744, Dante's *Purgatorio*, XV. 1. 5, and Milton's 'Il Penseroso', l. 82.

Young: Edward Young, author of *The Complaint: Or, Night Thoughts on Life, Death, and Immortality* (1742–5), one of the most popular long poems of the eighteenth century. Wollstonecraft refers to Young's address to the moon at the opening of Night the Third.

LETTER VI

35 *sufficient . . . evil*: Matthew 6: 34, 'Sufficient unto the day is the evil thereof.'

Cattegate: Kattegat is the area of sea between Denmark and the south of Sweden, joining the Skagerrak sea to the north. At this stage, Wollstonecraft is crossing the narrows now known as the Oslo fjord.

36 *Laurvig*: Larvik, a town famed for iron production from the seventeenth century.

Dr. Franklin: Benjamin Franklin, political theorist, diplomat, scientist, politician, and one of the Founding Fathers of the United States. Franklin was friendly with figures from Joseph Johnson's radical circle, including Joseph Priestley and Thomas Paine.

37 *cabriole*: or cabriolet, a light two-wheeled carriage drawn by a single horse.

38 *Norwegian miles . . . longer than the Swedish*: the old land mile in Norway and Sweden was 36,000 feet. As Norway and Sweden had different measures for a foot, in the former this was 11.295 km and in the latter 10.688 km.

Tonsberg: Tønsberg.

17th of July . . . gentleman: one of the few dates mentioned by Wollstonecraft. Judge Jacob Wulfsberg, a magistrate in Tønsberg, had been appointed a commissioner on the Ellefsen case. See Nyström, 25.

passing sweet: a reference to William Cowper's 'The Retirement', ll. 740–2, in *Poems* (1782), where the poet paraphrases the French moralist Jean de La Bruyère.

> How sweet, how passing sweet is solitude!
> But grant me still a friend in my retreat,
> Whom I may whisper, solitude is sweet.

39 *æolian harp . . . changing wind*: a stringed musical instrument which produces notes as air moves over it. It was a popular image for the mind and poetic inspiration among the Romantic poets, most famously in Coleridge's 'The Eolian Harp' (1795). Wollstonecraft may have been alluding to Cowper's use of this image in 'Expostulation', ll. 718–23.

The grave has closed over a dear friend: a reference to Fanny Skeys (née Blood), Wollstonecraft's friend from childhood who died in Portugal in 1785: see Introduction, p. x. Godwin quotes this passage at the close of chapter 3 in the *Memoirs* when discussing Mary's response to the death of Fanny.

LETTER VII

40 *king of Denmark . . . absolute monarch*: Norway had been brought under the rule of the Danish monarchy in the fourteenth century. In the seventeenth century the monarchy was made absolute and the various aristocratic assemblies abolished. Norwegians continued to think of themselves as a separate kingdom and the country retained a large degree of autonomy, including its own militia army, until the union was abolished at the Congress of Vienna (1814–15).

There are only two counts: Frederik Anton Wedel (1748–1811), Danish-Norwegian ambassador to London, was Count of Jarlsberg. Frederik Ahlefeldt-Laurvig (1760–1832) inherited the county of Larvik in 1791. It was sold to the crown in 1805.

Christiania and Fredericshall: Oslo was named Christiania from 1624 (Kristiania from the late nineteenth century) until 1925.

Prince Royal: the Danish Crown Prince Frederick (1768–1839) was the son of Queen Caroline Mathilde and King Christian VII (see the discussion of the Struensee/Matilda affair in the Introduction). The Crown Prince assumed the regency of Denmark between 1784 and 1808, during his father's mental illness, and passed a number of liberal reforms (see note to p. 13), including the abolition of serfdom in 1788. He then reigned as King of Denmark 1808–39 and of Norway 1808–14. The expedition in 1788 was the war with Sweden, ending in the battle of Kvistrum Bridge, mentioned in Letter V (see note to p. 28).

41 *Copenhagen*: from 1443 the Danish capital and centre of the joint monarchy.

commons: *allmenning* or Norwegian commons were lands over which the people could exercise certain traditional rights, such as grazing their livestock. Similar rights in England were being encroached upon by the enclosure movement. Throughout her comments on Norway, Wollstonecraft is impressed by the relative independence of the lower classes there.

42 *forbidden . . . to export corn or rye*: the 1670 Navigation Act required all Irish goods to pass through English ports, where excise duty was levied before they could be traded with the colonies. Wollstonecraft's mother was Irish, and in *A Short Residence* she draws a number of parallels between Anglo-Irish relations and the subordination of Norway to Denmark (see for instance her comments on 'the abject state of the Irish', p. 81).

42 *West Indies*: part of the slave trade triangle operating between Africa, the West Indies, and Europe. Denmark had colonies in the West Indies, but in January 1792 became the first European country to abolish the slave trade, when a royal ordinance declared its end with effect from 1803 (albeit not actually implemented until 1807). Thousands of Africans were transported before the ordinance came into effect and illicit slave trading continued from Danish ports until the 1840s, when slavery was abolished in the Danish colonies themselves: see Barton, 211–12. In 1794, Wollstonecraft had told Imlay of the positive response of one of her Parisian friends to the abolitionist sentiments in his account of America (see *Letters*, 266), but recent research suggests that in the 1780s Imlay had owned a part share in a slaving ship (see Verhoeven, chapter 4). Wollstonecraft finally mentions the slave trade directly as part of her general critique of the hypocrisy of commerce at the end of *A Short Residence*, p. 130.

the French revolution will have this effect: one of several places in the book (see note to p. 10 above) where—as in the *Historical and Moral View*—Wollstonecraft reaffirms her faith that for all its vicissitudes the French Revolution would have a generally positive effect on progress in Europe and beyond.

43 *he travelled through Norway*: Crown Prince Frederick led the Norwegian army into Sweden in 1788. See note to p. 40.

44 *castle, or rather arsenal*: Akershus, the fortress of Oslo.

eight hundred thousand: Coxe (1790), 132, arrives at a lower figure than Wollstonecraft's, that is, not more than 750,000. According to the census of 1769, the population of Norway was 723,000. In the next common census of 1801, Norway's population had risen to 883,000 (Dyrvik, 89–91).

45 *Bernstorff*: Count Andreas Peter Bernstorff (1735–97), Danish Foreign Minister 1784–97, a period during which he effectively fulfilled the role of Prime Minister to the Prince Regent. Despite his commitment to the Danish monarchy, his leadership was distinguished by its liberal reforms and a policy of armed neutrality rather than joining the anti-French coalitions. See also Letter XXI, where Wollstonecraft's attitude is rather less positive, perhaps because he failed to respond to her request for help in the Ellefsen case, but also because there she is assessing the Danish monarchy in the context of the Struensee–Matilda affair.

a step further in free-thinking: in fact, attempts by the Lutheran Church to rationalize the liturgy and prayer books met peasant resistance, and in 1796 the itinerant preacher Hans Nielsen Hauge began a movement of religious awakening: see Barton, 246–7. Wollstonecraft's publisher, Johnson, produced works by prominent free-thinking religious writers of the 1780s and 1790s, particularly the Unitarian Joseph Priestley. Unitarians were, like the Norwegian author mentioned here, distinguished by their rejection of the doctrine of the Trinity and the divinity of Christ.

German works on education: Danish literary circles were much influenced by German philosophy of education. Wollstonecraft herself had translated Christian Salzman's *Elements of morality for the use of Children* for Johnson in 1790.

no university: from the 1770s, with Struensee's relaxation of controls on the press, Norwegian pamphleteers and patriots were calling for their own separate university, calls which intensified in the 1790s, but which were only allowed with a royal decree of 1811. The university finally opened in 1813: see Barton, 73, 96, and 333–4. Clarke gives an account of Bernt Anker's applications to the court to obtain a university for Norway, section 2, 13–14.

46 *a salt work*: the Vallø salt-works near Tønsberg.

basons: an acceptable variant spelling of 'basins' in the eighteenth century, although not included in Samuel Johnson's *Dictionary*.

47 *The chapel of Windsor ... its present nice, clean state*: George III moved the royal residence back to Windsor Castle in 1789. Much of the castle, including St George's Chapel, was restored and modernized during George's reign. In a letter to Jane Arden, probably from late summer 1781, Wollstonecraft mentioned numerous visits to the 'cathedral' (*sic*) and the attention to dress and formalities in Windsor (see *Letters*, 33–4). Her recollection of the chapel reflects the contemporary taste for the Gothic and sublime, particularly in its Burkean emphasis on how its 'gloom increased its dimensions to the eye by hiding its parts'. By deflating the chapel's grandeur in this passage, Wollstonecraft seems to mock the illusions of Gothic superstition she and many radicals associated with the established Church.

48 *James the sixth, of Scotland, and first of England*: James I (1566–1625), who married Anne of Denmark, daughter of Frederick II. After a proxy marriage in August 1589, Anne attempted to sail for Scotland but storms forced her return to the coast of Norway. James gallantly sailed from Leith with a retinue to fetch her. They were married formally in Oslo in November and returned to Scotland in May 1590.

Ashes to ashes ... Dust to dust: the first lines of 'The Order for the Burial of the Dead' in *The Book of Common Prayer* (1549), alluding to Adam and Eve's fallen state in Genesis 3: 9.

contemplation of noble ruins ... exalts the mind: although such sentiments were often associated with sublime and picturesque tourism, the focus in the ensuing passage suggests that Wollstonecraft may have been influenced by republican variations upon this theme, in particular, Volney's *The Ruins, or a Survey of the Revolutions of Empires* (1791), which was published in translation by Joseph Johnson in 1792. Constantin François de Chasseboeuf, Comte de Volney (1757–1820), was a French historian and member of the National Assembly. The rousing invocation prefacing *The Ruins* similarly exalts reflection upon remains: 'Solitary ruins, sacred tombs, ye mouldering and silent walls, all hail! While the vulgar shrink from your aspect, my heart finds in the contemplation a thousand delicious sentiments, a thousand admirable recollections. . . . A while ago, the whole world bowed the neck in silence before the tyrants that oppressed it; and yet in that hopeless moment, you already proclaimed the truths that tyrants hold in abhorrence: mixing the dust of the proudest kings with that of the meanest slaves, you called upon us to contemplate this example of EQUALITY' (pp. xi–xii).

Opslo: an antiquated spelling of Oslo, in use by Clarke, section 2, 29, to describe the old quarter of Christiania.

LETTER VIII

49 *Tonsberg . . . one of the little sovereigns*: Wollstonecraft seems to refer to King Haakon Haakonson, who in the thirteenth century established a fortress in Tønsberg.

50 *Here I have frequently strayed . . . the awful throne of my Creator . . . its footstool*: this passage was one of several singled out by de La Tocnaye in his *Promenade en Suède* (1801), i. 29, for mockery of the influence of Sterne's sentimental style on Wollstonecraft's (see note below for one of Wollstonecraft's allusions to Sterne). The final sentence alludes to Isaiah 66: 1, 'Thus saith the Lord, The heaven is my throne, and the earth is my footstool.'

sink into sadness: this sentence was quoted by Wollstonecraft's friend Mary Hays in her novel *Memoirs of Emma Courtney* (1796), ii. 112.

Elysium: Milton, *Comus* (1637), l. 256. Comus compares the maiden's song to that of his mother Circe and 'the Sirens three', who 'as they sung, would take the prison'd soule | And lap it in Elysium'.

Maria, is it still so warm?: Mr Yorick's question to Maria upon her offer to dry his tear-sodden handkerchief in her bosom (Sterne, *A Sentimental Journey*, ii. 174).

embonpoint: well-nourished plumpness.

51 *chalybeat*: water containing iron, often from a spring, and taken for medicinal purposes.

life is more than a dream: Shakespeare, *The Tempest*, IV. i. 148–58.

young star fish: Wollstonecraft's reflections upon whether humans are merely 'animated dust' or spiritual beings may be related to the starfish via Buffon's account in the *Natural History* (1749–78) of the creature's surprising liveliness: 'All of this kind are formed of a semi-transparent, gelatinous substance, covered with a thin membrane, and, to an inattentive spectator, often appear like a lump of inanimate jelly, floating at random on the surface of the sea, or thrown by chance on shore at the departure of the tide. But, upon a more minute inspection, they will be found possessed of life and motion; they will be found to shoot forth their arms in every direction, in order to seize upon such insects as are near, and to devour them with great rapacity. . . . In summer, when the water of the sea is warmed by the heat of the sun, they float upon the surface, and in the dark, they send forth a kind of shining light, resembling that of phosphorus.' See *Buffon's Natural History Abridged*, 2 vols. (London, 1792), ii. 387–8.

52 *Lisbon*: Wollstonecraft travelled to Lisbon in 1785 to visit Fanny Skeys. See note to p. 39.

53 *I could not speak Danish*: Danish was the official language in Norway during the 'union'.

54 *joint expence*: perhaps a hint to Imlay with regard to his responsibilities towards Fanny.

55 *Danish literature . . . Copenhagen*: Wollstonecraft makes no distinction between Danish and Norwegian literature. Struensee's freeing of the press had stimulated a growing sense of the distinctiveness of Norwegian cultural identity, reflected in the intensifying demands for a university: see Barton, 96.

farmers use the thou and thee: 'thou' and 'thee' are the familiar forms. Wollstonecraft is making a typical observation on the relative development of manners and politeness in different parts of the country.

customs of a long standing: in *Vindication of the Rights of Men*, Wollstonecraft attacks Burke's emphasis on upholding custom and tradition, especially the culture of feudal deference and hierarchy. Here her emphasis is on more popular customs, including local traditions of child-care, but her middle-class radicalism still works in favour of an idea of rational progress and refinement over customary constraints.

Peruvian pair: descent from the sun god was claimed by the Inca dynasty of Peru. Wollstonecraft is probably referring to Manco-Capac and his sister-wife Mama Oella, possibly drawing on book II of her friend Joel Barlow's *The Vision of Columbus* (London, 1787); see especially his note pp. 44–5.

56 *Prometheus*: in Greek mythology, the Titan who stole fire from Zeus and gave it to humans. He was chained to a rock by Zeus in punishment for his transgression. The myth first appeared in Hesiod's *Theogony*, and was widely used by writers including Blake, Coleridge, and Byron during the Romantic period. Percy Shelley made extensive use of this figure in *Prometheus Unbound* (1820), as did Mary Shelley in *Frankenstein* (1818). Wollstonecraft humorously revisits the myth in Letter XVI.

I and my Frances: Fanny, her daughter.

LETTER IX

57 *Danish ambassador in London*: see note to p. 40.

tomb of the Capulets: the tomb in Verona where Romeo and Juliet died.

58 *tenants*: by the eighteenth century the institution of Norwegian crofters or 'husmenn' had gradually evolved into a 'rural proletariat' who rented land

and perhaps a cottage from a larger landowner. Typically the husmann would pay the rent with labour on the landowner's farm (Danielsen, 136–9, 186).

when Lutheranism was introduced: the Protestant Reformation was introduced to Norway when it came under Danish rule in 1536. Lutheranism became the official state religion in 1665 with the confirmation of the Danish monarchy as hereditary and absolute rulers.

59 *decadi*: In October 1793, a new revolutionary calendar was adopted by the French National Convention, under Jacobin leadership. The calendar, designed by Charles Gilbert Romme, divided each month into three weeks, lasting ten days, called *décades*. In place of Sunday, the tenth day, *décadi*, became the official day of relaxation and festivity, which Wollstonecraft contrasts to the more traditionally sombre Sabbath.

progress of Methodism: returning to Yorkshire in order to make her way to Scandinavia from Hull, Wollstonecraft visited the county where she had spent some of her childhood. Here and in the page that follows she implies that religious fanaticism and a renewed deference to aristocracy and social hierarchy were the products of a regressive response to the French Revolution in Britain. Norway may be less refined than Britain from Wollstonecraft's perspective, but retains for her the possibility of a progressive enlightenment away from 'aristocracy and fanaticism', p. 60.

morals of a place: Wollstonecraft deliberately substitutes the term 'morals' for the more obvious 'manners', insisting on the influence of social practices on moral behaviour.

60 *Rousseau's golden age of stupidity*: despite the celebration of the simple virtues of Norway in the preceding pages, Wollstonecraft is criticizing Rousseau's enthusiasm for the spartan and masculine virtues of primitive societies. Although the reveries that form such an important part of her book are clearly indebted to his *Reveries of the Solitary Walker* (see Favret, 104–7), her thoughts continually return to her need for 'the polished circles of the world', p. 61. Wollstonecraft repeatedly attacked Rousseau's theories in her *Vindication of the Rights of Woman*, where she claims that 'Rousseau exerts himself to prove that all *was* right originally: a crowd of authors that all *is* now right: and I, that all will *be* right . . . next to a state of Nature, Rousseau celebrates barbarism' (p. 22). See also references to the golden age in Letters I and XIV.

61 *similar reflections in America*: Imlay reflects on these and related matters in his *A Topographical Description*, 2nd edn. (London, 1793), 57–9. See Introduction, p. xiv.

LETTER X

62 *Dryden's fable of the flower and the leaf*: 'The Flower and the Leaf; or, The Lady in the Arbour', an allegory by Dryden in his *Fables Ancient and Modern* (1700), adapted from a poem formerly attributed to Chaucer.

The fable contrasts the brief pleasures of the flower with the laurel leaf of virtuous labour.

general good: the central standard of value in most republican and utilitarian thought. In *Enquiry Concerning Political Justice* (2nd edn., 1796), 122, for instance, Godwin laid out the view that 'Morality is that system of conduct which is determined by a consideration of the greatest general good: he is entitled to the highest moral approbation, whose conduct is, in the greatest number of instances, governed by views of benevolence, and made subservient to public utility.'

63 *mediators*: Clarke, 27, provides a more detailed account of the work of these mediators: 'there is also, in every parish, a Commission of Conciliation, before which every cause must be stated, previous to its going into a court of justice; and it is the office of the commissioners to mediate between the parties, and, if possible, to compromise matters. The party refusing to abide by the opinion of the commissioner is condemned to all the costs, if he do not afterwards appear upon trial that he was in the right.'

trials by jury: trial by jury was not introduced to Norway until the new constitution of 1814.

count of Laurvig: see note to p. 40.

65 *Helgeraac*: modern-day Helgeroa, a village on the coast a little way westwards from Larvik towards Risør.

Like the lone shrub . . . each blast: Oliver Goldsmith, *The Traveller; or, A Prospect of Society* (1764), ll. 103–4, a celebrated poem which was widely anthologized in the 1790s. Wollstonecraft slightly misquotes the following lines from memory.

> Here for a while, my proper cares resign'd,
> Here let me sit in sorrow for mankind,
> Like yon neglected shrub, at random cast,
> That shades the steep, and sighs at every blast. (ll. 102–4)

Goldsmith's exploration of the relationship between virtue and commerce obviously fits in with many of Wollstonecraft's reflections.

Virgin Land: modern Jomfruland, an elongated small island with its own distinctive flora and fauna, the outermost in the Kragerø archipelago, lying off the coast between Larvik and Risør.

66 *East Riisoer*: Risør, home town of Peder Ellefsen. Wollstonecraft confronted him there and extracted a partial confession.

Nootka Sound: a channel between the west coast of Canada and Vancouver Island, the subject to rival claims by Britain and Spain. In February 1789, Spain's attempt to enforce its sovereignty over the area led to a confrontation between the governments of the two nations known as the Nootka Crisis. A major war over the issue was averted by the three Nootka Conventions (1790, 1793, and 1794).

67 *queen's ware*: glazed domestic pottery.

LETTER X

68 *Portoer*: modern Portør.

a dollar: a rixdollar. See Wollstonecraft's supplementary note on the relative value of the currencies she met with on her journey.

American service . . . during the revolution: it seems the sailor had served on the American side during the War of Independence.

Rusoer: a misspelling of Risør.

69 *bastilled by nature*: the Bastille Saint-Antoine was a fortress and prison in south-east Paris, the fall of which to the Parisian crowd on 14 July 1789 symbolized the beginning of the French Revolution. The use of the verb 'bastilled' is unusual; it first appears in Young's *Night Thoughts*, IX. 1058. Wollstonecraft also used this form in chapter 10 of *Maria; or The Wrongs of Woman*, where the heroine recalls how 'Marriage had bastilled me for life'. Here Wollstonecraft reflects again on the extent to which the spartan conditions she finds in Norway may represent a prison-house more than a form of primitive liberty, although Gordon, 268, suggests her negative response to the town may have had something to do with the difficulties she encountered dealing with the Ellefsens.

generous juices of the heart: Wollstonecraft also refers to these 'generous juices' in chapters 5 and 12 of *A Vindication of the Rights of Woman* and in chapter 9 of *Maria*. In the former, she bemoans the education by which the benevolent social affections of boys 'are deadened by the selfish gratifications, which very early pollute the mind, and dry up the generous juices of the heart'.

70 *brake and briar*: Cowper, 'The Needless Alarm', l. 6, in *Poems*, ii (1795).

71 *most useful German productions lately published*: see note to p. 45 above. Wollstonecraft's writing suggests that she was also familiar with the work of Goethe, Kant, and Schiller among other contemporary German writers.

powers coalesced against France . . . dismembered Poland: Austria, Prussia, and Russia partitioned Poland in 1772, 1793, and 1795 in order to undermine the Polish reformist movement. The final partition was in response to an uprising led by General Tadeusz Kościuszko, a veteran of the American War of Independence. Kościuszko and the Polish national cause held great appeal for liberals and radicals in the 1790s.

72 *Shakspeare's magic island*: Prospero's island in *The Tempest*.

LETTER XII

73 *Elysian scenes*: in Greek mythology, the Elysian Fields were the resting place of those blessed by the gods. Wollstonecraft is describing the picturesque landscape on her descent into Tønsberg as a kind of paradise.

plans of happiness founded on virtue and principle: from Gothenburg Wollstonecraft writes to Imlay that she has 'damped that enthusiasm of character, which converts the grossest materials into a fuel, that imperceptibly feeds hopes, which aspire above common enjoyment': see Appendix 3, p. 142.

Moss: an important industrial town on the eastern side of Oslofjord. Coxe was shown the iron works belonging to Bernt Anker that Wollstonecraft does not have time to see (see Coxe (1790), 152). From Moss Wollstonecraft travelled overland north to Oslo before returning to head south for Sweden. For the Anker family, see note to p. 83.

Fannikin: Fanny, her daughter.

thick coming fears: see *Macbeth*, V. iii. 38, where Lady Macbeth's delusions are described as 'thick coming fancies'.

A calf . . . capital: *Hamlet*, III. ii. 101. A response to Polonius, who relates how he played Julius Caesar being killed by Brutus. Hamlet quips, 'it was a brute part of him to kill so capital a calf'.

74 *fop in the play*: William Wycherley's *The Country Wife* (1675), III. ii. 157–8. The buffoon Sparkish says to the rake Harcourt, 'for though I have known thee a great while, never go, if I do not love thee as well as a new acquaintance'.

LETTER XIII

76 *glebe land*: land assigned to a clergyman as part of his post.

77 *newspapers printed at Copenhagen*: Danish newspapers mostly consisted of reprinted material from foreign newspapers, so the accounts Wollstonecraft mentions may have been taken directly from hostile English reports.

tyrant's plea necessity: Milton, *Paradise Lost*, IV. 393–4, 'So spake the Fiend, and with necessitie, | The Tyrants plea, excus'd his devilish deeds.'

Robespierre was a monster: Maximilien Robespierre (1758–94), member of the National Convention and one of the most prominent in the Jacobin faction. An ardent admirer of Rousseau, he was a vocal supporter of the regicide and opponent of the Girondins. As a member of the Committee of Public Safety, he was the key figure in the Terror of 1793–4.

78 *effusions of a sensibility wounded almost to madness*: here Wollstonecraft foregrounds the emotional turmoil she suffered as Imlay abandoned her in favour of commercial pursuits and other women. In 1794 this despair had led her to unsuccessfully attempt suicide using laudanum. Upon her return to London from Scandinavia she found that Imlay had taken another mistress, and made another attempt at suicide by throwing herself into the Thames from Putney Bridge. Characteristically in this passage, Wollstonecraft's self-consciousness concerning her sensibility serves to regulate it.

79 *alum*: aluminium potassium sulphate. Imlay traded in alum, used in printing and dyeing. Alum was made by heating alumstone (alunite) with coal, keeping it exposed to air, and using hot water to remove the crystals which formed. The surrounding rocks would have been reddened by iron deposited by the residue. The process is described in detail by Clarke, section 2, 72–3, who also visited the works outside Christiania, which belonged to John Collet.

80 *capped with eternal snow . . . Mr. Coxe's description*: Coxe (1790), iii. 153. Coxe claims to describe the view beyond Oslo from a mountain top as he looks down on the city.

the people of Christiania rose: during the food shortages of 1795, it was rumoured that Bernt Anker had broken the prohibition against the export of grain in order to speculate on the continental market. The rioters attacked one of Anker's ships. The military were called out and four of the leaders of the rioters were arrested. The riots continued, however, and the Grand Bailiff entered into negotiations with the crowd to end the conflict with the result that the four leaders were freed.

an English frigate: Britain blockaded Scandinavian and Baltic ports to try to prevent trade with republican France. Imlay, of course, was deep in the business of evading the blockade.

81 *Grand Bailiff's lady*: the Danish monarchy was represented in Norway by four of these Grand Bailiffs (or 'Stiftsamtmann'). Here and on the next page, Wollstonecraft would seem to refer to Fredrik Julius Kaas (1758–1827) and his Norwegian wife Kristine, née Nilsen.

ancien régime: denotes the monarchical and aristocratic social and political system that operated in France until the Revolution, a term first recorded in English in 1794.

abject state of the Irish: one of several comments comparing the Norwegians under Danish rule to the Irish under British domination. In this passage she compares the power of the Norwegian bailiffs to the Anglo-Irish elite. Catholics were debarred from participation in political life.

82 *a man who has been confined six years*: Christian Jensen Lofthus (1750–97). In 1786 he had complained to the Crown Prince about the excessive taxation and other mistreatment of farmers by royal officials; attempts to arrest him sparked off a widespread peasant insurrection. Finally imprisoned the following year, he was chained to a rock in Akershus, where he died in 1797. Barton, 151–4.

83 *Hottentots*: a European name given to the African Khoikhoi tribe, who often appear in eighteenth-century writing as an example of the most primitive and savage state of mankind. The term had come to be used broadly to refer to any uncivilized people.

a pretty villa, and English garden: the garden belonged to Peder Anker (1749–1824), younger brother of Bernt Anker (1746–1805). The powerful Anker family entertained most foreign visitors to Christiania, including

Coxe and Clarke (with Malthus): both Coxe (1790), 158, and Clarke, section 2, 22–4, describe their visits to Peder's magnificent house and garden. The Ankers were a major source of information for Malthus. His travel diaries describe his conversations with them at length (*Malthus*, 98–9 and 105–6). Clarke, section 2, 4, describes Bernt Anker as someone whose 'character is so intimately connected with the history of *Christiana*, and of *Norway*, that no traveller, who has published an account of the country, during his life-time, has neglected to attend to it'. The family were Norwegian nationalists (and Anglophiles) who, according to Clarke, section 2, 27, 'spoke of the connection of Norway with Denmark as most fatal to the interests of the former'. Their commercial interests, however, meant they were no friends to those who supported popular rights, such as Loftus (see note to p. 82), which may explain why Wollstonecraft found it difficult to discover exactly what happened in the uprising.

LETTER XIV

84 *gothic*: Wollstonecraft's distaste for the Gothic again encodes a radical critique of Burkean conservatism: see note to p. 47. In *Vindication of the Rights of Men*, 2nd edn., 100, she asked, 'Why was it a duty to repair an ancient castle, built in barbarous ages, of Gothic materials? Why were the legislators obliged to rake among the heterogeneous ruins; to rebuild old walls, whose foundations could scarcely be explored, when a simple structure might be raised on the foundation of experience, the only valuable inheritance our forefathers could bequeath?

Dr. Price: Richard Price (1723–91), political radical and minister associated with rational dissent. Wollstonecraft became familiar with Price whilst living in Newington Green, where the latter was a minister at the Presbyterian chapel. He became a friend and mentor to her. Price's address to the London Society for Commemorating the Revolution in Great Britain in 1789, published as *Discourse on the Love of our Country* (1789), celebrated the French Revolution and spurred Burke to write the *Reflections*. See Introduction, p. xi.

86 *ever-smiling liberty*: Thomas Morell's words for a song from the first part of Handel's opera *Judas Maccabaeus* (1747). Wollstonecraft also quotes this song in *Maria; or the Wrongs of Woman*, chapter 12.

the nymph of the mountain: Milton's *L'Allegro* (1645), l. 36.

odels right: the allodial right of any lineal descendant to repurchase estates sold out of the family by paying the original price of purchase. The right protected the inheritance of property within the family against other forms of transfer, such as sale on the open market or gifts to the Church. In this sense, odel's right worked against the accumulation of larger properties. Eighteenth-century reforms had placed time limits on the right, as Wollstonecraft notes. The chapter added to the second edition of Malthus' *Essay on Population* (1803) identifies the odel's right as one of the major obstacles to the improvement of farms in Norway.

LETTER XV

87 *How I am altered . . . glowing colours*: these two sentences are taken almost complete from her letter to Imlay, written in Hull on 20 June 1795. See *Letters*, 304.

When the mind's free . . . delicate: see *King Lear*, III. iv. 11–12.

89 *cascade*: Holmes, 39–40, suggests that the description of the cascade outside Fredrikstad and the later one of the Trollhättan falls near Gothenburg in Letter XVII influenced Coleridge's poem 'Kubla Khan'. Clarke, section 1, 105, described them as having 'by no means answered the expectations excited by different descriptions of them already published', which would have included Wollstonecraft's.

90 *Geographical Grammars*: lurid tales of Norway's sea-monsters, Kraken, and mermen and women featured in numerous contemporary educational texts. See for example William Guthrie's *A New Geographical, Historical, and Commercial Grammar*, 2 vols. (1770), i. 96–8, still in print in 1795. 'Grammar' could be used as a title of any compendious book of information.

LETTER XVI

90 *Stromstad*: Wollstonecraft has crossed the border back into Sweden.

92 *Uddervalla*: Uddevalla, also visited by Coxe (1790), 128–9, a prosperous Swedish town on the coast, where the convention met in 1788 to agree to the evacuation of the Norwegian army from Sweden (saving Gothenburg from being sacked).

94 *Nestors*: Nestor, King of Pylos and father of Perseus, a veteran Argonaut and survivor of the Trojan War who, according to Homer's *Iliad*, outlived two generations and retained his strength. In both the *Iliad* and *Odyssey*, he is the elder statesman of the Greek army.

LETTER XVII

95 *Trollhættæ*: Trollhätte canal which connects Lake Vänern with Gothenburg and the Kattegat (with a view to connecting the latter with the Baltic) was completed in 1800, just after Clarke's visit: see his description section 1, 106–7.

97 *divorce*: Imlay's novel *The Emigrants*, 3, complains that 'the great difficulty there is in England, of obtaining a divorce' often forces 'women of the most virtuous inclinations into the gulf of ruin'. Later on in the novel, 154, further reflections on the same subject turn upon Queen Matilda of Denmark, whose fate preoccupied Wollstonecraft when she reached Denmark: see Introduction, pp. xx–xxi.

98 *Falckersberg*: Falkenberg.

Wales: the Wollstonecraft family had moved from Hoxton to Laugharne in South Wales in 1776. This was an unhappy time for Mary as she was separated from her close friend Fanny Blood.

LETTER XVIII

99 *rage for encampments*: Wollstonecraft is referring to the military encampments in Britain, established during the American War of Independence, which remained a notable presence into the French revolutionary wars. Prominent camps included Coxheath, Warley, Brighton, and Bagshot Heath. The military camps and exercises were highly visible and drew large numbers of spectators. Wollstonecraft's dry comment is typical of radical criticism of such spectacles.

the late fire: the royal palace Christianborg had been destroyed by fire in 1794 (see pp. 100–1). A much larger blaze, which started on 9 June 1795, destroyed about a quarter of Copenhagen. Having visited the city four years later, Clarke, section 1, 63, describes it as 'risen with renovated splendour from her ashes'.

101 *Prince Royal . . . would have stopt*: this critical account of Crown Prince Frederick contradicts the favourable one given in Letter VII.

domestic tyrants: the phrase, repeated on p. 107, that drew forth Clarke's defence of Norwegian married life (see Introduction), although on these pages Wollstonecraft is talking about the condition of Danish women. On p. 98 she refers to Swedish women as 'domestic drudges worn down by tyranny to servile submission'.

Bernstorff: see note to p. 45 above.

102 *Matilda*: (1751–75) George III's sister, and subsequently Matilda, Queen of Denmark and Norway (1766–72). See Introduction, pp. xx–xxi.

103 *Struensee*: see Introduction, pp. xx–xxi.

As flies to wanton boys . . . their sport: Gloucester in *King Lear*, IV. i. 37–8.

LETTER XIX

104 *Consequently executions . . . hardening the heart they ought to terrify*: criticism of public executions was common among progressive thinkers in the 1790s: see part I of Paine's *Rights of Man* (1791), 33, which notes that an execution displayed to the populace 'tortures their feelings or hardens their hearts' and tends to 'destroy tenderness or excite revenge; and by the base and false idea of governing men by terror, instead of reason, they become precedents'.

105 *had that society been well organized . . . renders it unjust*: Holmes, 291, traces an allusion to this passage in Mary Shelley's *Frankenstein*. On Mary Shelley's reading of her mother's book, see Introduction, pp. xxvii–xxviii.

Mr. Pitt: William Pitt the Younger (1759–1806), British Prime Minister from 1783 to 1801 and from 1804 until his death. Pitt's government was impatient at the neutrality of Denmark, and Struensee's sympathy for the French, hence the rumours that his emissaries had played a part in starting the fires of 1794 and 1795: see note to p. 99.

baseless fabric of a vision: see *The Tempest*, IV. i. 151.

Empiricism: 'quackery'. Only later in the nineteenth century did it come to have its modern meaning of practice based upon experiment and observation.

108 *national character*: on Wollstonecraft's reluctance to make generalizations about national character, see Introduction, p. xxi and note to p. 25.

the vanity and depravity of the French: in her *Historical and Moral View*, Wollstonecraft makes constant reference to the vanity and depravity of the French aristocracy, which she sees as a cause of the Revolution. The qualification of her views here reflects on her revision of her attitude to 'refinement' versus simplicity of manners as the book goes on.

virtuous enthusiasm: see note to Letter I, p. 10. Wollstonecraft often uses the word 'enthusiasm' in this sense, identifying it with heroic republican virtue, rather than the more common usage of the word to describe popular religious feeling associated with Methodism and other popular sects (what she calls 'fanaticism', p. 60). She represents herself as a victim of her own enthusiasm for virtue in the letter to Imlay of 3 July 1795: see Appendix 3, p. 142.

LETTER XX

109 *theatrical exhibitions*: Wollstonectaft's *Historical and Moral View*, 26, describes French theatres as 'schools for vanity', echoing the attack made in Rousseau's *Letter to d'Alembert* in defence of the Spartan virtues of his native Geneva. The qualification of Wollstonecraft's own earlier opinion here is in the vein of the reorientation of her attitude to 'refinement' away from Rousseauist ideas of virtue that runs throughout the book: see notes to pp. 60 and 108.

110 *Drinking . . . principal relaxation of the men*: see note to Letter III, p. 17.

the Mock Doctor: Molière's farce *Le Médecin malgré lui* (1666), in which an alcoholic woodcutter tries to pass himself off as a wise physician. Henry Fielding based *The Mock Doctor* (1732) on Molière's play.

ballat: 'ballet'. The Danish periodical *Svada* (1796) contains an article signed K.L.R. (probably Knud Lyhne Rahbek) defending the Danish theatre against Wollstonecraft's criticisms of 'a nation's theatre and public, just based on seeing one performance'. The article demonstrates just how quickly her book became available in Scandinavia. The editors are grateful to Gunnar Molden for this reference.

Rosembourg: Rosenborg Castle was begun as a summer palace for Christian IV in 1606–7 and was used as a royal residence until 1710. Subsequently it was used to house royal collections.

111 *Hirsholm*: site of Queen Matilda's favourite palace. Although far from unsympathetic to Matilda, Clarke describes it as exhibiting 'no marks of a good taste', section 1, 83.

112 *public library . . . Icelandic manuscripts*: the Royal Library, which had opened to the public in 1793, housed early Icelandic manuscripts, including the tales of Norse mythology in the *Edda*. Clarke records visiting both the Royal Library and the university library, also open to the public, and also rich in Icelandic manuscripts (see section 1, 71–2 and 79–80).

grows with its growth, and strengthens with its strength: Wollstonecraft slightly misquotes canto II of Alexander Pope's *An Essay on Man* (1734), ll. 133–6.

> As Man, perhaps, the moment of his breath,
> Receives the lurking principle of death;
> The young disease, that must subdue at length,
> Grows with his growth, and strengthens with his strength.

There are some good pictures . . . improvements in the art: Clarke, section 1, 75, thought the only picture worth noting was one by Salvator Rosa depicting Jonah preaching to the Ninevites. The 'splendid gallery' in Paris is the Louvre, opened as a public museum in August 1793.

Laplanders: or the indigenous Sámi people who live mostly in the northern parts of Norway, Sweden, Finland, and Russia. The term *Laplander* is today often considered derogatory.

113 *œconomical*: variant spelling of economical, meaning thrifty here, and with connotations of prudent household management.

monsieur le chien: there is a story that during his mental illness King Christian VII asked to have his dog made chamberlain. The editors are grateful for this information to Gunnar Molden.

LETTER XXI

114 *à la Necker*: Jacques Necker (1732–1804), Swiss-born French financier and statesman who was Louis XVI's Finance Minister 1776–81, during which time he made enemies through his efforts at fiscal reform, and again 1788–9, before his dismissal on the eve of the French Revolution. The popular outcry led Louis to recall him, and he continued to serve until 1790. His poor handling of the Estates-General and refusal to cooperate with Lafayette and Mirabeau during this time contributed to the worsening crisis. Wollstonecraft translated Necker's *De l'importance des opinions religieuses* (1788) for Joseph Johnson.

Lavater: Johann Kaspar Lavater (1741–1801), a Swiss pastor and poet, chiefly famous as the modern founder of physiognomy, the science of discerning personality from facial features. Lavater was a friend of Henry Fuseli, his schoolfellow at the Zurich Gymnasium, and in 1788 Joseph Johnson published a translation of his *Aphorisms on Man*. Initially enthusiastic about the French Revolution, by 1792 he was preaching against its irreligious excesses.

115 *Hamburg*: for Hamburg, where Wollstonecraft had thought she might rendezvous with Imlay at the end of her mission, see Introduction, pp. xvi–xvii.

116 *How dull, flat . . . should come to this*: Wollstonecraft misquotes *Hamlet*, I. ii. 133–7 from memory:

> How weary, stale, flat, and unprofitable
> Seem to me all the uses of this world!
> Fie on't, ah fie, fie! 'Tis an unweeded garden
> That grows to seed; things rank and gross in nature
> Possess it merely. That it should come to this.

LETTER XXII

116 *Corsoer . . . Great Belt*: modern day Korsør. The embarkation point on the west coast of the island of Zealand (a land journey across from Copenhagen) for the European mainland. The great and little belts are the straits between Denmark and the mainland, on either side of Fyn Island. The crossing is described in detail by Clarke, section 1, 55–6.

French having passed the Rhine: the French revolutionary armies took the Rhine from the Prussians in 1795.

117 *panier*: the hooped skirt in fashion in the eighteenth century. Wollstonecraft often commented on the restrictive function of women's fashion: see for instance her chapter on dress in *Thoughts on the Education of Daughters* (1787). Her own looser-fitting French attire seems to have attracted attention from Scandinavian women at several points in her journey.

gaité du cœur: 'gladness of heart'.

Little Belt: see note to p. 116.

118 *Ugolino*: Ugolino della Gherardesca (*c.*1220–89), Count of Donoratico, imprisoned in a tower with his sons and grandsons by the Archbishop of Pisa. They all starved to death, but Ugolino ate his dead children to ward off his fate. In Dante's *Inferno*, Ugolino eternally gnaws the skull of the Archbishop in the lowest ring of hell. The episode particularly fascinated English painters and poets, partly as an example of priestly cruelty. The first painting from Dante by an Englishman was *Count Ugolino* (1773) by Sir Joshua Reynolds.

120 *Holstein . . . Sleswick*: Schleswig and Holstein on the German mainland were duchies under Danish rule.

Charles of Hesse-Cassel: (1744–1836), second son of the Prince of Kassel, the future Frederick II, Landgrave of Hesse-Kassel, and Princess Mary of Great Britain, George II's daughter. Charles pursued a military career in Denmark and was royal governor of Schleswig-Holstein.

German despotism: Paine had dedicated part II of *Rights of Man* (1792) to the French general de Lafayette, hoping that the renewed French military campaign against Prussia and Austria might 'terminate in the extinction of German despotism' (p. vi). The phrase always contained an implied criticism of the British monarchy, who were still German princes. In the autumn of 1793 William Hodgson and Charles Pigott had been arrested on a charge of seditious words for calling George III a 'German hog butcher' for his pursuit of the war against France.

thousand ills which flesh is heir to: Wollstonecraft slightly misquotes *Hamlet*, III. i. 64–5, 'The heartache and the thousand natural shocks| That flesh is heir to.'

121 *Milton's devils*: in *Paradise Lost*, I. 423–30, Milton explains that the rebel angels can change size; they shrink to enter Pandaemonium (I. 775–98).

fauteuil: armchair.

All the world is a stage: see *As You Like It*, II. vii. 139.

human form, as well as face divine: see note to p. 24.

122 *an enemy to what is termed charity*: in *Vindication of the Rights of Men*, 2nd edn. 136, Wollstonecraft argues that to 'endeavour to make unhappy men resigned to their fate, is the tender endeavour of short-sighted benevolence, of transient yearnings of humanity; but to labour to increase human happiness by extirpating error, is a masculine godlike affection'.

laying up a treasure in heaven: Matthew 6: 20.

123 *Altona*: Altona, on the banks of the river Elbe, was a prosperous free port within the Danish territories of Schleswig-Holstein, easily close enough to Hamburg, about a mile, for Malthus to walk there for a social visit in 1799 (*Malthus*, 35).

LETTER XXIII

125 *other free towns*: in the Holy Roman Empire, the free imperial cities were formally ruled by the emperor, rather than by the immediate territorial ruler of the principality. Hamburg became a free city in 1189.

Mushroom fortunes: wealth which had sprung up rapidly. The term was associated with commerce and speculation. Here it is aimed at those who had made fortunes from the turmoil of war against revolutionary France: see Introduction, p. xiv. Clarke, section 1, 13, also notes the increased prosperity of Hamburg after the Revolution.

emigrants, 'fallen—fallen from their high estate': aristocrats who had fled the French Revolution: see Introduction, p. xvii. The quotation is from Dryden's *Alexander's Feast* (1697), IV. 77–8.

125 *croix de St. Louis*: a medal identifying the wearer as a member of the chivalric Order of St Louis. It was instituted by Louis XIV in April 1696 to honour exceptional military officers, and bears the name of his beatified ancestor Louis IX. In 1792, the revolutionary government withdrew the Order.

though heaven and earth their wishes crossed: Wollstonecraft slightly misquotes ll. 19–20 of 'Song I' by Anna Laetitia Barbauld, published in *Poems* (1773). The lyric, popularly named 'The Symptoms of Love', lists the marks by which 'true passion may be found': 'It is to hope, tho' hope were lost, | Tho' heaven and earth thy passion crost.'

126 *Madame La Fayette*: wife of Marie-Joseph-Motier, Marquis de Lafayette (1757–1834), who had fought in the American War of Independence and was a leading figure in the early stages of the French Revolution. He was charged with treason and fled to the Austrian side in 1792 when the Jacobins seized power in Paris. After the Marquis was imprisoned as a revolutionary, Madame Lafayette joined him in Austria and obtained his release in 1797.

a devil, who deserves the appellation of legion: Mark 5: 9 and Luke 8: 30.

Madame Genlis: Stéphanie Félicité Ducrest de Saint-Aubin, Comtesse de Genlis (1747–1830), playwright, novelist, and educationalist. Wollstonecraft quotes from her work in *The Female Reader* (1789). De Genlis's husband, the Marquis de Sillery, was an early Girondin victim of the guillotine in 1793. She fled France for Switzerland upon the fall of the Girondins.

traiteur: a manager of a restaurant or shop delivering cooked meals to order.

127 *ci-devant*: 'previously known as'; here referring to a noble whose titled distinctions were now suppressed by the Revolution.

ordinary: a public eating-house with fixed-price meals.

double louis d'or: the louis d'or was a French gold coin, introduced by Louis XIII in 1640, replaced by the franc in the 1790s.

the author of the American Farmer's Letters: J. Hector St John de Crèvecœur (1735–1813), author of the popular *Letters from an American Farmer* (1782). Crèvecœur had settled in America in 1769, but his prosperous life was interrupted by the War of Independence, in which he felt unable to choose sides, and he fled to France, returning in 1783 to find his farm burned and his wife murdered. He then settled in New York as French consul. Ill health forced him to return to France in 1790, but he avoided involvement in the Revolution and retired to Normandy, apart from brief visits to Germany, including a stay with his son over 1795–6 in Hamburg, where he encountered Wollstonecraft.

the wing-footed god: Hermes, amongst other things the god of travellers, commerce, thieves, tricksters, and liars.

128 *Cassandra*: a prophet of doom. In Greek legend, the daughter of Priam, King of Troy, cursed to foretell the future, including the fall of Troy, but not to be believed.

LETTER XXIV

128 *double—double, toil and trouble*: see *Macbeth*, IV. i. 10.

Klopstock's wife: Meta Möller, who in 1754 married Friedrich Gottlieb Klopstock (1724–1803) but died in 1758. Klopstock was a patriotic German poet and author of the epic *Der Messias* (1748-73). He met Wordsworth and Coleridge in Hamburg during 1798.

130 *owners of negro ships*: see note to p. 42 above.

justify the ways of God to man: see *Paradise Lost*, I. 26.

Take, O world! thy much indebted tear!: Young, *Night Thoughts*, I. 304. See note to p. 34.

The Oxford World's Classics Website

www.worldsclassics.co.uk

- Browse the full range of Oxford World's Classics online

- Sign up for our monthly e-alert to receive information on new titles

- Read extracts from the Introductions

- Listen to our editors and translators talk about the world's greatest literature with our Oxford World's Classics audio guides

- Join the conversation, follow us on Twitter at OWC_Oxford

- Teachers and lecturers can order inspection copies quickly and simply via our website

www.worldsclassics.co.uk

American Literature

British and Irish Literature

Children's Literature

Classics and Ancient Literature

Colonial Literature

Eastern Literature

European Literature

Gothic Literature

History

Medieval Literature

Oxford English Drama

Poetry

Philosophy

Politics

Religion

The Oxford Shakespeare

A complete list of Oxford World's Classics, including Authors in Context, Oxford English Drama, and the Oxford Shakespeare, is available in the UK from the Marketing Services Department, Oxford University Press, Great Clarendon Street, Oxford OX2 6DP, or visit the website at www.oup.com/uk/worldsclassics.

In the USA, visit www.oup.com/us/owc for a complete title list.

Oxford World's Classics are available from all good bookshops. In case of difficulty, customers in the UK should contact Oxford University Press Bookshop, 116 High Street, Oxford OX1 4BR.